ADVENTURES OF HUCKLEBERRY FINN AND ZOMBIE JIM

Also by W. Bill Czolgosz

Anna Karnivora

Eat @t Zero's

Persuasion . . . In Space (with Jane Austen)

Zombiefrieze (illustrated by Sean Simmans)

ADVENTURES OF HUCKLEBERRY FINN AND ZOMBIE JIM

MARK TWAIN

with

W. BILL CZOLGOSZ

G

GALLERY BOOKS

New York London Toronto Sydney

Gallery Books
A Division of Simon & Schuster, Inc.
1230 Avenue of the Americas
New York, NY 10020

This book is a work of fiction. Names, characters, places, and incidents either are products of the author's imagination or are used fictitiously. Any resemblance to actual events or locales or persons, living or dead, is entirely coincidental.

Published by arrangement with Coscom Entertainment

First Gallery Books trade paperback edition April 2011

Manufactured in the United States of America

10 9 8 7 6 5 4 3 2

Library of Congress Cataloging-in-Publication Data is available.

ISBN 978-1-4516-0978-3
ISBN 978-1-4516-1136-6 (ebook)

W. Bill Czolgosz dedicates this work to

Taylor & Haylee

Siblings. Friends. Persons of great importance.

NOTICE

Persons attempting to find a motive in this narrative will be prosecuted; persons attempting to find a moral in it will be banished; persons attempting to find a plot in it will be shot directly in the brain stem.

By Order of the Authors, Per G.G., Chief of Ordnance.

EXPLANATORY

In this book a number of dialects are used, to wit: the Missouri negro dialect; the extremest form of the backwoods Southwestern dialect; the ordinary "Pike County" dialect; the grizzled grumblings of the not dead, the nearly dead, and the certainly dead; and four modified varieties of this last. The shadings have not been done in a haphazard fashion, or by guesswork; but painstakingly, and with the trustworthy guidance and support of personal familiarity with these several forms of speech.

We make this explanation for the reason that without it many readers would suppose that all these characters were trying to talk alike and not succeeding.

The Authors.

"And with my own eyes I once saw the Sibyl at Cumae hanging in a great jar, and when the young men asked her, 'Sibyl, what do you want?' she said, 'I want to die.'"

—*Petronius,* Satyricon

ADVENTURES OF HUCKLEBERRY FINN AND ZOMBIE JIM

Scene: The Mississippi Valley

Time: 1839

CHAPTER I

The people used to own other people, an' they had a word for those people. Really mean. I think the only thing I was ever taught that managed to stick with me was that the widow better never hear that word come out of my mouth. Eventually, I learned that lesson good cause o' the whuppins I got when I tried it. Can't say I ever uttered it again. I believe not. All my days. Like I say, it was the widow's whuppin' what did it.

Other than that, she was always very kind. Strict, but kind.

I remember the widow now, sure I do. An' Miss Watson, too. An' pretty much everyone else. And that's sayin' a big deal 'cause the world was full-up of people in those times.

You don't know about me without you have read a book by the name of *The Undead Adventures of Tom Sawyer*; but that ain't no matter. That book was made by Mr. Mark Twain, and he told the truth, mainly. There was things which he stretched, but mainly he told the truth. That is nothing. I never seen anybody but lied one time or another, without it was Aunt Polly, or the widow, or maybe Mary. Aunt Polly—Tom's Aunt Polly, she is—and Mary, and the Widow Douglas is all told about in that book, which is mostly a true book, with some stretchers, as I said before.

Now the way that the book winds up is this: Tom and me found the bunderlugs that the robbers had put in the cave, and when we returned 'em to the traders it made us rich. There was almost a hundred of 'em, and th' reward money was plenty big. We got six thousand dollars apiece—all gold. It was an awful sight of money when it was piled up. Well, Judge Thatcher he took it and put it out at interest, and it fetched us a dollar a day apiece all the year round—more than a body could tell what to do with. The Widow Douglas she took me for her son, and allowed she would sivilize me; but it was rough living in the house all the time, considering how dismal regular and decent the widow was in all her ways; and so when I couldn't stand it no longer I lit out. I got into my old rags and my sugar-hogshead again, and was free and satisfied. But Tom Sawyer he hunted me up and said he was going to start his own band of robbers, and I might join if I would go back to the widow and be respectable. So I went back.

The widow she cried over me, and called me a poor lost lamb, and she called me a lot of other names, too, but she never meant no harm by it. She put me in them new clothes again, and I couldn't do nothing but sweat and sweat, and feel all cramped up. Well, then, the old thing commenced again. The widow rung a bell for supper, and you had to come to time. When you got to the table you couldn't go right to eating, but you had to wait for the widow to tuck down her head and grumble a little over the victuals, though there warn't really anything the matter with them—that is, nothing only everything was cooked by itself. In a barrel of odds and ends it is different; things get mixed up, and the juice kind of swaps around, and the things go better.

After supper she got out her book and learned me about Moses and the Bulrushers, and I was in a sweat to find out all about him; but by and by she let it out that Moses had been dead a considerable long time; so then I didn't care no more about him, because I don't take *much* stock in dead people.

I do mean that when I say it, about taking stock in dead people, *most* dead people, especially these days. Folks say the world is turned on its ear. I don't know about that. Sure thing it's at a considerable wobble, though.

Pretty soon afterward I wanted to smoke, and asked the widow to let me. But she wouldn't. She said it was a mean practice and wasn't clean, and I must try to not do it any more. That is just the way with some people. They get down on a thing when they don't know nothing about it. Here she was a-bothering about Moses, which was no kin to her, and no use to anybody, being gone, you see, yet finding a power of fault with me for doing a thing that had some good in it. And she took snuff, too; of course that was all right, because she done it herself.

Her sister, Miss Watson, a tolerable slim old maid, with goggles on, had just come to live with her, and took a set at me now with a spelling-book. She worked me middling hard for about an hour, and then the widow made her ease up. I couldn't stood it much longer. Then for an hour it was deadly dull, and I was fidgety. Miss Watson would say, "Don't put your feet up there, Huckleberry;" and "Don't scrunch up like that, Huckleberry—set up straight;" and pretty soon she would say, "Don't gap and stretch like that, Huckleberry—why don't you try to behave?" Then she told me all about the bad place, and I said I wished I was there. And then she told me how boys like me was more than likely than not to catch the fissythis, and I said fissythis weren't such a bad thing, 'cause at least I'd be having adventures. She got mad then, but I didn't mean no harm. All I wanted was to go somewheres; all I wanted was a change, I warn't particular. She said it was wicked to say what I said; said she wouldn't say it for the whole world; she was going to live so as to go to the good place. Well, I couldn't see no advantage in going where she was going, so I made up my mind I wouldn't try for it. But I never said so, because it would only make trouble, and wouldn't do no good.

Now she had got a start, and she went on and told me all about the good place. She said all a body would have to do there was to go around all day long with a harp and sing, forever and ever. I asked about if the folks with fissythis got to go there, too, and she said they surely did get to go, eventually, when their material selves were all over and done with. And I asked if that included the ones who had bit people and wreaked havoc and such, and she said it probably did, as long as their hearts was right before the pox took 'em. So I didn't think much of it. But I never said so. I asked her if she reckoned Tom Sawyer would go there, and she said not by a considerable sight. I was glad about that, because I wanted him and me to be together.

Miss Watson spelled fissythis like so: PHTHISIS. That never made a lick of sense to me. She said it could get into you just for breathing air blown in from the east, and that made even less sense. She said fissythis come from London or France, but those places might's well have been China. Tom told me Napoleon defeated all the pox over there and people was living healthier than ever. But I didn't know nothing about that for myself, nor how he pulled it off. I figured that Napoleon musta been a mighty big fella.

Miss Watson she kept pecking at me, and it got tiresome and lonesome. By and by they fetched the baggers in and had prayers, and then everybody was off to bed. I went up to my room with a piece of candle, and put it on the table. Then I set down in a chair by the window and tried to think of something cheerful, but it warn't no use. I felt so lonesome I most wished I was dead. The stars were shining, and the leaves rustled in the woods ever so mournful; and I heard an owl, away off, who-whooing about somebody that was maybe finally dead, and a whippowill and a dog crying about somebody that was going to catch the pox; and the wind was trying to whisper something to me, and I couldn't make out what it was, and so it made the cold shivers run over me. Then away out in the woods I heard that kind of a sound that a ghost makes when it wants to tell about something that's on its mind and can't make itself understood, and so can't rest easy in its grave, and has to go about that way every night grieving. I got so down-hearted and scared I did wish I had some company. Pretty soon a spider went crawling up my shoulder, and I flipped it off and it lit in the candle; and before I could budge it was all shriveled up. I didn't need anybody to tell me that that was an awful bad sign and would fetch me some bad luck, so I was scared and most shook the clothes off of me. I got up and turned around in my tracks three times and crossed my breast every time; and then I tied up a little lock of my hair with a thread to keep witches away. But I hadn't no confidence. You do that when you've lost a horseshoe that you've found, instead of nailing it up over the door, but I hadn't ever heard anybody say it was any way to keep off bad luck when you'd killed a spider.

I set down again, a-shaking all over, and got out my pipe for a smoke; for the house was all as still as death now, and so the widow wouldn't know. Well, after a long time I heard the clock away off in the town go boom—boom—boom—twelve licks; and all still again—stiller than ever. Pretty soon I heard a twig snap down in the dark amongst the trees—something was a stirring. I set still and listened. Directly I could just barely hear a "me-yow! me-yow!" down there. That was good! Says I, "me-yow! me-yow!" as soft as I could, and then I put out the light and scrambled out of the window on to the shed. Then I slipped down to the ground and crawled in among the trees, and, sure enough, there was Tom Sawyer waiting for me.

CHAPTER II

We went tiptoeing along a path amongst the trees back towards the end of the widow's garden, stooping down so as the branches wouldn't scrape our heads. When we was passing by the kitchen I fell over a root and made a noise. We scrouched down and laid still. Miss Watson's big bagger, named Jim, was setting in the kitchen door; we could see him pretty clear, because there was a light behind him. He got up and stretched his neck out about a minute, listening. Then he says, gurgling:

"Who dah?"

He listened some more; then he come tiptoeing down and stood right between us; we could a touched him, nearly. Well, likely it was minutes and minutes that there warn't a sound, and we all there so close together. There was a place on my ankle that got to itching, but I dasn't scratch it; and then my ear begun to itch; and next my back, right between my shoulders. Seemed like I'd die if I couldn't scratch. Well, I've noticed that thing plenty times since. If you are with the quality, or at a funeral, or trying to go to sleep when you ain't sleepy—if you are anywheres where it won't do for you to scratch, why you will itch all over in upwards of a thousand places. Pretty soon Jim says:

"Say, who is you? Whar is you? Dog my cats if I didn' hear sumf'n. Well, I know what I's goan to do: I's goan to set down here and listen tell I hears it agin."

So he set down on the ground betwixt me and Tom. He leaned his back up against a tree, and stretched his legs out till one of them most touched one of mine. My nose begun to itch. It itched till the tears come into my eyes. But I dasn't scratch. Then it begun to itch on the inside. Next I got to itching underneath. I didn't know how I was going to set still. This miserableness went on as much as six or seven minutes; but it seemed a sight longer than that. I was itching in eleven different places now. I reckoned I couldn't stand it more'n a minute longer, but I set my teeth hard and got ready to try. Just then Jim begun to breathe heavy; next he begun to snore and slobber—and then I was pretty soon comfortable again.

After the fissythis took him, Jim managed to keep parts of himself. He was called a half-bag or a some-bag, on account o' he could be made to understand things. That was his value. You couldn't trade or train a full bagger to do the things the black folks used to have to do. A full bagger is a damn problem. You got to go after the marbles in his head and knock 'em all out 'fore you can put him down.

New York City had itself a real crisis, more times than a once.

But a half-bagger, as the widow told me, still had the potential to be of some use to folks. He could listen and, even if he couldn't learn, he could still be put to the tasks he might have known in earlier times.

Tom he made a sign to me—kind of a little noise with his mouth—and we went creeping away on our hands and knees. When we was ten foot off Tom whispered to me, and wanted to tie Jim to the tree for fun. But I said no; he might wake and make a disturbance, and then they'd find out I warn't in. Then Tom said he hadn't got candles enough, and he would slip in the kitchen and get some more. I didn't want him to try. I said Jim might wake up and come. But Tom wanted to resk it; so we slid in there and got three candles, and Tom laid five cents on the table for pay. Then we got out, and I was in a sweat to get away; but nothing would do Tom but he must crawl to where Jim was, on his hands and knees, and play something on him. I waited, and it seemed a good while, everything was so still and lonesome.

As soon as Tom was back we cut along the path, around the garden fence, and by and by fetched up on the steep top of the hill the other side of the house. Tom said he slipped Jim's hat off of his head and hung it on a limb right over him, and Jim stirred a little, but he didn't wake. Afterwards Jim said the witches be witched him and put him in a trance, and rode him all over the State, and then set him under the trees again, and hung his hat on a limb to show who done it. And next time Jim told it he said they rode him down to New Orleans; and, after that, every time he told it he spread it more and more, till by and by he said they rode him all over the world, and tired him most to death, and his back was all over saddle-boils. Jim was monstrous proud about it, and he got so he wouldn't hardly notice the other baggers. Baggers would come miles to hear Jim tell about it, and he was more looked up to than any bagger in that country. Strange baggers would stand with their rotten mouths open and look him all over, same as if he was a wonder. Jim always kept that five-center piece round his neck with a string, and said it was a charm the devil give to him with his own hands, and told him he could cure anybody with it and fetch witches whenever he wanted to just by saying something to it; but he never told what it was he said to it. Baggers would come from all around there and give Jim anything they had, just for a sight of that five-center piece; but they wouldn't touch it, because the devil had had his hands on it, just like the devil had got his hands on them, once upon a time.

That's how Tom described it to me. It was the devil what made the fissythis pox. Them baggers what caught it made a special trip all the way to Hell 'fore they got to come back changed the way they was. He said they was charmed by the boyo, though I didn't figure charm had much to do with it.

Well, when Tom and me got to the edge of the hilltop we looked away down into the village and could see three or four lights twinkling, where there was sick folks, maybe; and the stars over us was sparkling ever so fine; and down by the village was the river, a whole mile broad, and awful still and grand. We went down the hill and found Jo Harper and Ben Rogers, and two or three more of the boys, hid in the old tanyard. So we unhitched a skiff and pulled down the river two mile and a half, to the big scar on the hillside, and went ashore.

We went to a clump of bushes, and Tom made everybody swear to keep the secret, and then showed them a hole in the hill, right in the thickest part of the bushes. Then we lit the candles, and crawled in on our hands and knees. We went about two hundred yards, and then the cave opened up. Tom poked about amongst the passages, and pretty soon ducked under a wall where you wouldn't a noticed that there was a hole. We went along a narrow place and got into a kind of room, all damp and sweaty and cold, and there we stopped. Tom says:

"Now, we'll start this band of robbers and call it Tom Sawyer's Gang. Everybody that wants to join has got to take an oath, and write his name in blood."

Everybody was willing. So Tom got out a sheet of paper

that he had wrote the oath on, and read it. It swore every boy to stick to the band, and never tell any of the secrets; and if anybody done anything to any boy in the band, whichever boy was ordered to kill that person and his family must do it, and he mustn't eat and he mustn't sleep till he had killed them and hacked a cross in their breasts, which was the sign of the band. And nobody that didn't belong to the band could use that mark, and if he did he must be sued; and if he done it again he must be killed. And if anybody that belonged to the band told the secrets, he must have his throat cut, and then have his carcass burnt up and the ashes scattered all around, so that not even the devil could send him back as a bagger, and his name blotted off of the list with blood and never mentioned again by the gang, but have a curse put on it and be forgot forever.

Everybody said it was a real beautiful oath, and asked Tom if he got it out of his own head. He said, some of it, but the rest was out of pirate-books and robber-books, and every gang that was high-toned had it. And there was even a couple of bag groups, smarter ones, the ones who worked in the tannery, who took a simplified form. Much less words, and easier to grunt.

Some thought it would be good to kill the *families* of boys that told the secrets. Tom said it was a good idea, so he took a pencil and wrote it in. Then Ben Rogers says:

"Here's Huck Finn, he hain't got no family; what you going to do 'bout him?"

"Well, hain't he got a father?" says Tom Sawyer.

"Yes, he's got a father, but you can't never find him these days. He used to lay drunk with the hogs in the tanyard, but he hain't been seen in these parts for a year or more."

They talked it over, and they was going to rule me out,

because they said every boy must have a family or somebody to kill, or else it wouldn't be fair and square for the others. Well, nobody could think of anything to do—everybody was stumped, and set still. I was most ready to cry; but all at once I thought of a way, and so I offered them Miss Watson—they could kill her. Everybody said:

"Oh, she'll do. That's all right. Huck can come in."

Then they all stuck a pin in their fingers to get blood to sign with, and I made my mark on the paper.

"Now," says Ben Rogers, "what's the line of business of this Gang?"

"Nothing only robbery and murder," Tom said.

"But who are we going to rob?—houses, or cattle, or—"

"Stuff! Stealing cattle and such things ain't robbery; it's burglary," says Tom Sawyer. "We ain't burglars. That ain't no sort of style. We are highwaymen. We stop stages and carriages on the road, with masks on, and kill the people and take their watches and money."

"Must we always kill the people?"

"Oh, certainly. It's best. Some authorities think different, but mostly it's considered best to kill them—except some that you bring to the cave here, and keep them till they're ransomed."

"Ransomed? What's that?"

"I don't know. But that's what they do. I've seen it in books; and so of course that's what we've got to do."

"But how can we do it if we don't know what it is?"

"Why, blame it all, we've *got* to do it. Don't I tell you it's in the books? Do you want to go to doing different from what's in the books, and get things all muddled up?"

"Oh, that's all very fine to *say*, Tom Sawyer, but how in the nation are these fellows going to be ransomed if we don't know how to do it to them?—that's the thing I want to get at. Now, what do you reckon it is?"

"Well, I don't know. But per'aps if we keep them till they're ransomed, it means that we keep them till they're dead."

"Now, that's something *like*. That'll answer. Why couldn't you said that before? We'll keep them till they're ransomed to death; and a bothersome lot they'll be, too—eating up everything, and always trying to get loose."

"How you talk, Ben Rogers. How can they get loose when there's a guard over them, ready to shoot them down if they move a peg?"

"A guard! Well, that *is* good. So somebody's got to set up all night and never get any sleep, just so as to watch them. I think that's foolishness. Why can't a body take a club and ransom them as soon as they get here?"

"Because it ain't in the books so—that's why. Now, Ben Rogers, do you want to do things regular, or don't you?—that's the idea. Don't you reckon that the people that made the books knows what's the correct thing to do? Do you reckon *you* can learn 'em anything? Not by a good deal. No, sir, we'll just go on and ransom them in the regular way."

"All right. I don't mind; but I say it's a fool way, anyhow. Say, do we kill the women, too?"

"Well, Ben Rogers, if I was as ignorant as you I wouldn't let on. Kill the women? No; nobody ever saw anything in the books like that. You fetch them to the cave, and you're always as polite as pie to them; and by and by they fall in love with you, and never want to go home any more."

"Well, if that's the way I'm agreed, but I don't take no stock in it. Mighty soon we'll have the cave so cluttered up with women, and fellows waiting to be ransomed, that there won't be no place for the robbers. But go ahead, I ain't got nothing to say."

"An' what about baggers an' such?"

"They's already worth a penny or two, and we can sell 'em up-river to the other pirates and bag traders."

"But they branded already."

"It don't matter with a bagger. You just get a foot on him and slice it away as soon as it was an oiled patch of garment. Ain't nothing to it. Cut his brand off and sell the bagger up-river, fresh as a daisy. Ain't nothin' simpler."

Little Tommy Barnes was asleep now, and when they waked him up he was scared, and cried, and said he wanted to go home to his ma, and didn't want to be a robber any more. Baggers always made him scared, anyway. He couldn't look at a fella with a bone hanging out without he'd take to wailing.

So they all made fun of him, and called him cry-baby, and that made him mad, and he said he would go straight and tell all the secrets. But Tom give him five cents to keep quiet, and said we would all go home and meet next week, and rob somebody and kill some people and get rich.

Ben Rogers said he couldn't get out much, only Sundays, and so he wanted to begin next Sunday; but all the boys said it would be wicked to do it on Sunday, and that settled the thing. They agreed to get together and fix a day as soon as they could, and then we elected Tom Sawyer first captain and Jo Harper second captain of the Gang, and so started home.

I clumb up the shed and crept into my window just before day was breaking. My new clothes was all greased up and clayey, and I was dog-tired.

CHAPTER III

Well, I got a good going-over in the morning from old Miss Watson on account of my clothes; but the widow she didn't scold, but only cleaned off the grease and clay, and looked so sorry that I thought I would behave awhile if I could. Then Miss Watson she took me in the closet and prayed, but nothing come of it. She told me to pray every day, and whatever I asked for I would get it. But it warn't so. I tried it. Once I got a fish-line, but no hooks. It warn't any good to me without hooks. I tried for the hooks three or four times, but somehow I couldn't make it work. By and by, one day, I asked Miss Watson to try for me, but she said I was a fool. She never told me why, and I couldn't make it out no way.

I set down one time back in the woods, and had a long think about it. I says to myself, if a body can get anything they pray for, why don't Deacon Winn get back the money he lost on pork? Why can't the widow get back her silver snuffbox that was stole? Why can't Miss Watson fat up? Why can't a folk cure themself of the fissythis? That must be the most spoken prayer in the whole world, except for Europe. And yet folks still getting it all the time. No, says I to my self, there ain't nothing in it. I went and told the widow about it, and she said the thing a body could get by praying for it was "spiritual gifts." This was too many for me, but she told me what she meant—I must help other people, and do everything I could for other people, and look out for them all the time, and never think about myself. This was including Miss Watson, as I took it. I went out in the woods and turned it over in my mind a long time, but I couldn't see no advantage about it—except for the other people; so at last I reckoned I wouldn't worry about it any more, but just let it go. Sometimes the widow would take me one side and talk about Providence in a way to make a body's mouth water; but maybe next day Miss Watson would take hold and knock it all down again. I judged I could see that there was two Providences, and a poor chap would stand considerable show with the widow's Providence, but if Miss Watson's got him there warn't no help for him any more. I thought it all out, and reckoned I would belong to the widow's if he wanted me, though I couldn't make out how he was a-going to be any better off then than what he was before, seeing I was so ignorant, and so kind of low-down and ornery.

Pap he hadn't been seen for more than a year, and that was comfortable for me; I didn't want to see him no more. He used to always whale me when he was sober and could get his hands on me; though I used to take to the woods most of the time when he was around. Well, about this time he was found in the river drownded, about twelve mile above town, so people said. They judged it was him, anyway; said this drownded man was just his size, and was ragged, and had uncommon long hair, which was all like pap; but they couldn't make nothing out of the face, because it had been in the water so long it warn't much like a face at all. They said he was floating on his back in the water. They took him and buried him on the bank. But I warn't comfortable long, because I happened to think of something.

I knowed mighty well that a drownded man don't float on his back, but on his face. So I knowed, then, that this warn't pap, but a woman dressed up in a man's clothes. So I was uncomfortable again. I judged the old man would turn up again by and by, though I wished he wouldn't.

We played robber now and then about a month, and then I resigned. All the boys did. We hadn't robbed nobody, hadn't killed any people, hadn't stole any baggers and sold 'em up-river, but only just pretended to do those things. We used to hop out of the woods and go charging down on hog-drivers and women in carts taking garden stuff to market, but we never hived any of them. Tom Sawyer called the hogs "ingots," and he called the turnips and stuff "julery," and we would go to the cave and powwow over what we had done, and how many people we had killed and marked. But I couldn't see no profit in it. One time Tom sent a boy to run about town with a blazing stick, which he called a slogan (which was the sign for the Gang to get together), and then he said he had got secret news by his spies that next day a whole parcel of Spanish merchants and rich A-rabs was going to camp in Cave Hollow with two hundred elephants, and four hundred baggers in fancy suits, and six hundred camels, and over a thousand "sumter" mules, all loaded down with di'monds, and they didn't have only a guard of four hundred soldiers, and so we would lay in ambuscade, as he called it, and kill the lot and scoop the things. He said we must slick up our swords and guns, and get ready. He never could go after even a turnip-cart but he must have the swords and guns all scoured up for it, though they was only lath and broomsticks, and you might scour at them till you rotted, and then they warn't worth a mouthful of ashes more than what they was before. I didn't believe we could lick such a crowd of Spaniards and A-rabs, but I wanted to see the camels and elephants, so I was on hand next day, Saturday, in the ambuscade; and when we got the word we rushed out of the woods and down the hill. But there warn't no Spaniards and A-rabs, and there warn't no camels nor no elephants, nor baggers in fancy suits. It warn't anything but a Sunday-school picnic, and only a primer-class at that. We busted it up, and chased the children up the hollow; but we never got anything but some doughnuts and jam, though Ben Rogers got a rag doll, and Jo Harper got a hymn-book and a tract; and then the teacher charged in, and made us drop everything and cut. I didn't see no di'monds, and I told Tom Sawyer so. He said there was loads of them there, anyway; and he said there was A-rabs there, too, and elephants and things. I said, why couldn't we see them, then? He said if I warn't so ignorant, but had read a book called Don Quixote, I would know without asking. He said it was all done by enchantment. He said there was hundreds of soldiers there, and elephants and treasure, and so on, but we had enemies which he called magicians; and they had turned the whole thing into an infant Sunday-school, just out of spite. I said, all right; then the thing for us to do was to go for the magicians. Tom Sawyer said I was a numskull.

"Why," said he, "a magician could call up a lot of genies, and they would hash you up like nothing before you could say Jack Robinson. They are as tall as a tree and as big around as a church."

"Well," I says, "s'pose we got some genies to help *us*—can't we lick the other crowd then?"

"How you going to get them?"

"I don't know. How do *they* get them?"

"Why, they rub an old tin lamp or an iron ring, and then

the genies come tearing in, with the thunder and lightning a-ripping around and the smoke a-rolling, and everything they're told to do they up and do it. They don't think nothing of pulling a shot-tower up by the roots, and belting a Sunday-school superintendent over the head with it—or any other man."

"Who makes them tear around so?"

"Why, whoever rubs the lamp or the ring. They belong to whoever rubs the lamp or the ring, and they've got to do whatever he says. If he tells them to build a palace forty miles long out of di'monds, and fill it full of chewing-gum, or whatever you want, and fetch an emperor's daughter from China for you to marry, they've got to do it—and they've got to do it before sun-up next morning, too. And more: they've got to waltz that palace around over the country wherever you want it, you understand."

"Well," says I, "I think they are a pack of flat-heads for not keeping the palace themselves 'stead of fooling them away like that. And what's more—if I was one of them I would see a man in Jericho before I would drop my business and come to him for the rubbing of an old tin lamp."

"How you talk, Huck Finn. Why, you'd *have* to come when he rubbed it, whether you wanted to or not."

"What! and I as high as a tree and as big as a church? All right, then; I *would* come; but I lay I'd make that man climb the highest tree there was in the country."

"Shucks, it ain't no use to talk to you, Huck Finn. You don't seem to know anything, somehow—perfect saphead."

I thought all this over for two or three days, and then I reckoned I would see if there was anything in it. I got an old tin lamp and an iron ring, and went out in the woods and rubbed and rubbed till I sweat like an Injun, calculating to build a palace and sell it; but it warn't no use, none of the genies come. So then I judged that all that stuff was only just one of Tom Sawyer's lies. I reckoned he believed in the A-rabs and the elephants, but as for me I think different. It had all the marks of a Sunday-school.

The time I asked Tom why baggers was called baggers, he said it was 'cause their lungs was tore out by the devil and been replaced with burlap satchels. But that was only after he had a minute or two to ponder it over.

"The dead still gotta breathe," he said.

Well, that didn't make a lick of sense to me. So I asked Miss Watson the same question, why baggers was called baggers, and she said it was 'cause you had to tie 'em up in a sack when they expired from the fissythis. That's how you would know if they come back dull, or keeping parts of themselves, or just plain ornery. If they was shriekin' and howlin' and rippin' like wolves to get out of the bag, you had to put 'em down quick, otherwise they'd jump around and start biting everyone. Gotta cut their heads off, or smash up their brains.

That's how it was done.

Most baggers, the ones folks bought and sold and traded, they was tame an' pleasant enough; not much fer wanting anything in the world. But you couldn't know which way they'd be until after they come back. Which is why the bag—so you didn't get hurt in findin' out.

When Sy Booth got the fissythis and was on his last breath, his brothers come and tied him up good and secure and left him that way for the night. In the morning they come back and he was almost like his old self. Quiet and friendly and the like, and not one to say much. So they let him come out of the bag, hobbled his left foot, and gave him as a gift to the Church, which he loved so much in life.

I still saw him from time to time, whacking at the weeds and not doing a very good job of it.

But when Sy Booth's widow succumbed to the pox, just a few weeks after Sy, it was a whole other different story. She come back raging like the devil himself, and if she hadn't been bagged and tied, a few fellas might've lost their eyes.

That's how it goes.

When I went back to Tom Sawyer with this new information, why baggers was called baggers, and how it was they got bagged-up just to see how gentle or not-gentle they come back, he told me he knowed it all along. I told him he was just whistling out of his ear, that he'd said the story about missing lungs and potato sacks, but he denied that on the souls of his ancestors and called me a rock-head.

"Never said no such thing," he said.

Oh, he was always a big fish.

CHAPTER IV

Well, three or four months run along, and it was well into the winter now. I had been to school most all the time and could spell and read and write just a little, and could say the multiplication table up to six times seven is thirty-five, and I don't reckon I could ever get any further than that if I was to live forever. I don't take no stock in mathematics, anyway.

At first I hated the school, but by and by I got so I could stand it. Whenever I got uncommon tired I played hookey, and the hiding I got next day done me good and cheered me up. So the longer I went to school the easier it got to be. I was getting sort of used to the widow's ways, too, and they warn't so raspy on me. Living in a house and sleeping in a bed pulled on me pretty tight mostly, but before the cold weather I used to slide out and sleep in the woods sometimes, and so that was a rest to me. I liked the old ways best, but I was getting so I liked the new ones, too, a little bit. The widow said I was coming along slow but sure, and doing very satisfactory. She said she warn't ashamed of me.

One morning I happened to turn over the salt-cellar at breakfast. I reached for some of it as quick as I could to throw over my left shoulder and keep off the bad luck, but Miss Watson was in ahead of me, and crossed me off. She says, "Take your hands away, Huckleberry; what a mess you are always making!" The widow put in a good word for me, but that warn't going to keep off the bad luck, I knowed that well enough. I started out, after breakfast, feeling worried and shaky, and wondering where it was going to fall on me, and what it was going to be. There is ways to keep off some kinds of bad luck, but this wasn't one of them kind; so I never tried to do anything, but just poked along low-spirited and on the watch-out.

I went down to the front garden and clumb over the stile where you go through the high board fence. There was an inch of new snow on the ground, and I seen somebody's tracks. They had come up from the quarry and stood around the stile a while, and then went on around the garden fence. It was funny they hadn't come in, after standing around so. I couldn't make it out. It was very curious, somehow. I was going to follow around, but I stooped down to look at the tracks first. I didn't notice anything at first, but next I did. There was a cross in the left boot-heel made with big nails, to keep off the devil.

I was up in a second and shinning down the hill. I looked over my shoulder every now and then, but I didn't see nobody. I was at Judge Thatcher's as quick as I could get there. He said:

"Why, my boy, you are all out of breath. Did you come for your interest?"

"No, sir," I says; "is there some for me?"

"Oh, yes, a half-yearly is in last night—over a hundred and fifty dollars. Quite a fortune for you. You had better let me invest it along with your six thousand, because if you take it you'll spend it."

"No, sir," I says, "I don't want to spend it. I don't want it at all—nor the six thousand, nuther. I want you to take it; I want to give it to you—the six thousand and all."

He looked surprised. He couldn't seem to make it out. He says:

"Why, what can you mean, my boy?"

I says, "Don't you ask me no questions about it, please. You'll take it—won't you?"

He says:

"Well, I'm puzzled. Is something the matter?"

"Please take it," says I, "and don't ask me nothing—then I won't have to tell no lies."

He studied a while, and then he says:

"Oho-o! I think I see. You want to *sell* all your property to me—not give it. That's the correct idea."

Then he wrote something on a paper and read it over, and says:

"There; you see it says 'for a consideration.' That means I have bought it of you and paid you for it. Here's a dollar for you. Now you sign it."

So I signed it, and left.

Miss Watson's bagger, Jim, had a hair-ball as big as your fist, which had been took out of the fourth stomach of an ox, and he used to do magic with it, back when he was alive. He said there was a black goblin inside of it, and it knowed everything. And Jim still knowed mostly how to use his magical appliances, for that was one of the parts of himself he managed to keep after meeting the boyo. So I went to him that night and told him pap was here again, for I found his tracks in the snow. What I wanted to know was, what he was going to do, and was he going to stay? Jim got out his hair-ball and said some nonsense over it, and then he held it up and dropped it on the floor. It fell pretty solid, and only rolled about an inch. Jim tried it again, and then another time, and it acted just the same. Jim got down on his knees, and put his ear against it and listened. But it warn't no use; he shook his head, meaning it wouldn't talk. He said sometimes it wouldn't talk without money. He was hard to understand when he talked. Like trying to hear words from the mouth of an old cow while she's chewing. I told him I had an old slick counterfeit quarter that warn't no good because the brass showed through the silver a little, and it wouldn't pass nohow, even if the brass didn't show, because it was so slick it felt greasy, and so that would tell on it every time. (I reckoned I wouldn't say nothing about the dollar I got from the judge.) I said it was pretty bad money, but maybe the hair-ball would take it, because maybe it wouldn't know the difference. Jim smelt it and bit it and rubbed it, and said he would manage so the hair-ball would think it was good. He said he would split open a raw Irish potato and stick the quarter in between and keep it there all night, and next morning you couldn't see no brass, and it wouldn't feel greasy no more, and so anybody in town would take it in a minute, let alone a hair-ball. Well, I knowed a potato would do that before, but I had forgot it.

Jim put the quarter under the hair-ball, and got down and listened again. This time he said the hair-ball was all right. He said it would tell my whole fortune if I wanted it to. I says, go on. So the hair-ball talked to Jim, and Jim told it to me. He says:

"Woof. Yo' ol' fatha don' know yit what he's gon' to do. Gruh. Sometimes he spec he'll go 'way, en den he spec he'll stay. De bes' way is to res' easy en let de ol' man take his own way. Grr. Dey's two angels hoverin' roun' 'bout him. One uv 'em is white en shiny, en da other one is black. De white one gits him to go right a little while, den de black one sail in en bust it all up. A body can't tell yit which one gon' to fetch him at de end. But you's all right. You gon' to have consid'able trouble in yo' life, en consid'able joy. Garrhh. Sometimes you gon' to git hurt, en sometimes you gon' to git sick; but every time you's gwyne to git well agin. Dey's two gals flyin' 'bout you in yo' life. One uv 'em's light en t'other one is dark. One is rich en t'other is po'. You gon' to marry de po' one frust en de rich one by en by. You wants to keep 'way fum de water as much as you kin, en don't run no resk, 'kase it's down in de bills dat you's gon' to git hung. Woof."

Jim sometimes woofed like that. Like an animal. It wasn't no thing with baggers. They made all kinds a'strange noises. If you din' know better, you might think it's the sound of goblins n' spirits n' such.

When I lit my candle and went up to my room that night there sat pap—his own self!

CHAPTER V

I *had* shut the door. Then I turned around and there he was. I used to be scared of him all the time, he tanned me so much. I reckoned I was scared now, too; but in a minute I see I was mistaken—that is, after the first jolt, as you may say, when my breath sort of hitched, he being so unexpected; but right away after I see I warn't scared of him worth bothring about.

He was most fifty, and he looked it. His hair was long and tangled and greasy, and hung down, and you could see his eyes shining through like he was behind vines. It was all black, no gray; so was his long, mixed-up whiskers. There warn't no color in his face, where his face showed; it was white; not like another man's white, but a white to make a body sick, a white to make a body's flesh crawl—a tree-toad white, a fish-belly white. Maybe even bagger white, as I seen some of them go. As for his clothes—just rags, that was all. He had one ankle resting on t'other knee; the boot on that foot was busted, and two of his toes stuck through, and he worked them now and then. I seen plenty of folks come back from Hell who looked a far sight better than he did. His hat was laying on the floor—an old black slouch with the top caved in, like a lid.

I stood a-looking at him; he set there a-looking at me, with his chair tilted back a little. I set the candle down. I noticed the window was up; so he had clumb in by the shed. He kept a-looking me all over. By and by he says:

"Starchy clothes—very. You think you're a good deal of a big-bug, *don't* you?"

"Maybe I am, maybe I ain't," I says.

"Don't you give me none o' your lip," says he. "You've put on considerable many frills since I been away. I'll take you down a peg before I get done with you. You're educated, too, they say—can read and write. You think you're better'n your father, now, don't you, because he can't? *I'll* take it out of you. Who told you you might meddle with such hifalut'n foolishness, hey?—who told you you could?"

"The widow. She told me."

"The widow, hey?—and who told the widow she could put in her shovel about a thing that ain't none of her business?"

"Nobody never told her."

"Well, I'll learn her how to meddle. And looky here—you drop that school, you hear? I'll learn people to bring up a boy to put on airs over his own father and let on to be better'n what *he* is. You lemme catch you fooling around that school again, you hear? Your mother couldn't read, and she couldn't write, nuther, before she died. None of the family couldn't before *they* died. I can't; and here you're a-swelling yourself up like this. I ain't the man to stand it—you hear? Say, lemme hear you read."

I took up a book and begun something about Julius Caesar and the old French wars. Talking about how Gull was divvied up into three pieces. When I'd read about a half a minute, he fetched the book a whack with his hand and knocked it across the house. He says:

"It's so. You can do it. I had my doubts when you told

me. Now looky here; you stop that putting on frills. I won't have it. I'll lay for you, my smarty; and if I catch you about that school I'll tan you good. First you know you'll get religion, too. I never see such a son."

He took up a little blue and yaller picture of some cows and a boy, and says:

"What's this?"

"It's something they give me for learning my lessons good."

He tore it up, and says:

"I'll give you something better—I'll give you a cowhide."

He set there a-mumbling and a-growling a minute, and then he says:

"*Ain't* you a sweet-scented dandy, though? A bed; and bedclothes; and a look'n'-glass; and a piece of carpet on the floor—and your own father got to sleep with the hogs in the tanyard. I never see such a son. I bet I'll take some o' these frills out o' you before I'm done with you. Why, there ain't no end to your airs—they say you're rich. Hey?—how's that?"

"They lie—that's how."

"Looky here—mind how you talk to me; I'm a-standing about all I can stand now—so don't gimme no sass. I've been in town two days, and I hain't heard nothing but about you bein' rich. I heard about it away down the river, too. That's why I come. You git me that money to-morrow—I want it."

"I hain't got no money."

"It's a lie. Judge Thatcher's got it. You git it. I want it."

"I hain't got no money, I tell you. You ask Judge Thatcher; he'll tell you the same."

"All right. I'll ask him; and I'll make him pungle, too, or

I'll know the reason why. Say, how much you got in your pocket? I want it."

"I hain't got only a dollar, and I want that to—"

"It don't make no difference what you want it for—you just shell it out."

He took it and bit it to see if it was good, and then he said he was going down town to get some whisky; said he hadn't had a drink all day. When he had got out on the shed he put his head in again, and cussed me for putting on frills and trying to be better than him; and when I reckoned he was gone he come back and put his head in again, and told me to mind about that school, because he was going to lay for me and lick me if I didn't drop that.

Next day he was drunk, and he went to Judge Thatcher's and bullyragged him, and tried to make him give up the money; but he couldn't, and then he swore he'd make the law force him. And he even hung a beatin' on the judge's favorite bagger, an old negro with just one eye, just to make his point.

The judge and the widow went to law to get the court to take me away from him and let one of them be my guardian; but it was a new judge that had just come, and he didn't know the old man; so he said courts mustn't interfere and separate families if they could help it; said he'd druther not take a child away from its father. So Judge Thatcher and the widow had to quit on the business.

That pleased the old man till he couldn't rest. He said he'd cowhide me till I was black and blue if I didn't raise some money for him. I borrowed three dollars from Judge Thatcher, and pap took it and got drunk, and went a-blowing around and cussing and whooping and carrying on; and beating on folks's helpless baggers, just for fun; and he kept it up all over town, with a tin pan, till most midnight; then they jailed him, and next day they had him before court, and jailed him again for a week. But he said *he* was satisfied; said he was boss of his son, and he'd make it warm for *him*.

When he got out the new judge said he was a-going to make a man of him. So he took him to his own house, and dressed him up clean and nice, and had him to breakfast and dinner and supper with the family, and was just old pie to him, so to speak. And after supper he talked to him about temperance and such things till the old man cried, and said he'd been a fool, and fooled away his life; but now he was a-going to turn over a new leaf and be a man nobody wouldn't be ashamed of, and he hoped the judge would help him and not look down on him. The judge said he could hug him for them words; so he cried, and his wife she cried again; pap said he'd been a man that had always been misunderstood before, and the judge said he believed it. The old man said that what a man wanted that was down was sympathy, and the judge said it was so; so they cried again. And when it was bedtime the old man rose up and held out his hand, and says:

"Look at it, gentlemen and ladies all; take a-hold of it; shake it. There's a hand that was the hand of a hog; but it ain't so no more; it's the hand of a man that's started in on a new life, and'll die before he'll go back. You mark them words—don't forget I said them. It's a clean hand now; shake it—don't be afeard."

So they shook it, one after the other, all around, and cried. The judge's wife she kissed it. Then the old man he signed a pledge—made his mark. The judge said it was the holiest time on record, or something like that. Then they tucked the old man into a beautiful room, which was the spare room, and in the night some time he got powerful thirsty and clumb out on to the porch-roof and slid down a stanchion and traded his new coat for a jug of forty-rod, and clumb back again and had a good old time; and towards daylight he crawled out again, drunk as a fiddler, and rolled off the porch and broke his left arm in two places, and was most froze to death when somebody found him after sun-up. And when they come to look at that spare room they had to take soundings before they could navigate it.

The judge he felt kind of sore. He said he reckoned a body could reform the old man with a shotgun, maybe, but he didn't know no other way. He said it'd be easier to reform a blood-hungry, wild-eyed bagger than it would be to reform pap. Those'd be the truest words I ever heard.

CHAPTER VI

Well, pretty soon the old man was up and around again, and then he went for Judge Thatcher in the courts to make him give up that money, and he went for me, too, for not stopping school. He catched me a couple of times and thrashed me, but I went to school just the same, and dodged him or outrun him most of the time. I didn't want to go to school much before, but I reckoned I'd go now to spite pap. That law trial was a slow business—appeared like they warn't ever going to get started on it; so every now and then I'd borrow two or three dollars off of the judge for him, to keep from getting a cowhiding. Every time he got money he got drunk; and every time he got drunk he raised Cain around town; and every time he raised Cain he got jailed. He was just suited—this kind of thing was right in his line.

He got to hanging around the widow's too much and so she told him at last that if he didn't quit using around there she would make trouble for him. Well, *wasn't* he mad? He said he would show who was Huck Finn's boss. So he watched out for me one day in the spring, and catched me, and took me up the river about three mile in a skiff, and crossed over to the Illinois shore where it was woody and there warn't no houses but an old log hut in a place where the timber was so thick you couldn't find it if you didn't know where it was.

This was fringe territory, y'see, all trees and shadows and full up of baggers that din' belong to nobody. You could see 'em wandering about, not a direction or clue 'bout what they was s'posed to be doin', but not actually causing ruckus, either. Like discarded dogs, I figger. Just roamin' the forest and not knowin' why.

Pap called 'em bunderlugs.

He'd say, "Fetch us water an' mind the bunderlugs, boy."

He kept me with him all the time, and I never got a chance to run off. We lived in that old cabin, and he always locked the door and put the key under his head nights. He had a gun which he had stole, I reckon, and we fished and hunted, and that was what we lived on. Every little while he locked me in and went down to the store, three miles, to the ferry, and traded fish and game for whisky, and fetched it home and got drunk and had a good time, and licked me. The widow she found out where I was by and by, and she sent a man over to try to get hold of me; but pap drove him off with the gun, and it warn't long after that till I was used to being where I was, and liked it—all but the cowhide part.

Still, he could take his aggressions out on the baggers, or bunderlugs, when the occasion took him. He might be mad as spit, but here comes another walkin' dead man in need of a good lickin'. And pap would give it to 'im, too. Them unbranded baggers was anyone's property, and there 'as no penalty for abusin' 'em. Not that pap woulda cared about penalties, nohow.

It was kind of lazy and jolly, laying off comfortable all day, smoking and fishing, and no books nor study. Two months or more run along, and my clothes got to be all rags and dirt, and I didn't see how I'd ever got to like it so well at the widow's, where you had to wash, and eat on a plate, and comb up, and go to bed and get up regular, and be forever bothering over a book, and have old Miss Watson pecking at you all the time. I didn't want to go back no more. I had stopped cussing, because the widow didn't like it; but now I took to it again because pap hadn't no objections. It was pretty good times up in the woods there, take it all around.

One time we had us a bad bunderlug, one of the kinds you wish never've been let out of the bag in the first place. Real dangerous and nasty, like a pack of whupped 'coons all bundled up into one person. All they do is bite and scratch and claw, and there was even a story or two about men having their brains scooped right out of their heads.

Sounds like a story that Tom'd tell, but it wasn't.

It was Arnold the blacksmith what got himself into a scrape with one of them full-baggers. Mean and vicious and just appeared at the shop as if he come out of nowhere. Well, blacksmith was a big ol' lobcock an' didn't reach for his hammer fast enough. Before he even knowed what hit him, that bunderlug was all upon him, and opening his skull to get at the good parts.

I heard that story from the widow.

When pap got himself into the same pickle, he weren't one to take no chances. This bagger come up out of the river, like a monster wrapped up in seaweeds, an' he didn't even have to bare his teeth 'fore pap knowed he was one of the bad ones.

"Get th' ax, boy," he calls out.

He put two shots in the bagger's head, and then hauled 'im up ashore to cut 'im down to smaller pieces. Pap was superstitious like that. He said the bad ones had the powers of the devil, an' it was smart thinkin' to buck 'em up into parts, so they cain't be causin' more troubles.

I din' argue with such thinkin'.

At times like that, pap was nearly bearable.

But by and by pap got too handy with his hick'ry, and I couldn't stand it. I was all over welts. He got to going away so much, too, and locking me in. Once he locked me in and was gone three days. It was dreadful lonesome, an' maybe just a little bit scared, too. I judged he had got drowned, and I wasn't ever going to get out any more. *Yes,* I was right scared. I made up my mind I would fix up some way to leave there. I had tried to get out of that cabin many a time, but I couldn't find no way. There warn't a window to it big enough for a dog to get through. I couldn't get up the chimbly; it was too narrow. The door was thick, solid oak slabs. Pap was pretty careful not to leave a knife or anything in the cabin when he was away; I reckon I had hunted the place over as much as a hundred times; well, I was most all the time at it, because it was about the only way to put in the time. But this time I found something at last; I found an old rusty wood-saw without any handle; it was laid in between a rafter and the clapboards of the roof. I greased it up and went to work. There was an old horse-blanket nailed against the logs at the far end of the cabin behind the table, to keep the wind from blowing through the chinks and putting the candle out. I got under the table and raised the blanket, and went to work to saw a section of the big bottom log out—big enough to let me through. Well, it was a good long job, but I was getting towards the end of it when I heard pap's gun in the woods. Shootin' baggers, again. I got rid of the signs of my work, and dropped the blanket and hid my saw, and pretty soon pap come in.

Pap warn't in a good humor—so he was his natural self. He said he was down town, and everything was going wrong. His lawyer said he reckoned he would win his lawsuit and get the money if they ever got started on the trial; but then there was ways to put it off a long time, and Judge Thatcher knowed how to do it. And he said people allowed there'd be another trial to get me away from him and give me to the widow for my guardian, and they guessed it would win this time. This shook me up considerable, because I didn't want to go back to the widow's any more and be so cramped up and sivilized, as they called it. Then the old man got to cussing, and cussed everything and everybody he could think of, and then cussed them all over again to make sure he hadn't skipped any, and after that he polished off with a kind of a general cuss all round, including a considerable parcel of people which he didn't know the names of, and so called them what's-his-name when he got to them, and went right along with his cussing.

He said he would like to see the widow get me. He said he would watch out, and if they tried to come any such game on him he knowed of a place six or seven mile off to stow me in, where they might hunt till they dropped and they couldn't find me. That made me pretty uneasy again, but only for a minute; I reckoned I wouldn't stay on hand till he got that chance.

The old man made me go to the skiff and fetch the things he had got. There was a fifty-pound sack of corn meal, and a side of bacon, ammunition, and a four-gallon jug of whisky, and an old book and two newspapers for wadding, besides some tow. I toted up a load, and went back and set down on the bow of the skiff to rest. I thought it all over, and I reckoned I would walk off with the gun and some lines, and take to the woods when I run away. I guessed I wouldn't stay in one place, but just tramp right across the country, mostly night times, and hunt and fish to keep alive, and so get so far away that the old man nor the widow couldn't ever find me any more. I judged I would saw out and leave that night if pap got drunk enough, and I reckoned he would. I got so full of it I didn't notice how long I was staying till the old man hollered and asked me whether I was asleep or drownded.

He was takin' a bit ill. Coughing like a dyin' dog and he had an infection up in his nose. Called it the bad humor. He said it smelled awful bad inside his own head and I believed him because I could smell it strong on my own, not anywhere close to his head. It was a strong, foul stench, like sulphur and phossyferous, and running out of him like yellowed water.

Bein' that way just made him more disagreeable than usual.

I got the things all up to the cabin, and then it was about dark. While I was cooking supper the old man took a swig or two and got sort of warmed up, and went to ripping again. He had been drunk over in town, and laid in the gutter all night, and he was a sight to look at. A body would a thought he was bunderlug, for sure—he was all mud and filth and flies and such. Whenever his liquor begun to work he most always went for the govment, this time he says:

"Call this a govment! why, just look at it and see what it's like. Here's the law a-standing ready to take a man's son away from him—a man's own son, which he has had all the trouble and all the anxiety and all the expense of raising. Yes, just as that man has got that son raised at last, and ready to go to work and begin to do suthin' for *him* and give him a rest, the law up and goes for him. And they call *that* govment! I got no rights at all. A damn half-bagger got more rights'n I do, that's the truth of it. That ain't all, nuther. The law backs that old Judge Thatcher up and helps him to keep me out o' my property. Here's what the law does: The law takes a man worth six thousand dollars and up'ards, and jams him into an old trap of a cabin like this, and lets him go round in clothes that ain't fitten for a hog. They call that govment! A man can't get his rights in a govment like this. Sometimes I've a mighty notion to just leave the country for good and all. Yes, and I *told* 'em so; I told old Thatcher so to his face. Lots of 'em heard me, and can tell what I said. Says I, for two cents I'd leave the blamed country and never come a-near it agin. Them's the very words. I says look at my hat—if you call it a hat—but the lid raises up and the rest of it goes down till it's below my chin, and then it ain't rightly a hat at all, but more like my head was shoved up through a jint o' stove-pipe. Look at it, says I—such a hat for me to wear—one of the wealthiest men in this town if I could git my rights.

"Wonderful govment, boy. Van Buren took his oppatunity, din' he, now? Free the negros and make the baggers do all the wuk. That's a fine idea, id'nit? Let the dead folks manage the flowers an' cook the beef, huh? Is that how you run a country? You run a country way a bagger has more rights than a white man? Who says I cain't go a-poundin' on a bagger? Whether he's half-bag or full-bag don' mean a lick to me. Turn the negro loose so he can own what I cain't?

"Oh, yes, this is a wonderful govment, wonderful. Why, looky here. There was a negro there from Ohio—a mulatter, most as white as a white man. He had the whitest shirt on you ever see, too, and the shiniest hat; and there ain't a man in that town that's got as fine clothes as what he had; and he had a gold watch and chain, and a silver-headed cane—the awfulest old gray-headed nabob in the State. And what do you think? They said he was a p'fessor in a college, and could talk all kinds of languages, and knowed everything. And that ain't the wust. They said he could *vote* when he was at home. Well, that let me out. Thinks I, what is the country a-coming to? It was 'lection day, and I was just about to go and vote myself if I warn't too drunk to get there; but when they told me there was a State in this country where they'd let that negro vote, I drawed out. I says I'll never vote agin. Them's the very words I said; they all heard me; and the country may rot for all me—I'll never vote agin as long as I live. And to see the cool way of that negro—why, he wouldn't a give me the road if I hadn't shoved him out o' the way. I says to the people, why ain't this negro put up at auction and sold anymores?—that's what I want to know. And what do you reckon they said? Why, they said they don't sell 'em no more, on account of the fissythis. There, now—that's a specimen. Free negros everywhere—"

Pap was agoing on so he never noticed where his old limber legs was taking him to, so he went head over heels over the tub of salt pork and barked both shins, and the rest of his speech was all the hottest kind of language—mostly hove at the negro and the bagger and the govment, though he give the tub some, too, all along, here and there. He hopped around the cabin considerable, first on one leg and then on the other, holding first one shin and then the other one, and at last he let out with his left foot all of a sudden and fetched the tub a rattling kick. But it warn't good judgment, because that was the boot that had a couple of his toes leaking out of the front end of it; so now he raised a howl that fairly made a body's hair raise, and down he went in the dirt, and rolled there, and held his toes; and the cussing he done then laid over anything he had ever done previous. He said so his own self afterwards. He had heard old Sowberry Hagan in his best days, and he said it laid over him, too; but I reckon that was sort of piling it on, maybe.

After supper pap took the jug, and said he had enough whisky there for two drunks and one delirium tremens. That was always his word. I judged he would be blind drunk in about an hour, and then I would steal the key, or saw myself out, one or t'other. He drank and drank, and tumbled down on his blankets by and by; but luck didn't run my way. He didn't go sound asleep, but was uneasy. He groaned and moaned and thrashed around this way and that for a long time. At last I got so sleepy I couldn't keep my eyes open all I could do, and so before I knowed what I was about I was sound asleep, and the candle burning.

I don't know how long I was asleep, but all of a sudden there was an awful scream and I was up. There was pap looking wild, and skipping around every which way and yelling about baggers. He said they was biting on his legs, trying to eat him up; and then he would give a jump and scream, and say one had bit him on the cheek—but I couldn't see no baggers. He started and run round and round the cabin, hollering "Git him off! Git him off! He's biting me on the neck!" I never see a man look so wild in the eyes. Pretty soon he was all fagged out, and fell down panting; then he rolled over and over wonderful fast, kicking things every which way, and striking and grabbing at the air with his hands, and screaming and saying there was devils and bunderlugs a-hold of him. He wore out by and by, and laid still a while, moaning. Then he laid stiller, and didn't make a sound. I could hear the owls and the wolves away off in the woods, and it seemed terrible still. He was laying over by the corner. By and by he raised up part way and listened, with his head to one side. He says, very low:

"Tramp—tramp—tramp; that's the dead; tramp—tramp—tramp; they'e coming after me, through them woods; but I won't go. Oh, they're here! don't touch me—don't! hands off—they're cold; let go. They want to git me, they do. Oh, let a poor devil alone!"

Then he went down on all fours and crawled off, begging them to let him alone, and he rolled himself up in his blanket and wallowed in under the old pine table, still a-begging; and then he went to crying. I could hear him through the blanket.

By and by he rolled out and jumped up on his feet looking wild, and he see me and went for me. He chased me round and round the place with a clasp-knife, calling me the Angel of Death, and saying he would kill me, and then I couldn't come for him no more. I begged, and told him I was only Huck; but he laughed *such* a screechy laugh, and roared and cussed, and kept on chasing me up. Once when I turned short and dodged under his arm he made a grab and got me by the jacket between my shoulders, and I thought I was gone; but I slid out of the jacket quick as lightning, and saved myself. Pretty soon he was all tired out, and dropped down with his back against the door, and said he would rest a minute and then kill me. He put his knife under him, and said he would sleep and get strong, and then he would see who was who.

So he dozed off pretty soon. By and by I got the old

split-bottom chair and clumb up as easy as I could, not to make any noise, and got down the gun. I slipped the ramrod down it to make sure it was loaded, then I laid it across the turnip barrel, pointing towards pap, and set down behind it to wait for him to stir. And how slow and still the time did drag along.

CHAPTER VII

"Git up! What you 'bout?"

I opened my eyes and looked around, trying to make out where I was. It was after sun-up, and I had been sound asleep. Pap was standing over me looking sour and sick, too. He says:

"What you doin' with this gun?"

I judged he didn't know nothing about what he had been doing, so I says:

"Somebody tried to get in, so I was laying for him."

"Why didn't you roust me out?"

"Well, I tried to, but I couldn't; I couldn't budge you."

"Well, all right. Don't stand there palavering all day, but out with you and see if there's a fish on the lines for breakfast. I'll be along in a minute."

He unlocked the door, and I cleared out up the river-bank. I noticed some pieces of limbs and such things floating down, and a sprinkling of bark; so I knowed the river had begun to rise. Pieces of people in there, too, on account of the graveyards bein' so full that folks was dumping their loved ones in the water, nowadays. And maybe some few of them pieces might still been a little bit alive and attached to some wailin' bagger who got himself too close to the edge.

I reckoned I would have great times now if I was over at the town. The June rise used to be always luck for me;

because as soon as that rise begins here comes cordwood floating down, and pieces of log rafts—sometimes a dozen logs together; so all you have to do is to catch them and sell them to the wood-yards and the sawmill.

I went along up the bank with one eye out for pap and t'other one out for what the rise might fetch along. Well, all at once here comes a canoe; just a beauty, too, about thirteen or fourteen foot long, riding high like a duck. I shot head-first off of the bank like a frog, clothes and all on, and struck out for the canoe. I just expected there'd be somebody laying down in it, because people often done that to fool folks, and when a chap had pulled a skiff out most to it they'd raise up and laugh at him, and a fellow might get an awful fright 'cause of all the unknown, unbranded baggers on the loose out there. But it warn't so this time. It was a drift-canoe sure enough, and I clumb in and paddled her ashore. Thinks I, the old man will be glad when he sees this—she's worth ten dollars. But when I got to shore pap wasn't in sight yet, and as I was running her into a little creek like a gully, all hung over with vines and willows, I struck another idea: I judged I'd hide her good, and then, 'stead of taking to the woods when I run off, I'd go down the river about fifty mile and camp in one place for good, and not have such a rough time tramping on foot.

It was pretty close to the shanty, and I thought I heard the old man coming all the time; but I got her hid; and then I out and looked around a bunch of willows, and there was the old man down the path a piece just drawing a bead on a bird with his gun. So he hadn't seen anything.

When he got along I was hard at it taking up a "trot" line. He abused me a little for being so slow; but I told him I fell in the river, and that was what made me so long.

I knowed he would see I was wet, and then he would be asking questions. We got five catfish off the lines and went home.

I saw a group of young baggers up in the woods. Children, a few of them, what died of the fissythis and now come back. They was no harm or trouble. Didn't seem to know a thing in the world, like their eyes was blind and their ears was deaf and their tongues was dumb; and they just went about in rings, like there was no mind at all, but at least they wasn't mean and ferocious. Maybe they was looking for their mammies. I couldn't guess, really. One of 'em, maybe the eldest of the bunch, looked to be in hard times. His right arm was hanging off by just a string, and the whole side of his face was caved in and festering black.

He wouldn't be long, I figured, until the bugs eat to his brain-stem and turn his lights all out.

While me an' pap laid off after breakfast to sleep up, both of us being about wore out, I got to thinking that if I could fix up some way to keep pap and the widow from trying to follow me, it would be a certainer thing than trusting to luck to get far enough off before they missed me; you see, all kinds of things might happen. Well, I didn't see no way for a while, but by and by pap raised up a minute to drink another barrel of water, and he says:

"Another time a man comes a-prowling round here you roust me out, you hear? Don't matter if he's alive or dead, you rouse me for sure. That man warn't here for no good. I'd a shot him. Next time you roust me out, you hear?"

Then he dropped down and went to sleep again, all sniffly and sniveling and hacking up a tempest; but what he had been saying give me the very idea I wanted. I says to myself, I can fix it now so nobody won't think of following me.

About twelve o'clock we turned out and went along up the bank. The river was coming up pretty fast, and lots of driftwood going by on the rise. By and by along comes part of a log raft—nine logs fast together. We went out with the skiff and towed it ashore. Then we had dinner. Anybody but pap would a waited and seen the day through, so as to catch more stuff; but that warn't pap's style. Nine logs was enough for one time; he must shove right over to town and sell. So he locked me in and took the skiff, and started off towing the raft about half-past three. I judged he wouldn't come back that night. I waited till I reckoned he had got a good start; then I out with my saw, and went to work on that log again. Before he was t'other side of the river I was out of the hole; him and his raft was just a speck on the water away off yonder.

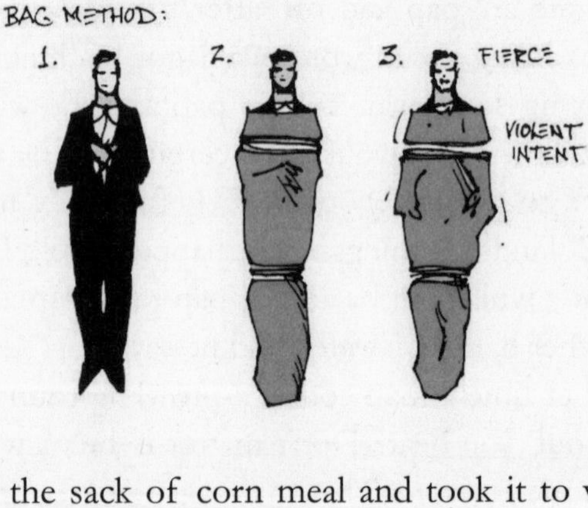

I took the sack of corn meal and took it to where the canoe was hid, and shoved the vines and branches apart and put it in; then I done the same with the side of bacon; then the whisky-jug. I took all the coffee and sugar there was, and all the ammunition; I took the wadding; I took the bucket and gourd; I took a dipper and a tin cup, and my old saw and two blankets, and the skillet and the coffee-pot. I took fish-lines and matches and other things—everything that was worth a cent. I cleaned out the place. I wanted an axe, but there wasn't any, only the one out at the woodpile, which pap liked to use for dis'embering baggers, and I knowed why I was going to leave that, as part o' my scheme. I fetched out the gun, and now I was done.

I had wore the ground a good deal crawling out of the hole and dragging out so many things. So I fixed that as good as I could from the outside by scattering dust on the place, which covered up the smoothness and the sawdust. Then I fixed the piece of log back into its place, and put two rocks under it and one against it to hold it there, for it was bent up at that place and didn't quite touch ground. If you stood four or five foot away and didn't know it was sawed, you wouldn't never notice it; and besides, this was the back of the cabin, and it warn't likely anybody would go fooling around there.

It was all grass clear to the canoe, so I hadn't left a track. I followed around to see. I stood on the bank and looked out over the river. All safe. So I took the gun and went up a piece into the woods, and was hunting around for some birds when I see the dead boy from the day b'fore; all alone now and looking more helpless than ever. I don't know where his playmates got off to and I doubt he did neither. His arm had finally dropped all the way off an' I could see that flies had made something of a hive out of his head.

Well, what's be the right thing for me to do? And what would his mammy tell me to do if she saw her little fella in such a dreadful situation? I knowed that killing a bagger wasn't exactly a crime, and I also knowed a thing or two 'bout what Tom Sawyer called mercy killing.

I shot this fellow and took him into camp.

I took the axe and smashed in the door. I beat it and hacked it considerable a-doing it. I fetched the boy in, and took him back nearly to the table and hacked into his throat with the axe, and laid him down on the ground to bleed; I say ground because it was ground—hard packed, and no boards. Well, next I took an old sack and put a lot of big rocks in it—all I could drag—and I started it from the boy, and dragged it to the door and through the woods down to the river and dumped it in, and down it sunk, out of sight. You could easy see that something had been dragged over the ground. I did wish Tom Sawyer was there; I knowed he would take an interest in this kind of business, and throw in the fancy touches. Nobody could spread himself like Tom Sawyer in such a thing as that.

Well, last I pulled out some of my hair, and blooded the axe good, and stuck it on the back side, and slung the axe in the corner. Then I took up the boy and held him to my breast with my jacket (so he couldn't drip) till I got a good piece below the house and then dumped him into the river. Now I thought of something else. So I went and got the bag of meal and my old saw out of the canoe, and fetched them to the house. I took the bag to where it used to stand, and ripped a hole in the bottom of it with the saw, for there warn't no knives and forks on the place—pap done everything with his clasp-knife about the cooking. Then I carried the sack about a hundred yards across the grass and through the willows east of the house, to a shallow lake that was five mile wide and full of rushes—and ducks too, you might say, in the season. There was a slough or a creek leading out of it on the other side that went miles away, I don't know where, but it didn't go to the river. The meal sifted out and made a little track all the way to the lake. I dropped pap's whetstone there too, so as to look like it had been done by accident. Then I tied up the rip in the meal sack with a string, so it wouldn't leak no more, and took it and my saw to the canoe again.

It was about dark now; so I dropped the canoe down the river under some willows that hung over the bank, and waited for the moon to rise. I made fast to a willow; then I took a bite to eat, and by and by laid down in the canoe to smoke a pipe and lay out a plan. I says to myself, they'll follow the track of that sackful of rocks to the shore and then drag the river for me. And they'll follow that meal track to the lake and go browsing down the creek that leads out of it to find the robbers that killed me and took the things. And if they happen to look in the river, they'll find the body of a boy who just might as well be me, and his face will be so ruined that they won't never tell the difference, anyway. Either way, they won't bother no more about me. All right; I can stop anywhere I want to. Jackson's Island is good enough for me; I know that island pretty well, and nobody ever comes there. And then I can paddle over to town nights, and slink around and pick up things I want. Jackson's Island's the place.

Felt a little bad about the dead boy, but then I reminded myself he was just a bagger, and no more human than a stick.

I was pretty tired, and the first thing I knowed I was asleep. When I woke up I didn't know where I was for a minute. I set up and looked around, a little scared. Then I remembered. The river looked miles and miles across. The moon was so bright I could a counted the drift logs that went a-slipping along, black and still, hundreds of yards out from shore. Everything was dead quiet, and it looked late, and *smelt* late. You know what I mean—I don't know the words to put it in.

I took a good gap and a stretch, and was just going to unhitch and start when I heard a sound away over the water. I listened. Pretty soon I made it out. It was that dull kind of a regular sound that comes from oars working in row-locks when it's a still night. I peeped out through the willow branches, and there it was—a skiff, away across the water. I couldn't tell how many was in it. It kept a-coming, and when it was abreast of me I see there warn't but one man in it. Think's I, maybe it's pap, though I warn't expecting him. He dropped below me with the current, and by and by he came a-swinging up shore in the easy water, and he went by so close I could a reached out the gun and touched him. Well, it *was* pap, sure enough—and sober, too, by the way he laid his oars.

I didn't lose no time. The next minute I was a-spinning down stream soft but quick in the shade of the bank. I made two mile and a half, and then struck out a quarter of a mile or more towards the middle of the river, because pretty soon I would be passing the ferry landing, and people might see me and hail me. I got out amongst the driftwood, and then laid down in the bottom of the canoe and let her float. I laid there, and had a good rest and a smoke out of my pipe, looking away into the sky; not a cloud in it. The sky looks ever so deep when you lay down on your back in the moonshine; I never knowed it before. And how far a body can hear on the water such nights! I heard people talking at the ferry landing. I heard what they said, too—every word of it. One man said it was getting towards the long days and the short nights now. T'other one said *this* warn't one of the short ones, he reckoned—and then they laughed, and he said it over again, and they laughed again; then they waked up another fellow and told him, and laughed, but he didn't laugh; he ripped out something brisk, and said let him alone. The first fellow said he 'lowed to tell it to his old woman—she would think it was pretty good; but he said that warn't nothing to some things he had said in his time. I heard one man say it was nearly three o'clock, and he hoped daylight wouldn't wait more than about a week longer. After that the talk got further and further away, and I couldn't make out the words any more; but I could hear the mumble, and now and then a laugh, too, but it seemed a long ways off.

And I heard the sounds that the bunderlugs make, which isn't always the same as what people make. Sometimes they can still know some of their words, like bagger Jim, but more often it was all mushy mouth and gibberish. I could hear 'em along the shore, back up in the trees, mumbling and groaning and saying pure nonsense. And then I started to think on how there seemed to be so many of them, these days, and not just a handful, like before.

Was I imaginin' that?

It sounded like whole lots out there in the darkness. Scores and scores, lost souls all of 'em, back from Hell and not necessar'ly pleased about it. The mild ones just muttering softly, but the mean ones makin' all that vicious racket. Sounded like piles of mean ones here and there. Sure musta been a whole lot of folks caught the fissythis in the time I been away from town.

I was away below the ferry now. I rose up, and there was Jackson's Island, about two mile and a half down stream, heavy timbered and standing up out of the middle of the river, big and dark and solid, like a steamboat without any lights. There warn't any signs of the bar at the head—it was all under water now.

It didn't take me long to get there. I shot past the head at a ripping rate, the current was so swift, and then I got into the dead water and landed on the side towards the Illinois shore. I run the canoe into a deep dent in the bank that I knowed about; I had to part the willow branches to get in; and when I made fast nobody could a seen the canoe from the outside.

I went up and set down on a log at the head of the island, and looked out on the big river and the black driftwood and away over to the town, three mile away, where there was three or four lights twinkling. A monstrous big lumber-raft was about a mile up stream, coming along down, with a lantern in the middle of it. I watched it come creeping down, and when it was most abreast of where I stood I heard a man say, "Stern oars, there! heave her head to stabboard!" I heard that just as plain as if the man was by my side.

There was a little gray in the sky now; so I stepped into the canoe, safely out of anyone's sight; and laid down for a nap before breakfast.

CHAPTER VIII

The sun was up so high when I waked that I judged it was after eight o'clock. I laid there in the *canoe* and the cool shade thinking about things, and feeling rested and ruther comfortable and satisfied. I went into the woods to take care of business. It was all peaceful and quiet under the trees, and not a soul in sight. I could see the sun out at one or two holes, but mostly it was big trees all about, and gloomy in there amongst them. There was freckled places on the ground where the light sifted down through the leaves, and the freckled places swapped about a little, showing there was a little breeze up there. A couple of squirrels set on a limb and jabbered at me very friendly.

I was powerful lazy and comfortable—didn't want to get up and cook breakfast. Well, I laid down in the forest and was dozing off again when I thinks I hears a deep sound of "boom!" away up the river. I rouses up, and rests on my elbow and listens; pretty soon I hears it again. I hopped up, and went and looked out at a hole in the leaves, and I see a bunch of smoke laying on the water a long ways up—about abreast the ferry. And there was the ferryboat full of people floating along down. I knowed what was the matter now. "Boom!" I see the white smoke squirt out of the ferryboat's side. You see, they was firing cannon over the water, trying to make my carcass come to the top.

I wondered if that li'l bagger boy was gonna surface any minute now.

I was pretty hungry, but it warn't going to do for me to start a fire, because they might see the smoke. So I set there and watched the cannon-smoke and listened to the boom. The river was a mile wide there, and it always looks pretty on a summer morning—so I was having a good enough time seeing them hunt for my remainders if I only had a bite to eat. Well, then I happened to think how they always put quicksilver in loaves of bread and float them off, because they always go right to the drownded carcass and stop there. So, says I, I'll keep a lookout, and if any of them's floating around after me I'll give them a show. I changed to the Illinois edge of the island to see what luck I could have, and I warn't disappointed. A big double loaf come along, and I most got it with a long stick, but my foot slipped and she floated out further. Of course I was where the current set in the closest to the shore—I knowed enough for that. But by and by along comes another one, and this time I won. I took out the plug and shook out the little dab of quicksilver, and set my teeth in. It was "baker's bread"—what the quality eat; none of your low-down corn-pone.

I got a good place amongst the leaves, and set there on a log, munching the bread and watching the ferry-boat, and very well satisfied. And then something struck me. I says, now I reckon the widow or the parson or somebody prayed that this bread would find me, and here it has gone and done it. So there ain't no doubt but there is something in that thing—that is, there's something in it when a body like the widow or the parson prays, but it don't work for me, and I reckon it don't work for only just the right kind.

I lit a pipe and had a good long smoke, and went on

watching. The ferryboat was floating with the current, and I allowed I'd have a chance to see who was aboard when she come along, because she would come in close, where the bread did. When she'd got pretty well along down towards me, I put out my pipe and went to where I fished out the bread, and laid down behind a log on the bank in a little open place. Where the log forked I could peep through.

By and by she come along, and she drifted in so close that they could a run out a plank and walked ashore. Most everybody was on the boat. Pap, and Judge Thatcher, and Bessie Thatcher, and Jo Harper, and Tom Sawyer, and his old Aunt Polly, and Sid and Mary, and plenty more. Everybody was talking about the murder, but the captain broke in and says:

"Look sharp, now; the current sets in the closest here, and maybe he's washed ashore and got tangled amongst the brush at the water's edge. I hope so, anyway."

I didn't hope so. They all crowded up and leaned over the rails, nearly in my face, and kept still, watching with all their might. I could see them first-rate, but they couldn't see me. Then the captain sung out:

"Stand away!" and the cannon let off such a blast right before me that it made me deef with the noise and pretty near blind with the smoke, and I judged I was gone. If they'd a had some bullets in, I reckon they'd a got the corpse they was after. Well, I see I warn't hurt, thanks to goodness. The boat floated on and went out of sight around the shoulder of the island. I could hear the booming now and then, further and further off, and by and by, after an hour, I didn't hear it no more. The island was three mile long. I judged they had got to the foot, and was giving it up. But they didn't yet a while. They turned around the foot of the island and started up the channel on the Missouri side, under steam, and booming once in a while as they went. I crossed over to that side and watched them. When they got abreast the head of the island they quit shooting and dropped over to the Missouri shore and went home to the town.

I knowed I was all right now. Nobody else would come a-hunting after me. I got my traps out of the canoe and made me a nice camp in the thick woods. I made a kind of a tent out of my blankets to put my things under so the rain couldn't get at them. I catched a catfish and haggled him open with my saw, and towards sundown I started my camp fire and had supper. Then I set out a line to catch some fish for breakfast.

When it was dark I set by my camp fire smoking, and feeling pretty well satisfied; but by and by it got sort of lonesome, and so I went and set on the bank and listened to the current swashing along, and counted the stars and drift logs and rafts that come down, and then went to bed; there ain't no better way to put in time when you are lonesome; you can't stay so, you soon get over it.

And so for three days and nights. No difference—just the same thing. But the next day I went exploring around down through the island. I was boss of it; no other folks or baggers or nothin'; it all belonged to me, so to say, and I wanted to know all about it; but mainly I wanted to put in the time. I found plenty strawberries, ripe and prime; and green summer grapes, and green razberries; and the green blackberries was just beginning to show. They would all come handy by and by, I judged.

Well, I went fooling along in the deep woods till I judged I warn't far from the foot of the island. I had my gun along, but I hadn't shot nothing; it was for protection from beasts and nasty bunderlugs; thought I would kill some game nigh home. About this time I mighty near stepped on a good-sized snake, and it went sliding off through the grass and flowers, and I after it, trying to get a shot at it. I clipped along, and all of a sudden I bounded right on to the ashes of a camp fire that was still smoking.

My heart jumped up amongst my lungs. I never waited for to look further, but uncocked my gun and went sneaking back on my tiptoes as fast as ever I could. Every now and then I stopped a second amongst the thick leaves and listened, but my breath come so hard I couldn't hear nothing else. I slunk along another piece further, then listened again; and so on, and so on. If I see a stump, I took it for a man; if I trod on a stick and broke it, it made me feel like a person had cut one of my breaths in two and I only got half, and the short half, too.

When I got to camp I warn't feeling very brash, there warn't much sand in my craw; but I says, this ain't no time to be fooling around. So I got all my traps into my canoe again so as to have them out of sight, and I put out the fire and scattered the ashes around to look like an old last year's camp, and then clumb a tree.

I reckon I was up in the tree two hours; but I didn't see nothing, I didn't hear nothing—I only *thought* I heard and seen as much as a thousand things. Well, I couldn't stay up there forever; so at last I got down, but I kept in the thick woods and on the lookout all the time. All I could get to eat was berries and what was left over from breakfast.

By the time it was night I was pretty hungry. So when it was good and dark I slid out from shore before moonrise and paddled over to the Illinois bank—about a quarter of a mile. I went out in the woods and cooked a supper, and

I had about made up my mind I would stay there all night when I hear a *plunkety-plunk, plunkety-plunk*, and says to myself, horses coming; and next I hear people's voices. I got everything into the canoe as quick as I could, and then went creeping through the woods to see what I could find out. I hadn't got far when I hear a man say:

"We better camp here if we can find a good place; the horses is about beat out. Let's look around."

I didn't wait, but shoved out and paddled away easy. I tied up in the old place, and reckoned I would sleep in the canoe again.

I didn't sleep much. I couldn't, somehow, for thinking. And every time I waked up I thought somebody had me by the neck. So the sleep didn't do me no good. By and by I says to myself, I can't live this way; I'm a-going to find out who it is that's here on the island with me; I'll find it out or bust. Well, I felt better right off.

So I took my paddle and slid out from shore just a step or two, and then let the canoe drop along down amongst the shadows. The moon was shining, and outside of the shadows it made it most as light as day. I poked along well on to an hour, everything still as rocks and sound asleep. Well, by this time I was most down to the foot of the island. A little ripply, cool breeze begun to blow, and that was as good as saying the night was about done. I give her a turn with the paddle and brung her nose to shore; then I got my gun and slipped out and into the edge of the woods. I sat down there on a log, and looked out through the leaves. I see the moon go off watch, and the darkness begin to blanket the river. But in a little while I see a pale streak over the treetops, and knowed the day was coming. So I took my gun and slipped off towards where I had run across that camp fire, stopping every minute or two to listen. But I hadn't no luck somehow; I couldn't seem to find the place. But by and by, sure enough, I catched a glimpse of fire away through the trees. I went for it, cautious and slow. By and by I was close enough to have a look, and there laid a man on the ground. It most give me the fantods. He had a blanket around his head, and his head was nearly in the fire. I set there behind a clump of bushes in about six foot of him, and kept my eyes on him steady. It was getting gray daylight now. Pretty soon he gapped and stretched himself and hove off the blanket, and it was Miss Watson's bagger Jim! I bet I was glad to see him. I says:

"Hello, Jim!" and skipped out.

He bounced up and stared at me wild with his dead doll eyes. Then he drops down on his knees, and puts his hands together and says:

"Is you like me, Huck? Is you a bagger or is you a ghos'? I hain't ever done no harm to a ghos'. I alwuz liked dead people, an' you know I be dead myself. I don' rememba that you catch the pox, so it mus' be that you come out a th' river as a ghos'."

Well, I warn't long making him understand I warn't no damn ghost or bunderlug. Never had no fissythis and surely never got drown or kilt. But I was ever so glad to see Jim. I warn't lonesome now. I told him I warn't afraid of *him* telling the people where I was. I talked along, but he only set there and looked at me; never said nothing. Then I says:

"It's good daylight. Le's get breakfast. Make up your camp fire good."

"What's de use er makin' up de camp fire to cook strawbries en sich truck? But you got a gun, hain't you? Den we kin git sumfn better den strawbries."

"Strawberries and such truck," I says. "Is that what you eatin'?"

"I couldn' git nuffn else," he says.

"Why, how long you been on the island, Jim?"

"I come heah de night arter you's killed."

"What, all that time?"

"Yes—indeedy."

"And ain't you had nothing but that kind of rubbage to eat?"

"No, sah—nuffn else."

"Well, is you starved?"

"I reck'n I could eat a hoss. I think I could. How long you ben on de islan'?"

"Since the night I got killed."

"No! W'y, what has you lived on? But you got a gun. Oh, yes, you got a gun. Dat's good. Now you kill sumfn en I'll make up de fire."

I don' figger to un'erstand how it all warks. Baggers don' need to eat, but they thinks they do. It's what Tom's Aunt Polly called a pattern; how they remembers eatin' so that's what they thinks they s'posed to be doing. Instink is another word for it. These baggers, these half baggers, th' good ones, they still likes to pretend they alive like ever'one else. An' so they eat and do the other thing too, except what comes out the bottom end idn't the same as what comes out of livin' folk. It's just like reg'lar food, but all half-chewed and kinda dry; like their body never got a dang thing out of it.

An' Jim was just like that, too. He warn't hungry, only thinks he was hungry. Bein' dead he don' need to eat, but no matter how much I tells it to him he don't understand a lick.

He says, "A hoss, Huck. I tells you I'd eat one."

So we went over to where the canoe was, and while he built a fire in a grassy open place amongst the trees, I fetched meal and bacon and coffee, and coffee-pot and frying-pan, and sugar and tin cups, and the bagger was set back considerable, because he reckoned it was all done with witchcraft. I catched a good big catfish, too, and Jim cleaned him with his knife, and fried him.

When breakfast was ready we lolled on the grass and eat it smoking hot. Jim laid it in with all his might, for he was most about starved. Then when we had got pretty well stuffed, we laid off and lazied. By and by Jim says:

"But looky here, Huck, who wuz it dat 'uz killed in dat shanty ef it warn't you?"

Then I told him the whole thing, how it was a li'l bunderlug fella who was already mostly roont, and he said it was smart. He said Tom Sawyer couldn't get up no better plan than what I had. He said:

"If he 'uz already mostly roont, you did him a fava."

"I reckon I did."

"No good kickin' 'round like that wif parts missin'. You got no dignity left. If I ever got to be like dat, missin' parts an' wif a broken head, I'd a ask some'un to finish me off fo' certain."

Then I says:

"How do you come to be here, Jim, and how'd you get here?"

He looked pretty uneasy, and didn't say nothing for a minute. Then he says:

"Maybe I better not tell."

"Why, Jim?"

"Well, dey's reasons. But you wouldn' tell on me ef I uz to tell you, would you, Huck?"

"Blamed if I would, Jim."

"Well, I b'lieve you, Huck. I—I run off."

"Jim!"

"But mind, you said you wouldn' tell—you know you said you wouldn' tell, Huck."

"Well, I did. I said I wouldn't, and I'll stick to it. Honest *injun*, I will. People would call me a low-down ungrateful zomby-lover and despise me for it—but that don't make no difference. I ain't a-going to tell, and I ain't a-going back there, anyways. So, now, le's know all about it."

"Well, you see, it 'uz dis way. Ole missus—dat's Miss Watson—she pecks on me all de time, en treats me pooty rough, but she awluz said she wouldn' sell me down to Orleans. But I noticed dey wuz a bagger trader roun' de place considable lately, en I begin to git oneasy. Well, one night I creeps to de do' pooty late, en de do' warn't quite shet, en I hear old missus tell de widder she gwyne to sell me down to Orleans, but she didn' want to, but she could git eight hund'd dollars for me, en it 'uz sich a big stack o' money she couldn' resis'. De widder she try to git her to say she wouldn' do it, but I never waited to hear de res'. I lit out mighty quick, I tell you.

"I tuck out en shin down de hill, en 'spec to steal a skift 'long de sho' som'ers 'bove de town, but dey wuz people a-stirring yit, so I hid in de ole tumble-down cooper-shop on de bank to wait for everybody to go 'way. Well, I wuz dah all night. Dey wuz somebody roun' all de time. 'Long 'bout six in de mawnin' skifts begin to go by, en 'bout eight er nine every skift dat went 'long wuz talkin' 'bout how yo' pap come over to de town en say you's killed. Dese las' skifts wuz full o' ladies en genlmen a-goin' over for to see de place. Sometimes dey'd pull up at de sho' en take a res' b'fo' dey started acrost, so by de talk I got to know all 'bout de killin'. I 'uz powerful sorry you's killed, Huck, but I ain't no mo' now.

"I laid dah under de shavin's all day. I 'uz hungry, but I warn't afeard; bekase I knowed ole missus en de widder wuz goin' to start to de camp-meet'n' right arter breakfas' en be gone all day, en dey knows I goes off wid de cattle 'bout daylight, so dey wouldn' 'spec to see me roun' de place, en so dey wouldn' miss me tell arter dark in de evenin'. De yuther servants wouldn' miss me, kase dey'd shin out en take holiday soon as de ole folks 'uz out'n de way.

"Well, when it come dark I tuck out up de river road, en went 'bout two mile er more to whah dey warn't no houses. I'd made up my mine 'bout what I's agwyne to do. You see, ef I kep' on tryin' to git away afoot, de dogs 'ud track me; ef I stole a skift to cross over, dey'd miss dat skift, you see, en dey'd know 'bout whah I'd lan' on de yuther side, en whah to pick up my track. So I says, a raff is what I's arter; it doan' *make* no track.

"I see a light a-comin' roun' de p'int bymeby, so I wade' in en shove' a log ahead o' me en swum more'n half way acrost de river, en got in 'mongst de drift-wood, en kep' my head down low, en kinder swum agin de current tell de raff come along. Den I swum to de stern uv it en tuck a-holt. It clouded up en 'uz pooty dark for a little while. So I clumb up en laid down on de planks. De men 'uz all 'way yonder in de middle, whah de lantern wuz. De river wuz a-risin', en dey wuz a good current; so I reck'n'd 'at by fo' in de mawnin' I'd be twenty-five mile down de river, en den I'd slip in jis b'fo' daylight en swim asho', en take to de woods on de Illinois side.

"But I didn' have no luck. When we 'uz mos' down to de

head er de islan' a man begin to come aft wid de lantern, I see it warn't no use fer to wait, so I slid overboard en struck out fer de islan'. Well, I had a notion I could lan' mos' anywhers, but I couldn't—bank too bluff. I 'uz mos' to de foot er de islan' b'fo' I found' a good place. I went into de woods en jedged I wouldn' fool wid raffs no mo', long as dey move de lantern roun' so. I had my pipe en a plug er dog-leg, en some matches in my cap, en dey warn't wet, so I 'uz all right."

"And so you ain't had no meat nor bread to eat all this time?"

"I gots powerful appytite, Huck."

"You dasn't even need to eat, Jim. I keep tellin' you."

"But you don't tell it to muh body, which makes me want to crave after mos' unnatural urges. I wants to eat things whuch th' Lord says you betta neva be eatin', if you know what I'm sayin'."

"Like Philistines an' such?"

"That'll do fine."

"Yer a strange bird, Jim."

"I wunderd it."

"Well, that's so. You've had to keep in the woods all the time, of course. Did you hear 'em shooting the cannon?"

"Oh, yes. I knowed dey was arter you. I see um go by heah—watched um thoo de bushes."

Some young birds come along, flying a yard or two at a time and lighting. Jim said it was a sign it was going to rain. He said it was a sign when young chickens flew that way, and so he reckoned it was the same way when young birds done it. I was going to catch some of them, but Jim wouldn't let me. He said it was death. He said his father laid mighty sick once, and some of them catched a bird, and his old granny said his father would die, and he did.

And Jim said you mustn't count the things you are going to cook for dinner, because that would bring bad luck. The same if you shook the table-cloth after sundown. And he said if a man owned a beehive and that man died, the bees must be told about it before sun-up next morning, or else the bees would all weaken down and quit work and die. Jim said bees wouldn't sting idiots; but I didn't believe that, because I had tried them lots of times myself, and they wouldn't sting me.

I had heard about some of these things before, but not all of them. Jim knowed all kinds of signs. He said he knowed most everything. Some things he knew when he was alive, and some things he din' know until after he met the devil. I said it looked to me like all the signs was about bad luck, and so I asked him if there warn't any good-luck signs. He says:

"Mighty few—an' *dey* ain't no use to a body. What you want to know when good luck's a-comin' for? Want to keep it off?" And he said: "Ef you's got hairy arms en a hairy breas', it's a sign dat you's agwyne to be rich. Well, dey's some use in a sign like dat, 'kase it's so fur ahead. You see, maybe you's got to be po' a long time fust, en so you might git discourage' en kill yo'sef 'f you didn' know by de sign dat you gwyne to be rich bymeby."

"Have you got hairy arms and a hairy breast, Jim?"

"What's de use to ax dat question? Don't you see I has?"

"Well, are you rich?"

"No, but I ben rich wunst, and gwyne to be rich agin. Wunst I had foteen dollars, but I tuck to specalat'n', en got busted out."

"What did you speculate in, Jim?"

"Well, fust I tackled stock."

"What kind of stock?"

"Why, live stock—cattle, you know. I put ten dollars in a cow. But I ain' gwyne to resk no mo' money in stock. De cow up 'n' died on my han's."

"So you lost the ten dollars."

"No, I didn't lose it all. I on'y los' 'bout nine of it. I sole de hide en taller for a dollar en ten cents."

"You had five dollars and ten cents left. Did you speculate any more?"

"Yes. You know that one-laigged negro dat friends wit' Misto Bradish? Well, he sot up a bank, en say anybody dat put in a dollar would git fo' dollars mo' at de en' er de year. Well, all de negros went in, but dey didn't have much. I wuz de on'y one dat had much. So I stuck out for mo' dan fo' dollars, en I said 'f I didn' git it I'd start a bank mysef. Well, o' course dat negro want' to keep me out er de business, bekase he says dey warn't business 'nough for two banks, so he say I could put in my five dollars en he pay me thirty-five at de en' er de year.

"So I done it. Den I reck'n'd I'd inves' de thirty-five dollars right off en keep things a-movin'. Dey wuz a characta name' Bob, dat had ketched a wood-flat, en his partner didn' know it; en I bought it off'n him en told him to take de thirty-five dollars when de en' er de year come; but somebody stole de wood-flat dat night, en nex day de one-laigged negro say de bank's busted. So dey didn' none uv us git no money."

"What did you do with the ten cents, Jim?"

"Well, I 'uz gwyne to spen' it, but I had a dream, en de dream tole me to give it to a negro name' Balum—Balum's Ass dey call him for short; he's one er dem chuckleheads, you know. But he's lucky, dey say, en I see I warn't lucky. De dream say let Balum inves' de ten cents en he'd make a raise for me. Well, Balum he tuck de money, en when he wuz in church he hear de preacher say dat whoever give to de po' len' to de Lord, en boun' to git his money back a hund'd times. So Balum he tuck en give de ten cents to de po', en laid low to see what wuz gwyne to come of it."

"Well, what did come of it, Jim?"

"Nuffn never come of it. I couldn' manage to k'leck dat money no way; en Balum he couldn'. I ain' gwyne to len' no mo' money 'dout I see de security. Boun' to git yo' money back a hund'd times, de preacher says! Ef I could git de ten *cents* back, I'd call it squah, en be glad er de chanst."

"Well, it's all right anyway, Jim; I don' think a bagger's allowed to be rich. You ain't allowed to own nothin' at all, as I un'erstand."

"Mebby it could happen."

"Mebby."

"Yes; en I's rich now, come to look at it. I owns mysef, en I's wuth eight hund'd dollars. I wisht I had de money, I wouldn' want no mo'."

Well, I din' know if he was still worth no eight hundred, but I din' tell him so. I reckon wit' so many bunderlugs runnin' round the bushes, a fella might as well go an' snatch up the one he wants an' not hafta pay a red cent. But then, too, Jim still had most o' himself an' could be put to good work. So mebby he was worth somethin', even if it warn't no eight hundred dollars.

Jim said eight hundred is what a good negro used to be worth.

I told him negros was all abolitioned on account of th' fissythis, an' one thing din' have nothin' to do with th' other. Negros was happy all up an' down the country, free for th' last two years. They was havin' their own property and incomes, and makin' babies to beat the band.

Negros thanks God for the fissythis, calls it the equalizer of men. An' I heard too of negros buyin' an' sellin' in baggers, which is fair cuz these slaves finally gets to own slaves an' they gets to feelin' impo'tant about it. Jim says:

"I uz a slave when I uz alive, an' then I get dead, an' I still gets to be a slave. Th' warld is a funny place."

Right 'bout this time the friendship boat arrived in New York. Joe Sink an' a bunch of negros mutineed an' turned out ornery, sayin' they wasn't gonna be anyone's slaves. And folks had to explain it to 'em that nobody wanted black slaves anyway; an' that negros'd been reprieved by bunderlugs; an' the whole thing was a big misunderstandin; and the President got himself involved; and someone tol' Joe Sink that there wouldn't even hafta be a trial, except for the fact that he went an' killed the ship's cook. An' someone else said the whole affair was a travesty anyway, and no one was supposed to be transporting African negros in the first place; and then there were all these men with pie on their faces; and the whole affair turned out to be a big ol' farce.

But me and Jim didn't know nothin' about it, at the time. How could we? Jim woulda liked thet story. He woulda called it excitin'.

CHAPTER IX

Jim had a bad smell if you sat with him for too long. I had a pretty bad smell, myself, but it wasn't nothing like Jim. Miss Watson used ta put the bucket to him an' make him stand in the shed 'til he uz dry. Myself, I always found it was just better to not be too close to him, or to stand in the breeze, or just to keep on movin'.

I wanted to go and look at a place right about the middle of the island that I'd found when I was exploring; so we started and soon got to it, because the island was only three miles long and a quarter of a mile wide.

This place was a tolerable long, steep hill or ridge about forty foot high. We had a rough time getting to the top, the sides was so steep and the bushes so thick. We tramped and clumb around all over it, and by and by found a good big cavern in the rock, most up to the top on the side towards Illinois. The cavern was as big as two or three rooms bunched together, and Jim could stand up straight in it. It was cool in there. Jim was for putting our traps in there right away, but I said we didn't want to be climbing up and down there all the time.

Jim said if we had the canoe hid in a good place, and had all the traps in the cavern, we could rush there if anybody was to come to the island, and they would never find us without dogs. And, besides, he said them little birds had said it was going to rain, and did I want the things to get wet?

So we went back and got the canoe, and paddled up abreast the cavern, and lugged all the traps up there. Then we hunted up a place close by to hide the canoe in, amongst the thick willows. We took some fish off of the lines and set them again, and begun to get ready for dinner.

The door of the cavern was big enough to roll a hogshead in, and on one side of the door the floor stuck out a little bit, and was flat and a good place to build a fire on. So we built it there and cooked dinner.

We spread the blankets inside for a carpet, and eat our dinner in there. We put all the other things handy at the back of the cavern. Pretty soon it darkened up, and begun to thunder and lighten; so the birds was right about it. Directly it begun to rain, and it rained like all fury, too, and I never see the wind blow so. It was one of these regular summer storms. It would get so dark that it looked all blue-black outside, and lovely; and the rain would thrash along by so thick that the trees off a little ways looked dim and spider-webby; and here would come a blast of wind that would bend the trees down and turn up the pale underside of the leaves; and then a perfect ripper of a gust would follow along and set the branches to tossing their arms as if they was just wild; and next, when it was just about the bluest and blackest—FST! it was as bright as glory, and you'd have a little glimpse of tree-tops a-plunging about away off yonder in the storm, hundreds of yards further than you could see before; dark as sin again in a second, and now you'd hear the thunder let go with an awful crash, and then go rumbling, grumbling, tumbling, down the sky towards the under side of the world, like rolling empty barrels down stairs—where it's long stairs and they bounce a good deal, you know.

"Jim, this is nice," I says. "I wouldn't want to be nowhere else but here. Pass me along another hunk of fish and some hot corn-bread."

"Well, you wouldn't a ben here 'f it hadn't a ben for Jim. You'd a ben down dah in de woods widout any dinner, en gittn' mos' drownded, too; dat you would, honey. Chickens knows when it's gwyne to rain, en so do de birds, chile."

The river went on raising and raising for ten or twelve days, till at last it was over the banks. The water was three or four foot deep on the island in the low places and on the Illinois bottom. On that side it was a good many miles wide, but on the Missouri side it was the same old distance across—a half a mile—because the Missouri shore was just a wall of high bluffs.

Daytimes we paddled all over the island in the canoe. It was mighty cool and shady in the deep woods, even if the sun was blazing outside. We went winding in and out amongst the trees, and sometimes the vines hung so thick we had to back away and go some other way. Well, on every old broken-down tree you could see rabbits and snakes and such things; and when the island had been overflowed a day or two they got so tame, on account of being hungry, that you could paddle right up and put your hand on them if you wanted to; but not the snakes and turtles—they would slide off in the water. The ridge our cavern was in was full of them. We could a had pets enough if we'd wanted them.

One night we catched a little section of a lumber raft—nice pine planks. It was twelve foot wide and about fifteen or sixteen foot long, and the top stood above water six or seven inches—a solid, level floor. We could see saw-logs go by in the daylight sometimes, but we let them go; we didn't show ourselves in daylight.

Another night when we was up at the head of the island, just before daylight, here comes a frame-house down, on the west side. She was a two-story, and tilted over considerable. We paddled out and got aboard—clumb in at an upstairs window. But it was too dark to see yet, so we made the canoe fast and set in her to wait for daylight.

The light begun to come before we got to the foot of the island. Then we looked in at the window. We could make out a bed, and a table, and two old chairs, and lots of things around about on the floor, and there was clothes hanging against the wall. There was something leaning against the wall in the far corner that looked like a man. So Jim says:

"Hello, you!"

But it didn't budge. So I hollered again, and then Jim says:

"De man ain't asleep—he's dead. You hold still—I'll go en see."

He went over, and touched him and looked, and says:

"It's a dead man. Yes, indeedy; naked, too. He's all taken by pox; his nose still draining awfulness. But he got himself a bullet-hole too, like some'un had a cause to shoot 'im. I reck'n he's ben dead two er three days. You best stay apart, Huck, and doan' look at his face—it's too gashly."

I didn't look at him at all. Jim throwed some old rags over him, but he needn't done it; I didn't want to see him. I went into t'other room to look for salvageables. There was heaps of old greasy cards scattered around over the floor, and old whisky bottles, and a couple of masks made out of black cloth; and all over the walls was the ignorantest kind of words and pictures made with charcoal. There was two old dirty calico dresses, and a sun-bonnet, and some women's underclothes hanging against the wall, and some men's clothing, too.

I heard Jim cry out, and other sounds, too. I was too afeared to go look. I knowed without knowin' what was goin' on. That dead man wasn't all completely dead. He was a bagger, like Jim, and mebby full-bag, too. Not gentle and still keeping pieces of his former self. This fella was mean, and he shrieked like the boyo. Jim yells:

"You stay *'way,* Huck! You just stay 'way!"

An' I heard things breaking, and glass going smash, and the sound of bodies rolling against the wall and across the floor.

"He's a hungry one!" Jim yells.

I crouched in the corner and put my hands over my ears. I didn't know what else to do. Fright overtook me, I reckon. No control over that.

Soon enough all went quiet and there came a splashing noise. Some'un went into the drink. An' the body that came around the corner could have been either one o' them, but I was damn pleased to see it was Jim. Says he:

"I broke his neck, surely I did. An' now he be on his way to the bottom of the river, an' den back to Hell."

So, we put the things I collected into the canoe—it might come good. There was a boy's old speckled straw hat on the floor; I took that, too. And there was a bottle that had had milk in it, and it had a rag stopper for a baby to suck. We would a took the bottle, but it was broke. There was a seedy old chest, and an old hair trunk with the hinges broke. They stood open, but there warn't nothing left in them that was any account. The way things was scattered about we reckoned the people left in a hurry, and warn't fixed so as to carry off most of their stuff.

Jim had scrapes down his one cheek and a long trail o' yella snot down the other. He said that was courtesy of the man who was now in th' river. He said he was a nasty one, and wouldn't a made a good servant fer anyone. He says:

"Mind that some o' dem might try to eat you, Huck."

I says, "Thet's what pap used to think. I figgered he was all full up of beans. Why would anyone want ta eat somebody?"

"It a bad desire, I tell you."

"Would you wan' eat me, Jim?"

"No, but I could 'magine it."

"'Magine eating me? Thet's bunky."

"I wouldn' do it 'cause you my friend an' I be civilized an' all, but I be lyin' to you if I said the' warn't pat o' me that din' think it might be nice to take jus' a li'l taste."

"Lay off now, Jim,'fore I bean you one."

He laughed 'bout that.

We got an old tin lantern, and a butcher-knife without any handle, and a bran-new Barlow knife worth two bits in any store, and a lot of tallow candles, and a tin candlestick, and a gourd, and a tin cup, and a ratty old bedquilt off the bed, and a reticule with needles and pins and beeswax and buttons and thread and all such truck in it, and a hatchet and some nails, and a fishline as thick as my little finger with some monstrous hooks on it, and a roll of buckskin, and a leather dog-collar, and a horseshoe, and some vials of medicine that didn't have no label on them; and just as we was leaving I found a tolerable good curry-comb, and Jim he found a ratty old fiddle-bow, and a wooden leg. The straps was broke off of it, but, barring that, it was a good enough leg, though it was too long for me and not long enough for Jim, and we couldn't find the other one, though we hunted all around.

And so, take it all around, we made a good haul. When we was ready to shove off we was a quarter of a mile below the island, and it was pretty broad day; so I made Jim lay down in the canoe and cover up with the quilt, because if he set up people could tell he was a bagger a good ways off, mostly on account of his eyes, and the way the flies buzzed around his big dead head. I paddled over to the Illinois shore, and drifted down most a half a mile doing it. I crept up the dead water under the bank, and hadn't no accidents and didn't see nobody. We got home all safe.

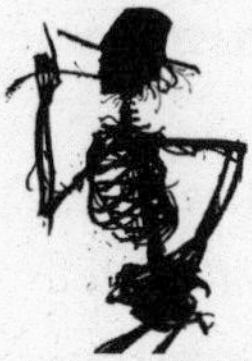

CHAPTER X

After breakfast I wanted to talk more about the bagger in the house and guess out how he come to be like that, whether he was more dead from the bullet or more dead from the fissythis, and if he was still walkin' around on the bottom of the river, but Jim didn't want to. He said it would fetch bad luck; and besides, he said, he might come and ha'nt us; he said a man that warn't buried was more likely to go a-ha'nting around than one that was planted and comfortable. That sounded pretty reasonable, so I didn't say no more; but I couldn't keep from studying over it and wishing I knowed who shot the man, and what they done it for.

"He not alive on da river bottom," Jim said. "I kin tell you dat."

We rummaged the clothes we'd got, and found eight dollars in silver sewed up in the lining of an old blanket overcoat. Jim said he reckoned the people in that house stole the coat, because if they'd a knowed the money was there they wouldn't a left it. I said I reckoned they killed him, too; but Jim didn't want to talk about that. I says:

"Now you think it's bad luck; but what did you say when I fetched in the snake-skin that I found on the top of the ridge day before yesterday? You said it was the worst bad luck in the world to touch a snake-skin with my hands. Well, here's your bad luck! We've raked in all this truck and eight dollars besides. I wish we could have some bad luck like this every day, Jim."

"Never you mind, honey, never you mind. Don't you git too peart. It's a-comin'. Mind I tell you, it's a-comin'."

It did come, too. It was a Tuesday that we had that talk. Well, after dinner Friday we was laying around in the grass at the upper end of the ridge, and got out of tobacco. I went to the cavern to get some, and found a rattlesnake in there. I killed him, and curled him up on the foot of Jim's blanket, ever so natural, thinking there'd be some fun when Jim found him there. Well, by night I forgot all about the snake, and when Jim flung himself down on the blanket while I struck a light the snake's mate was there, and bit him.

He didn't yell or nothin'.

He was barefooted, and the snake bit him right on the heel. That all comes of my being such a fool as to not remember that wherever you leave a dead snake its mate always comes there and curls around it. Jim told me to chop off the snake's head and throw it away, and then skin the body and roast a piece of it. I done it, and he eat it and said it would help take away his other cravens. He made me take off the rattles and tie them around his wrist, too. He said that was a good-luck charm and Lord knew we needed more good luck. Then I slid out quiet and throwed the snakes clear away amongst the bushes; for I warn't going to let Jim find out it was all my fault, not if I could help it. I as't him:

"Don' it hurt?"

He says, "I don' feel too much, Huck. Stuff is all dead inside o' me. Sumtimes I'm not even sure I'm here. I gots to touch myself to know, an' even dat don't always work."

I know from pap's stories that getting' bit by a rattler

feels like someone stickin' a white-hot poker up inside you. An' here was Jim just sittin' like a dull lobcock, not really very upset at all, like pap woulda bin.

Still, Jim was troubled a bit. He reminded me of the young bagger what I shot, an' how he was all rough and missin' parts. He says he had to worry 'bout the same problem for himself. He says, "If'n my foot gits 'nfected, it might just fall off of me. And then I be hoppin' 'round like a fool."

I says, "Aren't you alreafy infected? With death, I mean?"

"I doubt it's the same, Huck."

"It smells about the same to me."

Jim sucked and sucked at the whisky jug, thinkin' that fillin' himself with spirit might ward off the bad humors. His foot swelled up a wee bit, and some black juice oozed out. He din' get drunk though, an' when he relieved himself it was still pure whisky what came out of him.

Jim stayed laid up for four days and nights. He din' wanna take no chances. He said he wanted to keep his feet as long as possible. There was no serious swelling. I made up my mind I wouldn't ever take a-holt of a snake-skin again with my hands, now that I see what had come of it. Jim said he reckoned I would believe him next time. And he said that handling a snake-skin was such awful bad luck that maybe we hadn't got to the end of it yet. He said he druther see the new moon over his left shoulder as much as a thousand times than take up a snake-skin in his hand. Well, I was getting to feel that way myself, though I've always reckoned that looking at the new moon over your left shoulder is one of the carelessest and foolishest things a body can do. Old Hank Bunker done it once, and bragged about it; and in less than two years he got drunk and fell off of the shot-tower, and spread himself out so that he was just a kind of a layer, as you may say; and they slid him edgeways between two barn doors for a coffin, and buried him so, so they say, but I didn't see it. Pap told me. But anyway it all come of looking at the moon that way, like a fool.

Well, the days went along, and the river went down between its banks again; and about the first thing we done was to bait one of the big hooks with a skinned rabbit and set it and catch a catfish that was as big as a man, being six foot two inches long, and weighed over two hundred pounds. We couldn't handle him, of course; he would a flung us into Illinois. We just set there and watched him rip and tear around till he drownded. We found a brass button in his stomach and a round ball, and lots of rubbage. We split the ball open with the hatchet, and there was a spool in it. Jim said he'd had it there a long time, to coat it over so and make a ball of it. It was as big a fish as was ever catched in the Mississippi, I reckon. Jim said he hadn't ever seen a bigger one. He would a been worth a good deal over at the village. They peddle out such a fish as that by the pound in the market-house there; everybody buys some of him; his meat's as white as snow and makes a good fry.

Next morning I said it was getting slow and dull, and I wanted to get a stirring up some way. I said I reckoned I would slip over the river and find out what was going on. Jim liked that notion; but he said I must go in the dark and look sharp. Then he studied it over and said, couldn't I put on some of them old things and dress up like a girl? That was a good notion, too. So we shortened up one of the calico gowns, and I turned up my trouser-legs to my knees and got into it. Jim hitched it behind with the hooks, and it was a fair fit. I put on the sun-bonnet and tied it under my chin, and then for a body to look in and see my face was like looking down a joint of stove-pipe. Jim said nobody would know me, even in the daytime, hardly. I practiced around all day to get the hang of the things, and by and by I could do pretty well in them, only Jim said I didn't walk like a girl; and he said I must quit pulling up my gown to get at my britches-pocket. I took notice, and done better.

I started up the Illinois shore in the canoe just after dark.

I started across to the town from a little below the ferry-landing, and the drift of the current fetched me in at the bottom of the town. I tied up and started along the bank. There was a light burning in a little shanty that hadn't been lived in for a long time, and I wondered who had took up quarters there. I slipped up and peeped in at the window. There was a woman about forty year old in there knitting by a candle that was on a pine table. I didn't know her face; she was a stranger, for you couldn't start a face in that town that I didn't know. Now this was lucky, because I was weakening; I was getting afraid I had come; people might know my voice and find me out. But if this woman had been in such a little town two days she could tell me all I wanted to know; so I knocked at the door, and made up my mind I wouldn't forget I was a girl.

She had herself a half-bagger. An old man who was missing his legs b'neath the knees. The very thing Jim feared for himself. An' he just sat on the porch, useless like a sack of mulch, baking in the sun and not even botherin' to swat the flies offa himself. I couldn't imagine the point of keeping a bagger like that one. What could he do? Not much, to my mind. Not much at all.

CHAPTER XI

"Come in," says the woman, and I did. She says: "Take a cheer."

I done it. She looked me all over with her little shiny eyes, and says:

"What might your name be?"

"Sarah Williams."

"Where 'bouts do you live? In this neighborhood?"

"No'm. In Hookerville, seven mile below. I've walked all the way and I'm all tired out. I see you got yourself a bagger for a doorman."

"It's my father, sad to say. I don't work him, but I'm loathe to finish him off, either. Too attached to him. He don't even know where he is. There's not much of himself left, but he don't bite."

"I don't bite neither, ma'am. I'm fancy and I'm civilized."

"Hungry, too, I reckon, after such a trek. I'll find you something."

"No'm, I ain't hungry. I was so hungry I had to stop two miles below here at a farm; so I ain't hungry no more. It's what makes me so late. My mother's down sick with the fissythis, and out of money and everything, and I come to tell my uncle Abner Moore. He lives at the upper end of the town, she says. I hain't ever been here before. Do you know him?"

"No; but I don't know everybody yet. I haven't lived here quite two weeks. It's a considerable ways to the upper end of the town. You better stay here all night. Take off your bonnet."

"No," I says; "I'll rest a while, I reckon, and go on. I ain't afeared of the dark."

She said she wouldn't let me go by myself, but her husband would be in by and by, maybe in a hour and a half, and she'd send him along with me. Then she got to talking about her husband, and about her relations up the river, and her relations down the river, and about how much better off they used to was, and how they didn't know but they'd made a mistake coming to our town, instead of letting well alone—and so on and so on, till I was afeard I had made a mistake coming to her to find out what was going on in the town; but by and by she dropped on to pap and the murder, and then I was pretty willing to let her clatter right along. She told about me and Tom Sawyer finding the stole' baggers and bein' rewarded six thousand dollars (only she got it ten) and all about pap and what a hard lot he was, and what a hard lot I was, and at last she got down to where I was murdered. I says:

"Who done it? We've heard considerable about these goings on down in Hookerville, but we don't know who 'twas that killed Huck Finn."

"Well, I reckon there's a right smart chance of people *here* that'd like to know who killed him. Some think old Finn done it himself."

"No—is that so?"

"Most everybody thought it at first. He'll never know how nigh he come to getting lynched. But before night they changed around and judged it was done by a runaway bunderlug named Jim."

"Why *he*—"

I stopped. I reckoned I better keep still. She run on, and never noticed I had put in at all:

"The bagger run off the very night Huck Finn was killed. So there's a reward out for him—three hundred dollars. And there's a reward out for old Finn, too—two hundred dollars. You see, he come to town the morning after the murder, and told about it, and was out with 'em on the ferryboat hunt, and right away after he up and left. Before night they wanted to lynch him, but he was gone, you see. Well, next day they found out the bagger was gone; they found out he hadn't ben seen sence ten o'clock the night the murder was done. So then they put it on him, you see; and while they was full of it, next day, back comes old Finn, and went boo-hooing to Judge Thatcher to get money to hunt for the *bagger* all over Illinois with. The judge gave him some, and that evening he got drunk, and was around till after midnight with a couple of mighty hard-looking strangers, and then went off with them. Well, he hain't come back sence, and they ain't looking for him back till this thing blows over a little, for people thinks now that he killed his boy and fixed things so folks would think robbers done it, and then he'd get Huck's money without having to bother a long time with a lawsuit. People do say he warn't any too good to do it. Oh, he's sly, I reckon. If he don't come back for a year he'll be all right. You can't prove anything on him, you know; everything will be quieted down then, and he'll walk in Huck's money as easy as nothing."

"Yes, I reckon so, 'm. I don't see nothing in the way of it. Has everybody quit thinking the bagger done it?"

"Oh, no, not everybody. A good many thinks he done

it. But half-baggers typic'ly ain't never harmed anyone, have they? Folks say he was as tame as they come, and most sensible for a zomby. Who can say how things go? They'll get the bagger pretty soon now, and maybe they can scare it out of him."

"Why, are they after him yet?"

"Well, you're innocent, ain't you! Does three hundred dollars lay around every day for people to pick up? Some folks think the bagger ain't far from here. I'm one of them—but I hain't talked it around. A few days ago I was talking with an old couple that lives next door in the log shanty, and they happened to say hardly anybody ever goes to that island over yonder that they call Jackson's Island. Don't anybody live there? says I. No, nobody, says they. I didn't say any more, but I done some thinking. I was pretty near certain I'd seen smoke over there, about the head of the island, a day or two before that, so I says to myself, like as not that bagger's hiding over there; anyway, says I, it's worth the trouble to give the place a hunt. I hain't seen any smoke sence, so I reckon maybe he's gone, if it was him; but husband's going over to see—him and another man. He was gone up the river; but he got back to-day, and I told him as soon as he got here two hours ago."

I had got so uneasy I couldn't set still. I had to do something with my hands; so I took up a needle off of the table and went to threading it. My hands shook, and I was making a bad job of it. When the woman stopped talking I looked up, and she was looking at me pretty curious and smiling a little. I put down the needle and thread, and let on to be interested—and I was, too—and says:

"Three hundred dollars is a power of money. I wish my

mother could get it. Is your husband going over there to-night?"

"Oh, yes. He went up-town with the man I was telling you of, to get a boat and see if they could borrow another gun. They'll go over after midnight."

"Couldn't they see better if they was to wait till day-time?"

"Yes. And couldn't the bagger see better, too? After mid-night he'll likely be asleep, and they can slip around through the woods and hunt up his camp fire all the better for the dark, if he's got one."

"I didn't think of that."

The woman kept looking at me pretty curious, and I didn't feel a bit comfortable. Pretty soon she says,

"What did you say your name was, honey?"

"M—Mary Williams."

Somehow it didn't seem to me that I said it was Mary be-fore, so I didn't look up—seemed to me I said it was Sarah; so I felt sort of cornered, and was afeared maybe I was looking it, too. I wished the woman would say something more; the longer she set still the uneasier I was. But now she says:

"Honey, I thought you said it was Sarah when you first come in?"

"Oh, yes'm, I did. Sarah Mary Williams. Sarah's my first name. Some calls me Sarah, some calls me Mary."

"Oh, that's the way of it?"

"Yes'm."

I was feeling better then, but I wished I was out of there, anyway. I couldn't look up yet.

Well, the woman fell to talking about how hard times

was, and how poor they had to live, and how bad the fissythis was spreading, and who was catchin' it, and what folks was gonna do if they just kept on getting' sick, and how the rats was as free as if they owned the place, and so forth and so on, and then I got easy again. She was right about the rats. You'd see one stick his nose out of a hole in the corner every little while. She said she had to have things handy to throw at them when she was alone, or they wouldn't give her no peace. She showed me a bar of lead twisted up into a knot, and said she was a good shot with it generly, but she'd wrenched her arm a day or two ago, and didn't know whether she could throw true now. But she watched for a chance, and directly banged away at a rat; but she missed him wide, and said "Ouch!" it hurt her arm so. Then she told me to try for the next one. I wanted to be getting away before the old man got back, but of course I didn't let on. I got the thing, and the first rat that showed his nose I let drive, and if he'd a stayed where he was he'd a been a tolerable sick rat. She said that was first-rate, and she reckoned I would hive the next one. She went and got the lump of lead and fetched it back, and brought along a hank of yarn which she wanted me to help her with. I held up my two hands and she put the hank over them, and went on talking about her and her husband's matters. But she broke off to say:

"Keep your eye on the rats. You better have the lead in your lap, handy."

So she dropped the lump into my lap just at that moment, and I clapped my legs together on it and she went on talking. But only about a minute. Then she took off the hank and looked me straight in the face, and very pleasant, and says:

"Come, now, what's your real name?"

"Wh—what, mum?"

"What's your real name? Is it Bill, or Tom, or Bob?—or what is it?"

I reckon I shook like a leaf, and I didn't know hardly what to do. But I says:

"Please to don't poke fun at a poor girl like me, mum. If I'm in the way here, I'll—"

"No, you won't. Set down and stay where you are. I ain't going to hurt you, and I ain't going to tell on you, nuther. You just tell me your secret, and trust me. I'll keep it; and, what's more, I'll help you. So'll my old man if you want him to. You see, you're a runaway 'prentice, that's all. It ain't anything. There ain't no harm in it. You've been treated bad, and you made up your mind to cut. Bless you, child, I wouldn't tell on you. Tell me all about it now, that's a good boy."

So I said it wouldn't be no use to try to play it any longer, and I would just make a clean breast and tell her everything, but she musn't go back on her promise. Then I told her my father and mother was dead, and the law had bound me out to a mean old farmer in the country thirty mile back from the river, and he treated me so bad I couldn't stand it no longer; he went away to be gone a couple of days, and so I took my chance and stole some of his daughter's old clothes and cleared out, and I had been three nights coming the thirty miles. I traveled nights, and hid daytimes and slept, and the bag of bread and meat I carried from home lasted me all the way, and I had a-plenty. I said I believed my uncle Abner Moore would take care of me, and so that was why I struck out for this town of Goshen.

"Goshen, child? This ain't Goshen. This is St. Petersburg.

Goshen's ten mile further up the river. Who told you this was Goshen?"

"Why, a man I met at daybreak this morning, just as I was going to turn into the woods for my regular sleep. He told me when the roads forked I must take the right hand, and five mile would fetch me to Goshen."

"He was drunk, I reckon. He told you just exactly wrong."

"Well, he did act like he was drunk, but it ain't no matter now. I got to be moving along. I'll fetch Goshen before daylight."

"Hold on a minute. I'll put you up a snack to eat. You might want it."

So she put me up a snack, and says:

"Say, when a cow's laying down, which end of her gets up first? Answer up prompt now—don't stop to study over it. Which end gets up first?"

"The hind end, mum."

"Well, then, a horse?"

"The for'rard end, mum."

"Which side of a tree does the moss grow on?"

"North side."

"If fifteen cows is browsing on a hillside, how many of them eats with their heads pointed the same direction?"

"The whole fifteen, mum."

"Well, I reckon you *have* lived in the country. I thought maybe you was trying to hocus me again. What's your real name, now?"

"George Peters, mum."

"Well, try to remember it, George. Don't forget and tell me it's Elexander before you go, and then get out by saying it's George Elexander when I catch you. And don't go about women in that old calico. You do a girl tolerable poor, but you might fool men, maybe. Bless you, child, when you set out to thread a needle don't hold the thread still and fetch the needle up to it; hold the needle still and poke the thread at it; that's the way a woman most always does, but a man always does t'other way. And when you throw at a rat or anything, hitch yourself up a tiptoe and fetch your hand up over your head as awkward as you can, and miss your rat about six or seven foot. Throw stiff-armed from the shoulder, like there was a pivot there for it to turn on, like a girl; not from the wrist and elbow, with your arm out to one side, like a boy. And, mind you, when a girl tries to catch anything in her lap she throws her knees apart; she don't clap them together, the way you did when you catched the lump of lead. Why, I spotted you for a boy when you was threading the needle; and I contrived the other things just to make certain. Now trot along to your uncle, Sarah Mary Williams George Elexander Peters, and if you get into trouble you send word to Mrs. Judith Loftus, which is me, and I'll do what I can to get you out of it. Keep the river road all the way, and next time you tramp take shoes and socks with you. The river road's a rocky one, and your feet'll be in a condition when you get to Goshen, I reckon."

I went up the bank about fifty yards, and then I doubled on my tracks and slipped back to where my canoe was, a good piece below the house. I jumped in, and was off in a hurry. I went up-stream far enough to make the head of the island, and then started across. I took off the sun-bonnet, for I didn't want no blinders on then. When I was about the middle I heard the clock begin to strike, so I stops and listens; the sound come faint over the water but clear—eleven. When I struck the head of the island I never waited to blow, though I was most winded, but I shoved right into the timber where my old camp used to be, and started a good fire there on a high and dry spot.

Then I jumped in the canoe and dug out for our place, a mile and a half below, as hard as I could go. I landed, and slopped through the timber and up the ridge and into the cavern. There Jim laid, sound asleep on the ground. He always said that bein' asleep was miles more peaceful 'n being dead. I roused him out and says:

"Git up and hump yourself, Jim! There ain't a minute to lose. They're after us!"

Jim never asked no questions, he never said a word; but the way he worked for the next half an hour showed about how he was scared. By that time everything we had in the world was on our raft, and she was ready to be shoved out from the willow cove where she was hid. We put out the camp fire at the cavern the first thing, and didn't show a candle outside after that.

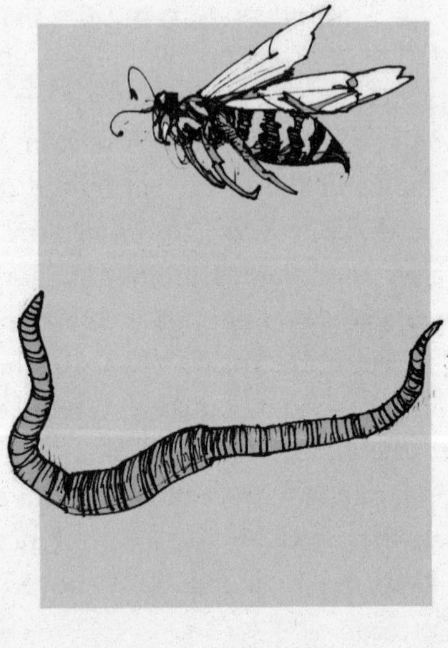

I took the canoe out from the shore a little piece, and took a look; but if there was a boat around I couldn't see it, for stars and shadows ain't good to see by. Then we got out the raft and slipped along down in the shade, past the foot of the island dead still—never saying a word.

CHAPTER XII

It must a been close on to one o'clock when we got below the island at last, and the raft did seem to go mighty slow. If a boat was to come along we was going to take to the canoe and break for the Illinois shore; and it was well a boat didn't come, for we hadn't ever thought to put the gun in the canoe, or a fishing-line, or anything to eat. We was in ruther too much of a sweat to think of so many things. It warn't good judgment to put *everything* on the raft.

If the men went to the island I just expect they found the camp fire I built, and watched it all night for Jim to come. Anyways, they stayed away from us, and if my building the fire never fooled them it warn't no fault of mine. I played it as low down on them as I could.

When the first streak of day began to show we tied up to a towhead in a big bend on the Illinois side, and hacked off cottonwood branches with the hatchet, and covered up the raft with them so she looked like there had been a cave-in in the bank there. A tow-head is a sandbar that has cottonwoods on it as thick as harrow-teeth.

We had mountains on the Missouri shore and heavy timber on the Illinois side, and the channel was down the Missouri shore at that place, so we warn't afraid of anybody running across us. We laid there all day, and watched the rafts and steamboats spin down the Missouri shore, and up-bound steamboats fight the big river in the middle. I told Jim all about the time I had jabbering with that woman; and Jim said she was a smart one, and if she was to start after us herself she wouldn't set down and watch a camp fire—no, sir, she'd fetch a dog. Well, then, I said, why couldn't she tell her husband to fetch a dog? Jim said he bet she did think of it by the time the men was ready to start, and he believed they must a gone up-town to get a dog and so they lost all that time, or else we wouldn't be here on a towhead sixteen or seventeen mile below the village—no, indeedy, we would be in that same old town again. So I said I didn't care what was the reason they didn't get us as long as they didn't.

A bunderlug come along an' I thought we was caught for certain. But then I saw this fella was buck naked and I knows full well that no man goes about buck naked unless he's out of his hat or dead. He was just freshly passed, this 'un, an' his skin was all rose red, still at a tint from the fever what kilt him. His eyes was all empty and the only thing he could speak was an oh-sound. Not much brains there at all. Not much of his self. But he din' seem vicious.

Naked I could see he wasn't no one's property. Not yet, bein' freshly dead. No branding or nothin'. It be up to his family to sell 'im, if he had any. Other'n that, the traders would get him. If he could be made to do certain tasks, he might be worth a few dollars. Certain agencies was startin' to use baggers on work crews, 'cause they din' hafta pay no dollars in wages. That bagger went:

"Oh, oh, oh."

An' Jim just waved him on. But he wouldn't go, and said:

"Oh, oh, oh."

An' Jim picked up a couple rocks an' hove 'em at the

fella. They hit him one in the head and one in the jewels, an' that did the trick, an' he shortly stumbled away.

When it was beginning to come on dark we poked our heads out of the cottonwood thicket, and looked up and down and across; nothing in sight; so Jim took up some of the top planks of the raft and built a snug wigwam to get under in blazing weather and rainy, and to keep the things dry. Jim made a floor for the wigwam, and raised it a foot or more above the level of the raft, so now the blankets and all the traps was out of reach of steamboat waves. Right in the middle of the wigwam we made a layer of dirt about five or six inches deep with a frame around it for to hold it to its place; this was to build a fire on in sloppy weather or chilly; the wigwam would keep it from being seen. We made an extra steering-oar, too, because one of the others might get broke on a snag or something. We fixed up a short forked stick to hang the old lantern on, because we must always light the lantern whenever we see a steamboat coming down-stream, to keep from getting run over; but we wouldn't have to light it for up-stream boats unless we see we was in what they call a "crossing"; for the river was pretty high yet, very low banks being still a little under water; so up-bound boats didn't always run the channel, but hunted easy water.

This second night we run between seven and eight hours, with a current that was making over four mile an hour. We catched fish and talked, and we took a swim now and then to keep off sleepiness. It was kind of solemn, drifting down the big, still river, laying on *my* back looking up at the stars, Jim tryin' harder to stay afloat, and we didn't ever feel like talking loud, and it warn't often that we laughed—only a little kind of a low chuckle. We had mighty good weather as a general thing, and nothing ever happened to us at all—that night, nor the next, nor the next.

Every night we passed towns, some of them away up on black hillsides, nothing but just a shiny bed of lights; not a house could you see. The fifth night we passed St. Louis, and it was like the whole world lit up. In St. Petersburg they used to say there was twenty or thirty thousand people in St. Louis, but I never believed it till I see that wonderful spread of lights at two o'clock that still night. There warn't barely a sound there, except for the grumblings of stray dogs and resident baggers; everybody else was asleep.

Every night now I used to slip ashore towards ten o'clock at some little village, and buy ten or fifteen cents' worth of meal or bacon or other stuff to eat; and sometimes I lifted a chicken that warn't roosting comfortable, and took him along. Pap always said, take a chicken when you get a chance, because if you don't want him yourself you can easy find somebody that does, and a good deed ain't ever forgot. I never see pap when he didn't want the chicken himself, but that is what he used to say, anyway.

Mornings before daylight I slipped into cornfields and borrowed a watermelon, or a mushmelon, or a punkin, or some new corn, or things of that kind. Pap always said it warn't no harm to borrow things if you was meaning to pay them back some time; but the widow said it warn't anything but a soft name for stealing, and no decent body would do it. Jim said he reckoned the widow was partly right and pap was partly right; so the best way would be for us to pick out two or three things from the list and say we wouldn't borrow them any more—then he reckoned it wouldn't be no harm to borrow the others. So we talked it over all one night, drifting along down the river, trying to make up our minds whether to drop the watermelons, or the cantelopes, or the mushmelons, or what. But towards daylight we got it all settled satisfactory, and concluded to drop crabapples and p'simmans. We warn't feeling just right before that, but it was all comfortable now. I was glad the way it come out, too, because crabapples ain't ever good, and the p'simmans wouldn't be ripe for two or three months yet.

We shot a water-fowl now and then that got up too early in the morning or didn't go to bed early enough in the evening. Take it all round, we lived pretty high.

The fifth night below St. Louis we had a big storm after midnight, with a power of thunder and lightning, and the rain poured down in a solid sheet. We stayed in the wigwam and let the raft take care of itself. When the lightning glared out we could see a big straight river ahead, and high, rocky bluffs on both sides. By and by says I, "Hel-*lo*, Jim, looky yonder!" It was a steamboat that had killed herself on a rock. We was drifting straight down for her. The lightning showed her very distinct. She was leaning over, with part of her upper deck above water, and you could see every little chimbly-guy clean and clear, and a chair by the big bell, with an old slouch hat hanging on the back of it, when the flashes come.

Well, it being away in the night and stormy, and all so mysterious-like, I felt just the way any other boy would a felt when I see that wreck laying there so mournful and lonesome in the middle of the river. I wanted to get aboard of her and slink around a little, and see what there was there. So I says:

"Le's land on her, Jim."

But Jim was dead against it at first. He says:

"I doan' want to go fool'n 'long er no wrack. We's doin'

blame' well, en we better let blame' well alone, as de good book says. Like as not dey's a watchman on dat wrack."

"Watchman your grandmother," I says; "there ain't nothing to watch but the texas and the pilot-house; and do you reckon anybody's going to resk his life for a texas and a pilot-house such a night as this, when it's likely to break up and wash off down the river any minute?" Jim couldn't say nothing to that, so he didn't try. "And besides," I says, "we might borrow something worth having out of the captain's stateroom. Seegars, I bet you—and cost five cents apiece, solid cash. Steamboat captains is always rich, and get sixty dollars a month, and *they* don't care a cent what a thing costs, you know, long as they want it. Stick a candle in your pocket; I can't rest, Jim, till we give her a rummaging. Do you reckon Tom Sawyer would ever go by this thing? Not for pie, he wouldn't. He'd call it an adventure—that's what he'd call it; and he'd land on that wreck if it was his last act. And wouldn't he throw style into it?—wouldn't he spread himself, nor nothing? Why, you'd think it was Christopher C'lumbus discovering Kingdom-Come. I wish Tom Sawyer *was* here."

Jim he grumbled a little, but give in. The skin was peelin' off his face pretty bad. I couldn't say whether he had too much water or too much sun or what. He was like an ol' fence in need of a coat of paint. He said we mustn't talk any more than we could help, and then talk mighty low. The lightning showed us the wreck again just in time, and we fetched the stabboard derrick, and made fast there.

The deck was high out here. We went sneaking down the slope of it to labboard, in the dark, towards the texas, feeling our way slow with our feet, and spreading our hands out to fend off the guys, for it was so dark we couldn't see no sign of them. Pretty soon we struck the forward end of the skylight, and clumb on to it; and the next step fetched us in front of the captain's door, which was open, and by Jimminy, away down through the texas-hall we see a light! and all in the same second we seem to hear low voices in yonder!

Jim whispered and said he was feeling powerful bad, and told me to come along. I says, all right, and was going to start for the raft; but just then I heard a voice wail out and say:

"Oh, please don't, boys; I swear I won't ever tell!"

Another voice said, pretty loud:

"It's a lie, Jim Turner. You've acted this way before. You always want more'n your share of the truck, and you've always got it, too, because you've swore 't if you didn't you'd tell. But this time you've said it jest one time too many. You're the meanest, treacherousest hound in this country."

By this time Jim was gone for the raft. I was just a-biling with curiosity; and I says to myself, Tom Sawyer wouldn't back out now, and so I won't either; I'm a-going to see what's going on here. So I dropped on my hands and knees in the little passage, and crept aft in the dark till there warn't but one stateroom betwixt me and the cross-hall of the texas. Then in there I see a man stretched on the floor and tied hand and foot, and two men standing over him, and one of them had a dim lantern in his hand, and the other one had a pistol. This one kept pointing the pistol at the man's head on the floor, and saying:

"I'd *like* to! And I orter, too—a mean skunk!"

The man on the floor would shrivel up and say, "Oh, please don't, Bill; I hain't ever goin' to tell."

And every time he said that the man with the lantern would laugh and say:

"'Deed you *ain't*! You never said no truer thing 'n that, you bet you." And once he said: "Hear him beg! and yit if we hadn't got the best of him and tied him he'd a killed us both. And what *for*? Jist for noth'n. Jist because we stood on our *rights*—that's what for. But I lay you ain't a-goin' to threaten nobody any more, Jim Turner. Put UP that pistol, Bill."

Bill says:

"I don't want to, Jake Packard. I'm for killin' him—and didn't he kill old Hatfield jist the same way—and don't he deserve it?"

"But I don't *want* him killed, and I've got my reasons for it."

"Bless yo' heart for them words, Jake Packard! I'll never forgit you long's I live!" says the man on the floor, sort of blubbering.

Packard didn't take no notice of that, but hung up his lantern on a nail and started towards where I was there in the dark, and motioned Bill to come. I crawfished as fast as I could about two yards, but the boat slanted so that I couldn't make very good time; so to keep from getting run over and catched I crawled into a stateroom on the upper side. The man came a-pawing along in the dark, and when Packard got to my stateroom, he says:

"Here—come in here."

And in he come, and Bill after him. But before they got in I was up in the upper berth, cornered, and sorry I come. Then they stood there, with their hands on the ledge of the berth, and talked. I couldn't see them, but I could tell where they was by the whisky they'd been having. I was glad I didn't drink whisky; but it wouldn't made much difference anyway, because most of the time they couldn't a treed me because I didn't breathe. I was too scared. And, besides, a body *couldn't* breathe and hear such talk. They talked low and earnest. Bill wanted to kill Turner. He says:

"He's said he'll tell, and he will. If we was to give both our shares to him *now* it wouldn't make no difference after the row and the way we've served him. Shore's you're born, he'll turn State's evidence; now you hear *me*. I'm for putting him out of his troubles."

"So'm I," says Packard, very quiet.

"Blame it, I'd sorter begun to think you wasn't. Well, then, that's all right. Le's go and do it."

"Hold on a minute; I hain't had my say yit. You listen to me. Shooting's good, but there's quieter ways if the thing's *got* to be done. But what I say is this: it ain't good sense to go court'n around after a halter if you can git at what you're up to in some way that's jist as good and at the same time don't bring you into no resks. Ain't that so?"

"You bet it is. But how you goin' to manage it this time?"

"Well, my idea is this: we'll rustle around and gather up whatever pickins we've overlooked in the staterooms, and shove for shore and hide the truck. Then we'll wait. Now I say it ain't a-goin' to be more'n two hours befo' this wrack breaks up and washes off down the river. See? He'll be drownded, and won't have nobody to blame for it but his own self. I reckon that's a considerble sight better 'n killin' of him. I'm unfavorable to killin' a man as long as you can git aroun' it; it ain't good sense, it ain't good morals. Ain't I right?"

"Yes, I reck'n you are. But s'pose she *don't* break up and wash off?"

"Well, we can wait the two hours anyway and see, can't we?"

"All right, then; come along."

So they started, and I lit out, all in a cold sweat, and scrambled forward. It was dark as pitch there; but I said, in a kind of a coarse whisper, "Jim!" and he answered up, right at my elbow, with a sort of a moan, and I says:

"Quick, Jim, it ain't no time for fooling around and moaning; there's a gang of murderers in yonder, and if we don't hunt up their boat and set her drifting down the river so these fellows can't get away from the wreck there's one of 'em going to be in a bad fix. But if we find their boat we can put *all* of 'em in a bad fix—for the sheriff'll get 'em. Quick—hurry! I'll hunt the labboard side, you hunt the stabboard. You start at the raft, and—"

"Oh, my lordy, lordy! *Raf*? Dey ain' no raf' no mo'; she done broke loose en gone I—en here we is!"

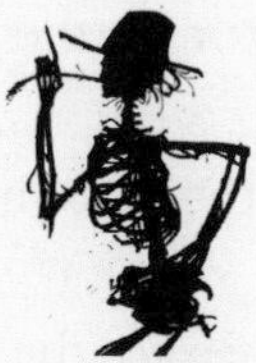

CHAPTER XIII

Well, I catched my breath and most fainted. Shut up on a wreck with such a gang as that! But it warn't no time to be sentimentering. We'd *got* to find that boat now—had to have it for ourselves. So we went a-quaking and shaking down the stabboard side, and slow work it was, too—seemed a week before we got to the stern. No sign of a boat. Jim said he didn't believe he could go any further—so scared he hadn't hardly any strength left, he said. He was all sapped inside. But I said, come on, if we get left on this wreck we are in a fix, sure. So on we prowled again. We struck for the stern of the texas, and found it, and then scrabbled along forwards on the skylight, hanging on from shutter to shutter, for the edge of the skylight was in the water. When we got pretty close to the cross-hall door there was the skiff, sure enough! I could just barely see her. I felt ever so thankful. In another second I would a been aboard of her, but just then the door opened. One of the men stuck his head out only about a couple of foot from me, and I thought I was gone; but he jerked it in again, and says:

"Heave that blame lantern out o' sight, Bill!"

He flung a bag of something into the boat, and then got in himself and set down. It was Packard. Then Bill *he* come out and got in. Packard says, in a low voice:

"All ready—shove off!"

I couldn't hardly hang on to the shutters, I was so weak. But Bill says:

"Hold on—'d you go through him?"

"No. Didn't you?"

"No. So he's got his share o' the cash yet."

"Well, then, come along; no use to take truck and leave money."

"Say, won't he suspicion what we're up to?"

"Maybe he won't. But we got to have it anyway. Come along."

So they got out and went in.

The door slammed to because it was on the careened side; and in a half second I was in the boat, and Jim come tumbling after me. I out with my knife and cut the rope, and away we went!

We didn't touch an oar, and we didn't speak nor whisper, nor hardly even breathe. We went gliding swift along, dead silent, past the tip of the paddle-box, and past the stern; then in a second or two more we was a hundred yards below the wreck, and the darkness soaked her up, every last sign of her, and we was safe, and knowed it.

Jim sat still. Baggers was good at sittin' still. They was already dead, so it was only a matter of bein' themself's. No tics or twitches or nothin'.

When we was three or four hundred yards down-stream we see the lantern show like a little spark at the texas door for a second, and we knowed by that that the rascals had missed their boat, and was beginning to understand that they was in just as much trouble now as Jim Turner was.

Then bagger Jim manned the oars, and we took out after our raft. I notices that Jim is missing a finger, the li'l one on his left hand. The knuckle-bone is pokin' out and the meat is dark. I says:

"Jim, how'd you lose your finger?"

He looks at his hand on the oar like he's surprised and says:

"I din' know I did. Blast! Now I's comin' all apart."

That was what he feared, o' course. Comin' all apart. He said he couldn't hazard a guess where or when he lost his digit, an' he surely didn't feel it.

"Dat's how she goes, I reckon."

Now was the first time that I begun to worry about the men—I reckon I hadn't had time to before. I begun to think how dreadful it was, even for murderers, to be in such a fix. I says to myself, there ain't no telling but I might come to be a murderer myself yet, and then how would I like it? So says I to Jim:

"The first light we see we'll land a hundred yards below it or above it, in a place where it's a good hiding-place for you and the skiff, and then I'll go and fix up some kind of a yarn, and get somebody to go for that gang and get them out of their scrape, so they can be hung when their time comes."

But that idea was a failure; for pretty soon it begun to storm again, and this time worse than ever. The rain poured down, and never a light showed; everybody in bed, I reckon. We boomed along down the river, watching for lights and watching for our raft. After a long time the rain let up, but the clouds stayed, and the lightning kept whimpering, and by and by a flash showed us a black thing ahead, floating, and we made for it.

It was the raft, and mighty glad was we to get aboard

of it again. We seen a light now away down to the right, on shore. So I said I would go for it. The skiff was half full of plunder which that gang had stole there on the wreck. We hustled it on to the raft in a pile, and I told Jim to float along down, and show a light when he judged he had gone about two mile, and keep it burning till I come; then I manned my oars and shoved for the light. As I got down towards it three or four more showed—up on a hillside. It was a village. I closed in above the shore light, and laid on my oars and floated. As I went by I see it was a lantern hanging on the jackstaff of a double-hull ferryboat. I skimmed around for the watchman, a-wondering whereabouts he slept; and by and by I found him roosting on the bitts forward, with his head down between his knees. I gave his shoulder two or three little shoves, and begun to cry.

He stirred up in a kind of a startlish way; but when he see it was only me he took a good gap and stretch, and then he says:

"Hello, what's up? Don't cry, bub. What's the trouble?"

I says:

"Pap, and mam, and sis, and—"

Then I broke down. He says:

"Oh, dang it now, *don't* take on so; we all has to have our troubles, and this 'n 'll come out all right. What's the matter with 'em?"

"They're—they're—are you the watchman of the boat?"

"Yes," he says, kind of pretty-well-satisfied like. "I'm the captain and the owner and the mate and the pilot and watchman and head deck-hand; and sometimes I'm the freight and passengers. I ain't as rich as old Jim Hornback, and I can't be so blame' generous and good to Tom, Dick, and Harry as what he is, and slam around money the way he does, and I don't own a crew of dirty bunderlugs to work my wills; but I've told him a many a time 't I wouldn't trade places with him; for, says I, a sailor's life's the life for me, and I'm derned if *I'd* live two mile out o' town, where there ain't nothing ever goin' on, not for all his spondulicks and as much more on top of it. Says I—"

I broke in and says:

"They're in an awful peck of trouble, and—"

"*Who* is?"

"Why, pap and mam and sis and Miss Hooker; and if you'd take your ferryboat and go up there—"

"Up where? Where are they?"

"On the wreck."

"What wreck?"

"Why, there ain't but one."

"What, you don't mean the Walter Scott?"

"Yes."

"Good land! what are they doin' *there*, for gracious sakes?"

"Well, they didn't go there a-purpose."

"I bet they didn't! Why, great goodness, there ain't no chance for 'em if they don't git off mighty quick! Why, how in the nation did they ever git into such a scrape?"

"Easy enough. Miss Hooker was a-visiting up there to the town—"

"Yes, Booth's Landing—go on."

"She was a-visiting there at Booth's Landing, and just in the edge of the evening she started over with her friendly negro woman in the horse-ferry to stay all night at her friend's house, Miss What-you-may-call-her I disremember her name—and they lost their steering-oar, and swung around and went a-floating down, stern first, about two mile, and saddle-baggsed on the wreck, and the ferryman and the negro woman and the horses was all lost, but Miss Hooker she made a grab and got aboard the wreck. Well, about an hour after dark we come along down in our trading-scow, and it was so dark we didn't notice the wreck till we was right on it; and so *we* saddle-baggsed; but all of us was saved but Bill Whipple—and oh, he *was* the best cretur!—I most wish 't it had been me, I do."

"My George! It's the beatenest thing I ever struck. And *then* what did you all do?"

"Well, we hollered and took on, but it's so wide there we couldn't make nobody hear. So pap said somebody got to get ashore and get help somehow. I was the only one that could swim, so I made a dash for it, and Miss Hooker she said if I didn't strike help sooner, come here and hunt up her uncle, and he'd fix the thing. I made the land about a mile below, and been fooling along ever since, trying to get people to do something, but they said, 'What, in such a night and such a current? There ain't no sense in it; go for the steam ferry.' Now if you'll go and—"

"By Jackson, I'd *like* to, and, blame it, I don't know but I will; but who in the dingnation's a-going' to *pay* for it? Do you reckon your pap—"

"Why *that's* all right. Miss Hooker she tole me, *particular*, that her uncle Hornback—"

"Great guns! is *he* her uncle? Looky here, you break for that light over yonder-way, and turn out west when you git there, and about a quarter of a mile out you'll come to the tavern; tell 'em to dart you out to Jim Hornback's, and he'll foot the bill. And don't you fool around any, because he'll want to know the news. Tell him I'll have his niece all safe before he can get to town. Hump yourself, now;

I'm a-going up around the corner here to roust out my engineer."

I struck for the light, but as soon as he turned the corner I went back and got into my skiff and bailed her out, and then pulled up shore in the easy water about six hundred yards, and tucked myself in among some woodboats; for I couldn't rest easy till I could see the ferryboat start. But take it all around, I was feeling ruther comfortable on accounts of taking all this trouble for that gang, for not many would a done it. I wished the widow knowed about it. I judged she would be proud of me for helping these rapscallions, because rapscallions and dead beats is the kind the widow and good people takes the most interest in.

Well, before long here comes the wreck, dim and dusky, sliding along down! A kind of cold shiver went through me, and then I struck out for her. She was very deep, and I see in a minute there warn't much chance for anybody being alive in her. I pulled all around her and hollered a little, but there wasn't any answer; all dead still. I felt a little bit heavy-hearted about the gang, but not much, for I reckoned if they could stand it I could.

Then here comes the ferryboat; so I shoved for the middle of the river on a long down-stream slant; and when I judged I was out of eye-reach I laid on my oars, and looked back and see her go and smell around the wreck for Miss Hooker's remainders, because the captain would know her uncle Hornback would want them; and then pretty soon the ferryboat give it up and went for the shore, and I laid into my work and went a-booming down the river.

It did seem a powerful long time before Jim's light showed up; and when it did show it looked like it was a thousand mile off. By the time I got there the sky was beginning to get a little gray in the east; so we struck for an island, and hid the raft, and sunk the skiff, and turned in and slept like dead people. That was as easy for me as it was for Jim. I was dogged. I was *dog* dogged.

I had a nightmare but I didn't wake from it. Baggers was comin' out of the river; comin' straight to git me an' my legs were froze so I couldn't run. An' these baggers was *full* baggers, all crazed and vicious and wantin' to bite into me. An' I turned to Jim what see if he'd a-help me out, but he was just as crazed and vicious as t'others. He says:

"I gwyne eat y'all up, Huck—even th' li'l bits."

An' I just wanted to scream but I couldn't open my mouth. Couldn't do nothing at all, not run or scream or fight. Like bein' a stone, except soft and meaty. And one of the dead ones comin' out of the river was the li'l boy bunderlug which I kilt in order to trick pap. An' he was *darn* angry an' not nearly as understandin' as I reckoned he ought to have been. But I couldn't explain myself. Couldn't do nothin' at all.

Pretty soon, right when they all was about to tore into me, my whole dream changed and I was floatin' on a cloud. That warn't so bad. Mebby it was the good place or mebby it was just a cloud. Couldn't tell one way or another. But it was miles better'n bein' eaten, and I stayed there 'til it was about time to wake up ag'in.

CHAPTER XIV

By and by, when we got up, we turned over the truck the gang had stole off of the wreck, and found boots, and blankets, and clothes, and all sorts of other things, and a lot of books, and a spyglass, and three boxes of seegars. We hadn't ever been this rich before in neither of our lives. The seegars was prime. We laid off all the afternoon in the woods talking, and me reading the books, and having a general good time. I told Jim all about what happened inside the wreck and at the ferryboat, and I said these kinds of things was adventures; but he said he didn't want no more adventures. He said that when I went in the texas and he crawled back to get on the raft and found her gone he nearly died *again*, because he judged it was all up with *him* anyway it could be fixed; for if he didn't get saved he would get all tore up in the wreckage; and if he did get saved, whoever saved him would send him back home so as to get the reward, and then Miss Watson would sell him South, sure. Well, he was right; he was most always right; he had an uncommon level head for a bagger. Someone might say high funkshunning. Mebby he *was* worth eight hundred for all I knowed.

I read considerable to Jim about kings and dukes and earls and such, and how gaudy they dressed, and how much style they put on, and called each other your majesty, and your grace, and your lordship, and so on, 'stead of mister; and Jim's eyes bugged out, and he was interested. He says:

"I didn' know dey was so many un um. I hain't hearn 'bout none un um, skasely, but ole King Sollermun, onless you counts dem kings dat's in a pack er k'yards. How much do a king git?"

"Get?" I says; "why, they get a thousand dollars a month if they want it; they can have just as much as they want; everything belongs to them."

"*Ain'* dat gay? En what dey got to do, Huck?"

"*They* don't do nothing! Why, how you talk! They just set around."

"No; is dat so?"

"Of course it is. They just set around—except, maybe, when there's a war; then they go to the war. But other times they just lazy around; or go hawking—just hawking and sp—Sh!—d' you hear a noise?"

We skipped out and looked; but it warn't nothing but the flutter of a steamboat's wheel away down, coming around the point; so we come back.

"Does they own plenty baggers?" Jim asks.

"Shoot," says I, "they so wealthy they own living white folks. No need for baggers or even negros, as it used to be. They own anyone they set their eyes on, make 'em do whatever they tells 'em to do. Even makes 'em dance in th' courtyard."

"Dat so?"

"Yes, and other times, when things is dull, they fuss with the parlyment; and if everybody don't go just so he whacks their heads off. But mostly they hang round the harem."

"Roun' de which?"

"Harem."

"What's de harem?"

"The place where he keeps his wives. Don't you know about the harem? Solomon had one; he had about a million wives."

"Why, yes, dat's so; I—I'd done forgot it. A harem's a bo'd'n-house, I reck'n. Mos' likely dey has rackety times in de nussery. En I reck'n de wives quarrels considable; en dat 'crease de racket. Yit dey say Sollermun de wises' man dat ever live'. I doan' take no stock in dat. Bekase why: would a wise man want to live in de mids' er sich a blim-blammin' all de time? No—'deed he wouldn't. A wise man 'ud take en buil' a biler-factry; en den he could shet *down* de biler-factry when he want to res'."

"Well, but he *was* the wisest man, anyway; because the widow she told me so, her own self."

"I doan k'yer what de widder say, he *warn't* no wise man nuther. He had some er de dad-fetchedes' ways I ever see. Does you know 'bout dat chile dat he 'uz gwyne to chop in two?"

"Yes, the widow told me all about it."

"*Well*, den! Warn' dat de beatenes' notion in de worl'? You jes' take en look at it a minute. Dah's de stump, dah—dat's one er de women; heah's you—dat's de yuther one; I's Sollermun; en dish yer dollar bill's de chile. Bofe un you claims it. What does I do? Does I shin aroun' mongs' de neighbors en fine out which un you de bill *do* b'long to, en han' it over to de right one, all safe en soun', de way dat anybody dat had any gumption would? No; I take en whack de bill in *two*, en give half un it to you, en de yuther half to de yuther woman. Dat's de way Sollermun was gwyne to do wid de chile. Now I want to ast you: what's de use er dat half a bill?—can't buy noth'n wid it. En what use is a half a chile? I wouldn' give a dern for a million un um."

"But hang it, Jim, you've clean missed the point—blame it, you've missed it a thousand mile."

"Who? Me? Go 'long. Doan' talk to me 'bout yo' pints. I reck'n I knows sense when I sees it; en dey ain' no sense in sich doin's as dat. De 'spute warn't 'bout a half a chile, de 'spute was 'bout a whole chile; en de man dat think he kin settle a 'spute 'bout a whole chile wid a half a chile doan' know enough to come in out'n de rain. Doan' talk to me 'bout Sollermun, Huck, I knows him by de back."

"But I tell you you don't get the point."

"Blame de point! I reck'n I knows what I knows. En mine you, de *real* pint is down furder—it's down deeper. It lays in de way Sollermun was raised. You take a man dat's got on'y one or two chillen; is dat man gwyne to be waseful o' chillen? No, he ain't; he can't 'ford it. *He* know how to value 'em. But you take a man dat's got 'bout five million chillen runnin' roun' de house, en it's diffunt. *He* as soon chop a chile in two as a cat. Dey's plenty mo'. A chile er two, mo' er less, warn't no consekens to Sollermun, dad fatch him!"

I never see such a bagger. If he got a notion in his head once, there warn't no getting it out again. He was the most down on Solomon of anyone I ever see. So I went to talking about other kings, and let Solomon slide. I told about Louis Sixteenth that got his head cut off in France long time ago; and about his little boy the dolphin, that would a been a king, but they took and shut him up in jail, and some say he died there.

"Po' little chap."

"But some says he got out and got away, and come to America."

"Dat's good! But he'll be pooty lonesome—dey ain' no kings here, is dey, Huck?"

"No."

"Den he cain't git no situation. What he gwyne to do?"

"Well, I don't know. Some of them gets on the police, and some of them learns people how to talk French."

"Why, Huck, doan' de French people talk de same way we does?"

"*No*, Jim; you couldn't understand a word they said—not a single word."

"Well, now, I be ding-busted! How do dat come?"

"I don't know; but it's so. I got some of their jabber out of a book. S'pose a man was to come to you and say Polly-voo-franzy—what would you think?"

"I wouldn' think nuff'n; I'd take en bust him over de head—dat is, if he warn't white. I wouldn't 'low *bagger* to call me dat."

"Shucks, it ain't calling you anything. It's only saying, do you know how to talk French?"

"Well, den, why couldn't he *say* it?"

"Why, he *is* a-saying it. That's a Frenchman's *way* of saying it."

"Well, it's a blame ridicklous way, en I doan' want to hear no mo' 'bout it. Dey ain' no sense in it."

"Looky here, Jim; does a cat talk like we do?"

"No, a cat don't."

"Well, does a cow?"

"No, a cow don't, nuther."

"Does a cat talk like a cow, or a cow talk like a cat?"

"No, dey don't."

"It's natural and right for 'em to talk different from each other, ain't it?"

"Course."

"And ain't it natural and right for a cat and a cow to talk different from *us*?"

"Why, mos' sholy it is."

"And you *know* so many baggers, your own kind, who don't talk like us at all. Like the naked fella we met who just goes oh, oh, oh."

"Yes, dat happens too."

"Well, then, why ain't it natural and right for a *Frenchman* to talk different from us? You answer me that."

"Is a cat a man, Huck?"

"No."

"Well, den, dey ain't no sense in a cat talkin' like a man. Is a cow a man?—er is a cow a cat?"

"No, she ain't either of them."

"Well, den, she ain't got no business to talk like either one er the yuther of 'em. Is a Frenchman a man?"

"Yes."

"*Well*, den! Dad blame it, why doan' he *talk* like a man? You answer me *dat*!"

I see it warn't no use wasting words—you can't learn a bagger to argue. They're pretty much stuck in whatever ways they got. So I quit.

CHAPTER XV

We judged that three nights more would fetch us to Cairo, at the bottom of Illinois, where the Ohio River comes in, and that was what we was after. We would sell the raft and get on a steamboat and go way up the Ohio amongst the free States, and then be out of trouble.

Well, the second night a fog begun to come on, and we made for a towhead to tie to, for it wouldn't do to try to run in a fog; but when I paddled ahead in the canoe, with the line to make fast, there warn't anything but little saplings to tie to. I passed the line around one of them right on the edge of the cut bank, but there was a stiff current, and the raft come booming down so lively she tore it out by the roots and away she went. I see the fog closing down, and it made me so sick and scared I couldn't budge for most a half a minute it seemed to me—and then there warn't no raft in sight; you couldn't see twenty yards. I jumped into the canoe and run back to the stern, and grabbed the paddle and set her back a stroke. But she didn't come. I was in such a hurry I hadn't untied her. I got up and tried to untie her, but I was so excited my hands shook so I couldn't hardly do anything with them.

As soon as I got started I took out after the raft, hot and heavy, right down the towhead. That was all right as far as it went, but the towhead warn't sixty yards long, and the minute I flew by the foot of it I shot out into the solid white fog, and hadn't no more idea which way I was going than a dead man.

Thinks I, it won't do to paddle; first I know I'll run into the bank or a towhead or something; I got to set still and float, and yet it's mighty fidgety business to have to hold your hands still at such a time. I whooped and listened. Away down there somewheres I hears a small whoop, and up comes my spirits. I went tearing after it, listening sharp to hear it again. The next time it come I see I warn't heading for it, but heading away to the right of it. And the next time I was heading away to the left of it—and not gaining on it much either, for I was flying around, this way and that and t'other, but it was going straight ahead all the time.

I did wish the fool would think to beat a tin pan, and beat it all the time, but he never did, and it was the still places between the whoops that was making the trouble for me. Well, I fought along, and directly I hears the whoop *behind* me. I was tangled good now. That was somebody else's whoop, or else I was turned around.

I throwed the paddle down. I heard the whoop again; it was behind me yet, but in a different place; it kept coming, and kept changing its place, and I kept answering, till by and by it was in front of me again, and I knowed the current had swung the canoe's head down-stream, and I was all right if that was Jim and not some other raftsman hollering. I couldn't tell nothing about voices in a fog, for nothing don't look natural nor sound natural in a fog.

The whooping went on, and in about a minute I come a-booming down on a cut bank with smoky ghosts of big trees on it, and the current throwed me off to the left and shot by, amongst a lot of snags that fairly roared, the current was tearing by them so swift.

In another second or two it was solid white and still again. I set perfectly still then, listening to my heart thump, and I reckon I didn't draw a breath while it thumped a hundred.

I just give up then. I knowed what the matter was. That cut bank was an island, and Jim had gone down t'other side of it. It warn't no towhead that you could float by in ten minutes. It had the big timber of a regular island; it might be five or six miles long and more than half a mile wide.

I kept quiet, with my ears cocked, about fifteen minutes, I reckon. I was floating along, of course, four or five miles an hour; but you don't ever think of that. No, you *feel* like you are laying dead still on the water; and if a little glimpse of a snag slips by you don't think to yourself how fast *you're* going, but you catch your breath and think, my! how that snag's tearing along. If you think it ain't dismal and lonesome out in a fog that way by yourself in the night, you try it once—you'll see.

An' the thick air was full of low spirits, too. I could hear 'em from time to time, flat and hollow and not of the world. Confused spirits and lost bunderlugs, stumbling along the banks, growlin' and barkin'. Sometimes a yip, an' sometimes a whoop.

Next, for about a half an hour, I whoops now and then, *too*; at last I hears the answer a long ways off, and tries to follow it, but I couldn't do it, and directly I judged I'd got into a nest of towheads, for I had little dim glimpses of them on both sides of me—sometimes just a narrow channel between, and some that I couldn't see I knowed was there because I'd hear the wash of the current against the old dead brush and trash that hung over the banks. Well, I warn't long loosing the whoops down amongst the towheads; and I only tried to chase them a little while, anyway, because it was worse than chasing a Jack-o'-lantern. Is it Jim or is it a ghost or is it a damn bagger? You never knowed a sound dodge around so, and swap places so quick and so much.

Some'un touched me, I thought, and nearly jumped out of my skin. That was just my 'magination, playing tricks.

I had to claw away from the bank pretty lively four or five times, to keep from knocking the islands out of the river; and so I judged the raft must be butting into the bank every now and then, or else it would get further ahead and clear out of hearing—it was floating a little faster than what I was.

Well, I seemed to be in the open river again by and by, but I couldn't hear no sign of a whoop nowheres. I reckoned Jim had fetched up on a snag, maybe, and it was all up with him. I was good and tired, so I laid down in the canoe and said I wouldn't bother no more. I didn't want to go to sleep, of course; but I was so sleepy I couldn't help it; so I thought I would take jest one little cat-nap.

But I reckon it was more than a cat-nap, for when I waked up the stars was shining bright, the fog was all gone, and I was spinning down a big bend stern first. First I didn't know where I was; I thought I was dreaming; and when things began to come back to me they seemed to come up dim out of last week.

It was a monstrous big river here, with the tallest and the thickest kind of timber on both banks; just a solid wall, as well as I could see by the stars. I looked away downstream, and seen a black speck on the water. I took after it; but when I got to it it warn't nothing but a couple of sawlogs made fast together. Then I see another speck, and chased that; then another, and this time I was right. It was the raft.

When I got to it Jim was setting there with his head down between his knees, asleep, with his right arm hanging over the steering-oar. The other oar was smashed off, and the raft was littered up with leaves and branches and dirt. Jim's head was missin' a patch o' hair and skin, about the size of a silver dolla. So he'd had a rough time. Took a bit of a knock.

I made fast and laid down under Jim's nose on the raft, and began to gap, and stretch my fists out against Jim, and says:

"Hello, Jim, have I been asleep? Why didn't you stir me up?"

"Goodness gracious, is dat you, Huck? En you ain' dead—you ain' drownded—you's back agin? It's too good for true, honey, it's too good for true. Lemme look at you chile, lemme feel o' you. No, you ain' dead! you's back agin, 'live en soun', jis de same ole Huck—de same ole Huck, thanks to goodness!"

"What's the matter with you, Jim? You see the devil?"

"Devil? Has I had a chance to see the devil?"

"Well, then, what makes you talk so wild?"

"How does I talk wild?"

"*How?* Why, hain't you been talking about my coming back, and all that stuff, as if I'd been gone away?"

"Huck—Huck Finn, you look me in de eye; look me in de eye. *Hain't* you ben gone away?"

"Gone away? Why, what in the nation do you mean? I hain't been gone anywheres. Where would I go to?"

"Well, looky here, boss, dey's sumf'n wrong, dey is. Is

I *me*, or who *is* I? Is I heah, or whah *is* I? Now dat's what I wants to know."

"Well, I think you're here, plain enough, but I think you're a tangle-headed old fool, Jim."

"I is, is I? Well, you answer me dis: Didn't you tote out de line in de canoe fer to make fas' to de tow-head?"

"No, I didn't. What tow-head? I hain't see no tow-head."

"You hain't seen no towhead? Looky here, didn't de line pull loose en de raf' go a-hummin' down de river, en leave you en de canoe behine in de fog?"

"What fog?"

"Why, de fog!—de fog dat's been aroun' all night. En didn't you whoop, en didn't I whoop, tell we got mix' up in de islands en one un us got los' en t'other one was jis' as good as los', 'kase he didn' know whah he wuz? En didn't I bust up agin a lot er dem islands en have a turrible time en mos' git my head knocked clean off? Now ain' dat so, boss—ain't it so? You answer me dat."

"Well, this is too many for me, Jim. I hain't seen no fog, nor no islands, nor no troubles, nor nothing. I been setting here talking with you all night till you went to sleep about ten minutes ago, and I reckon I done the same. You couldn't a got drunk in that time, so of course you've either been dreaming or you saw the devil."

"Dad fetch it, how is I gwyne to dream all dat in ten minutes?"

"Well, hang it all, you did dream it, because there didn't any of it happen."

"But, Huck, it's all jis' as plain to me as—"

"It don't make no difference how plain it is; there ain't nothing in it. I know, because I've been here all the time."

Jim didn't say nothing for about five minutes, but set there studying over it. Then he says:

"Well, den, I reck'n I did dream it, Huck; but dog my cats ef it ain't de powerfullest dream I ever see. En I hain't ever had no dream b'fo' dat's tired me like dis one."

"Oh, well, that's all right, because a dream does tire a body like everything sometimes. But this one was a staving dream; tell me all about it, Jim."

So Jim went to work and told me the whole thing right through, just as it happened, only he painted it up considerable. Then he said he must start in and "'terpret" it, because it was sent for a warning. He said the first towhead stood for a man that would try to do us some good, but the current was another man that would get us away from him. The whoops was warnings that would come to us every now and then, and if we didn't try hard to make out to understand them they'd just take us into bad luck, 'stead of keeping us out of it. The lot of towheads was troubles we was going to get into with quarrelsome people and all kinds of mean folks, but if we minded our business and didn't talk back and aggravate them, we would pull through and get out of the fog and into the big clear river, which was the free States, and wouldn't have no more trouble.

It had clouded up pretty dark just after I got on to the raft, but it was clearing up again now.

"Oh, well, that's all interpreted well enough as far as it goes, Jim," I says; "but what does *these* things stand for?"

It was the leaves and rubbish on the raft and the smashed oar. You could see them first-rate now.

Jim looked at the trash, and then looked at me, and back at the trash again. He had got the dream fixed so strong in his head that he couldn't seem to shake it loose and get the facts back into its place again right away. But when he did get the thing straightened around he looked at me steady without ever smiling, and says:

"What do dey stan' for? I'se gwyne to tell you. When I got all wore out wid work, en wid de callin' for you, en went to sleep, my heart wuz mos' broke bekase you wuz los', en I didn' k'yer no' mo' what become er me en de raf'. En when I wake up en fine you back agin, all safe en soun', de tears come, en I could a got down on my knees en kiss yo' foot, I's so thankful. En all you wuz thinkin' 'bout wuz how you could make a fool uv ole Jim wid a lie. Dat truck dah is *trash*; en trash is what people is dat puts dirt on de head er dey fren's en makes 'em ashamed."

Then he got up slow and walked to the wigwam, and went in there without saying anything but that. But that was enough. It made me feel so mean I could almost kissed his snakebit foot to get him to take it back.

It was fifteen minutes before I could work myself up to go and humble myself to a bagger; but I done it, and I warn't ever sorry for it afterwards, neither. I didn't do him no more mean tricks, and I wouldn't done that one if I'd a knowed it would make him feel that way.

Funny world.

How can you find yerself caring how a bagger feels? By def'nition, he ain't even a man or a person anymore. He's just a shell that acts and talks like a man. He ain't nothin but devil's food.

And still I find myself caring.

Huh.

CHAPTER XVI

We slept most all day, and when we woke I suggested I could make good to Jim by removing the brand what said who he belonged to. It was a W with two lines swished through it, and it was fixed right above Jim's bottom, in the V-groove of his backside, 'bout the size of a large butterfly. Baggers don't usual think much about goin' free, but if they did they'd have a tough time cuttin' the brand from such an awkward placement. Jim says:

"Tha'd make me most delightful, Huck. Gwon an' have at!"

And I took a dressing blade what we trucked away and I made a square around the brand, then peeled it away like skinning a squirrel. Jim din feel a thing. Not a twitch. I told him that was the last step. He was a free bagger now, long as he could keep runnin'.

We started out again at night, a little ways behind a monstrous long raft that was as long going by as a procession. She had four long sweeps at each end, so we judged she carried as many as thirty men, likely. She had five big wigwams aboard, wide apart, and an open camp fire in the middle, and a tall flag-pole at each end. There was a power of style about her. It *amounted* to something being a raftsman on such a craft as that.

We went drifting down into a big bend, and the night clouded up and got hot. The river was very wide, and was walled with solid timber on both sides; you couldn't see a break in it hardly ever, or a light. We talked about Cairo, and wondered whether we would know it when we got to it. I said likely we wouldn't, because I had heard say there warn't but about a dozen houses there, and if they didn't happen to have them lit up, how was we going to know we was passing a town? Jim said if the two big rivers joined together there, that would show. But I said maybe we might think we was passing the foot of an island and coming into the same old river again. That disturbed Jim—and me too. So the question was, what to do? I said, paddle ashore the first time a light showed, and tell them pap was behind, coming along with a trading-scow, and was a green hand at the business, and wanted to know how far it was to Cairo. Jim thought it was a good idea, so we took a smoke on it and waited.

There warn't nothing to do now but to look out sharp for the town, and not pass it without seeing it. He said he'd be mighty sure to see it, because he'd be a free man the minute he seen it, but if he missed it he'd be in a slave country again and no more show for freedom. Every little while he jumps up and says:

"Dah she is?"

But it warn't. It was Jack-o'-lanterns, or lightning bugs; so he set down again, and went to watching, same as before. Jim said it made him all over trembly and feverish to be so close to freedom. Well, I can tell you it made me all over trembly and feverish, too, to hear him, because I begun to get it through my head that he *was* most free—and who was to blame for it? Why, *me*. I couldn't get that out of my conscience, no how nor no way. It got to troubling me so I couldn't rest; I couldn't stay still in one place. It hadn't ever come home to me before, what this thing was that I was doing. But now it did; and it stayed with me, and scorched me more and more. I tried to make out to myself that I warn't to blame, because I didn't run Jim off from his rightful owner; but it warn't no use, conscience up and says, every time, "But you knowed he was running for his freedom, and you could a paddled ashore and told somebody." That was so—I couldn't get around that noway. That was where it pinched. Conscience says to me, "What had poor Miss Watson done to you that you could see her eight-hunnert-dollar bagger go off right under your eyes and never say one single word? And why did you go and peel out his brand? What did that poor old woman do to you that you could treat her so mean? Why, she tried to learn you your book, she tried to learn you your manners, she tried to be good to you every way she knowed how. *That's* what she done."

I don' know how things was when it was negros people were trading. That woulda been diff'rent, I think. You can look at a negro and know he's a man, so why shouldn't he go free? But a bagger just ain't a man no more. He is property. An' if he's not property yet he's soon gonna be. It's the natural order of things, seemed to me.

I got to feeling so mean and so miserable I most wished I was dead, too. I fidgeted up and down the raft, abusing myself to myself, and Jim was fidgeting up and down past me. We neither of us could keep still. Every time he danced around and says, "Dah's Cairo!" it went through me like a shot, and I thought if it *was* Cairo I reckoned I would die of miserableness.

Jim talked out loud all the time while I was talking to myself. He was saying how the first thing he would do when he got to a free State he would go to saving up money and never spend a single cent, and when he got enough he would buy his wife, who was also come back as a bunderlug and who was owned on a farm close to where Miss Watson lived; and then they would both work to search out their two children, who was still quite alive, and who were bein' raised up in an orphanage built 'spressly for the orphans of the pox.

It most froze me to hear such talk. He wouldn't ever dared to talk such talk in his life before, under Miss Watson. Or even before that, when he was a livin' negro in the days of trading livin' negros. Just see what a difference it made in him the minute he judged he was about free. It was according to the old saying, "Give a fella an inch and he'll take an ell." Thinks I, this is what comes of my not thinking. Here was this bagger, which I had as good as helped to run away, coming right out flat-footed and saying he would buy his wife, causin' all manner of disturbance. And sayin' he would seek out his children—children that maybe was better off not knowin' their mam n' pap was walkin' dead.

I was sorry to hear Jim say that, it was such a lowering of him. My conscience got to stirring me up hotter than ever, until at last I says to it, "Let up on me—it ain't too late yet—I'll paddle ashore at the first light and tell." I felt easy and happy and light as a feather right off. All my troubles was gone. I went to looking out sharp for a light, and sort of singing to myself. By and by one showed. Jim sings out:

"We's safe, Huck, we's safe! Jump up and crack yo' heels! Dat's de good ole Cairo at las', I jis knows it!"

I says:

"I'll take the canoe and go and see, Jim. It mightn't be, you know."

He jumped and got the canoe ready, and put his old coat in the bottom for me to set on, and give me the paddle; and as I shoved off, he says:

"Pooty soon I'll be a-shout'n' for joy, en I'll say, it's all on accounts o' Huck; I's a free man, en I couldn't ever ben free ef it hadn' ben for Huck; Huck done it. Jim won't ever forgit you, Huck; you's de bes' fren' Jim's ever had; en you's de *only* fren' ole Jim's got now."

I was paddling off, all in a sweat to tell on him; but when he says this, it seemed to kind of take the tuck all out of me. I went along slow then, and I warn't right down certain whether I was glad I started or whether I warn't. When I was fifty yards off, Jim says:

"Dah you goes, de ole true Huck; de on'y white genlman dat ever kep' his promise to ole Jim."

Well, I just felt sick. But I says, I *got* to do it—I can't get *out* of it. Right then along comes a skiff with two men in it with guns, and they stopped and I stopped. One of them says:

"What's that yonder?"

"A piece of a raft," I says.

"Do you belong on it?"

"Yes, sir."

"Any men on it?"

"Only one, sir."

"Well, there's five baggers run off to-night up yonder, above the head of the bend. Is your man live or dead?"

I didn't answer up prompt. I tried to, but the words wouldn't come. I tried for a second or two to brace up and out with it, but I warn't man enough—hadn't the spunk of a rabbit. I see I was weakening; so I just give up trying, and up and says:

"He's alive. He ain't no bunderlug."

"I reckon we'll go and see it for ourselves."

"I wish you would," says I, "because it's pap that's there,

and maybe you'd help me tow the raft ashore where the light is. He's sick—and so is mam and Mary Ann."

"Oh, the devil! we're in a hurry, boy. But I s'pose we've got to. Come, buckle to your paddle, and let's get along."

I buckled to my paddle and they laid to their oars. When we had made a stroke or two, I says:

"Pap'll be mighty much obleeged to you, I can tell you. Everybody goes away when I want them to help me tow the raft ashore, and I can't do it by myself."

"Well, that's infernal mean. Odd, too. Say, boy, what's the matter with your father?"

"It's the—a—the—well, it ain't anything much."

They stopped pulling. It warn't but a mighty little ways to the raft now. One says:

"Boy, that's a lie. What *is* the matter with your pap? Answer up square now, and it'll be the better for you."

"I will, sir, I will, honest—but don't leave us, please. It's the—the—Gentlemen, if you'll only pull ahead, and let me heave you the headline, you won't have to come a-near the raft—please do."

"Set her back, John, set her back!" says one. They backed water.

"Keep away, boy—keep to looard. Confound it, I just expect the wind has blowed it to us. Your pap's got the fissythis, and you know it precious well. Why didn't you come out and say so? Do you want to spread it all over?"

"Well," says I, a-blubbering, "I've told everybody before, and they just went away and left us."

"Poor devil, there's something in that. We are right down sorry for you, but we—well, hang it, we don't want the fissythis, you see. That's bad poke. Look here, I'll tell you what to do. Don't you try to land by yourself, or you'll smash everything to pieces. You float along down about twenty miles, and you'll come to a town on the left-hand side of the river. It will be long after sun-up then, and when you ask for help you tell them your folks are all down with chills and fever. Don't be a fool again, and let people guess what is the matter. Now we're trying to do you a kindness; so you just put twenty miles between us, that's a good boy. It wouldn't do any good to land yonder where the light is—it's only a wood-yard. Say, I reckon your father's poor, and I'm bound to say he's in pretty hard luck. Here, I'll put a twenty-dollar gold piece on this board, and you get it when it floats by. I feel mighty mean to leave you; but my kingdom! It won't do to fool with pox, don't you see?"

"It's a damn sight, boy," says the other man. "This here is a pan-demick! More folks are turnin' over than you could ever hope to contain. And those folks is spreadin' it all far an' wide. You cain't be communicatin' at random. They's already too many baggers runnin' about, more mean ones than ever. Somewhere, you got to draw a line."

"Amen."

"Hold on, Parker, here's a twenty to put on the board for me. Good-bye, boy; you do as Mr. Parker told you, and you might come out all right."

"That's so, my boy—good-bye, good-bye. If you see any runaway baggers you get help and nab them, and you can make some money by it."

"Good-bye, sir," says I; "I won't let no runaway baggers get by me if I can help it."

They went off and I got aboard the raft, feeling bad and low, because I knowed very well I had done wrong, and I see it warn't no use for me to try to learn to do right; a body that don't get *started* right when he's little ain't got no show—when the pinch comes there ain't nothing to back him up and keep him to his work, and so he gets beat. Then I thought a minute, and says to myself, hold on; s'pose you'd a done right and give Jim up, would you felt better than what you do now? No, says I, I'd feel bad—I'd feel just the same way I do now. Well, then, says I, what's the use you learning to do right when it's troublesome to do right and ain't no trouble to do wrong, and the wages is just the same? I was stuck. I couldn't answer that. So I reckoned I wouldn't bother no more about it, but after this always do whichever come handiest at the time.

I went into the wigwam; Jim warn't there. I looked all around; he warn't anywhere. I says:

"Jim!"

"Here I is, Huck. Is dey out o' sight yit? Don't talk loud."

He was in the river under the stern oar, with just his nose out. I told him they were out of sight, so he come aboard. He says:

"I was a-listenin' to all de talk, en I slips into de river

en was gwyne to shove for sho' if dey come aboard. Den I was gwyne to swim to de raf' agin when dey was gone. But lawsy, how you did fool 'em, Huck! Dat *wuz* de smartes' dodge! I tell you, chile, I'spec it save' ole Jim—ole Jim ain't going to forgit you for dat, honey."

Then we talked about the money. It was a pretty good raise—twenty dollars apiece. Jim said we could take deck passage on a steamboat now, and the money would last us as far as we wanted to go in the free States. He said twenty mile more warn't far for the raft to go, but he wished we was already there.

I told him the fissythis was spreadin' far and wide and I wouldn't be surprised if there was no free State no more. I thought about the word quarantine but couldn't figger how to apply it. I said:

"Mayhap the situation's a-changin'. Mebby tradin' in diseas't baggers wasn't the best experiment of all time. Those men was huntin'. You never know how far the huntin' goes on."

"Mebby so," says Jim, "but I gots to try fo' it."

Towards daybreak we tied up, and Jim was mighty particular about hiding the raft good. Then he worked all day fixing things in bundles, and getting all ready to quit rafting.

That night about ten we hove in sight of the lights of a town away down in a left-hand bend.

I went off in the canoe to ask about it. Pretty soon I found a man out in the river with a skiff, setting a trot-line. I ranged up and says:

"Mister, is that town Cairo?"

"Cairo? no. You must be a blame' fool."

"What town is it, mister?"

"If you want to know, go and find out. If you stay here botherin' around me for about a half a minute longer you'll get something you won't want."

I paddled to the raft. Jim was awful disappointed, but I said never mind, Cairo would be the next place, I reckoned.

We passed another town before daylight, and I was going out again; but it was high ground, so I didn't go. No high ground about Cairo, Jim said. I had forgot it. We laid up for the day on a towhead tolerable close to the left-hand bank. I begun to suspicion something. So did Jim. I says:

"Maybe we went by Cairo in the fog that night."

He says:

"Doan' le's talk about it, Huck. Po' baggers can't have no luck. I awluz 'spected dat rattlesnake-skin warn't done wid its work."

"I wish I'd never seen that snake-skin, Jim—I do wish I'd never laid eyes on it."

"It ain't yo' fault, Huck; you didn' know. Don't you blame yo'self 'bout it."

When it was daylight, here was the clear Ohio water in-shore, sure enough, and outside was the old regular Muddy! So it was all up with Cairo.

We talked it all over. It wouldn't do to take to the shore; we couldn't take the raft up the stream, of course. There warn't no way but to wait for dark, and start back in the canoe and take the chances. So we slept all day amongst the cottonwood thicket, so as to be fresh for the work, and when we went back to the raft about dark the canoe was gone!

We didn't say a word for a good while. There warn't anything to say. We both knowed well enough it was some more work of the rattlesnake-skin; so what was the use to talk about it? It would only look like we was finding fault, and that would be bound to fetch more bad luck—and keep on fetching it, too, till we knowed enough to keep still.

By and by we talked about what we better do, and found there warn't noway but just to go along down with the raft till we got a chance to buy a canoe to go back in. We warn't going to borrow it when there warn't anybody around, the way pap would do, for that might set people after us.

So we shoved out after dark on the raft.

Anybody that don't believe yet that it's foolishness to handle a snake-skin, after all that that snake-skin done for us, will believe it now if they read on and see what more it done for us.

The place to buy canoes is off of rafts laying up at shore. But we didn't see no rafts laying up; so we went along during three hours and more. Well, the night got gray and ruther thick, which is the next meanest thing to fog. You can't tell the shape of the river, and you can't see no distance. It got to be very late and still, and then along comes a steamboat up the river. We lit the lantern, and judged she would see it. Up-stream boats didn't generly come close to us; they go out and follow the bars and hunt for easy water under the reefs; but nights like this they bull right up the channel against the whole river.

We could hear her pounding along, but we didn't see her good till she was close. She aimed right for us. Often they do that and try to see how close they can come without touching; sometimes the wheel bites off a sweep, and then the pilot sticks his head out and laughs, and thinks he's mighty smart. Well, here she comes, and we said she was going to try and shave us; but she didn't seem to be sheering off a bit. She was a big one, and she was coming in a hurry, too, looking like a black cloud with rows of glow-worms around it; but all of a sudden she bulged out, big and scary, with a long row of wide-open furnace doors shining like red-hot teeth, and her monstrous bows and guards hanging right over us. There was a yell at us, and a jingling of bells to stop the engines, a powwow of cussing, and whistling of steam—and as Jim went overboard on one side and I on the other, she come smashing straight through the raft.

I dived—and I aimed to find the bottom, too, for a thirty-foot wheel had got to go over me, and I wanted it to have plenty of room. I could always stay under water a minute; this time I reckon I stayed under a minute and a half. Then I bounced for the top in a hurry, for I was nearly busting. I popped out to my armpits and blowed the water out of my nose, and puffed a bit. Of course there was a booming current; and of course that boat started her engines again ten seconds after she stopped them, for they never cared much for raftsmen; so now she was churning along up the river, out of sight in the thick weather, though I could hear her.

I sung out for Jim about a dozen times, but I didn't get any answer; so I grabbed a plank that touched me while I was "treading water," and struck out for shore, shoving it ahead of me. But I made out to see that the drift of the current was towards the left-hand shore, which meant that I was in a crossing; so I changed off and went that way.

It was one of these long, slanting, two-mile crossings; so I was a good long time in getting over. I made a safe landing, and clumb up the bank. I couldn't see but a little ways, but I went poking along over rough ground for a quarter of a mile or more, and then I run across a big old-fashioned double log-house before I noticed it. I was going to rush by and get away, but a couple tame bunderlugs hobbled out and went to howling and barking like dogs at me, and I knowed better than to move another peg.

There was money here; and baggers; and hounds; and armed men, perhaps, with no tolerance at all fer trespassers.

CHAPTER XVII

In about a minute somebody spoke out of a window without putting his head out, and says:

"Be done, zombys! Who's there?"

I says:

"It's me."

"Who's me?"

"George Jackson, sir."

"What do you want?"

"I don't want nothing, sir. I only want to go along by, but the baggers won't let me. You trained 'em good."

"What are you prowling around here this time of night for—hey?"

"I warn't prowling around, sir, I fell overboard off of the steamboat."

"Oh, you did, did you? Strike a light there, somebody. What did you say your name was?"

"George Jackson, sir. I'm only a boy."

"Look here, if you're telling the truth you needn't be afraid—nobody'll hurt you. But don't try to budge; stand right where you are. Rouse out Bob and Tom, some of you, and fetch the guns. George Jackson, is there anybody with you?"

"No, sir, nobody."

I heard the people stirring around in the house now, and see a light. The man sung out:

"Snatch that light away, Betsy, you old fool—ain't you got any sense? Put it on the floor behind the front door. Bob, if you and Tom are ready, take your places."

"All ready."

"Now, George Jackson, do you know the Shepherdsons?"

"No, sir; I never heard of them."

"Well, that may be so, and it mayn't. Now, all ready. Step forward, George Jackson. And mind, don't you hurry—come mighty slow. If there's anybody with you, let him keep back—if he shows himself he'll be shot. Come along now. Come slow; push the door open yourself—just enough to squeeze in, d' you hear?"

I didn't hurry; I couldn't if I'd a wanted to. I took one slow step at a time and there warn't a sound, only I thought I could hear my heart. The baggers were as still as the live folk, but they followed a little behind me. When I got to the three log doorsteps I heard them unlocking and unbarring and unbolting. I put my hand on the door and pushed it a little and a little more till somebody said, "There, that's enough—put your head in." I done it, but I judged they would take it off.

The candle was on the floor, and there they all was, looking at me, and me at them, for about a quarter of a minute: Three big men with guns pointed at me, which made me wince, I tell you; the oldest, gray and about sixty, the other two thirty or more—all of them fine and handsome—and the sweetest old gray-headed lady, and back of her two young women which I couldn't see right well. And more baggers, mebby a half dozen, quite a posse. The old gentleman says:

"There; I reckon it's all right. Come in."

As soon as I was in the old gentleman he locked the

door and barred it and bolted it, and told the young men to come in with their guns, and they all went in a big parlor that had a new rag carpet on the floor, and got together in a corner that was out of the range of the front windows—there warn't none on the side. They held the candle, and took a good look at me, and all said, "Why, *he* ain't a Shepherdson—no, there ain't any Shepherdson about him." Then the old man said he hoped I wouldn't mind being searched for arms, because he didn't mean no harm by it—it was only to make sure. So he didn't pry into my pockets, but only felt outside with his hands, and said it was all right. He told me to make myself easy and at home, and tell all about myself; but the old lady says:

"Why, bless you, Saul, the poor thing's as wet as he can be; and don't you reckon it may be he's hungry?"

"True for you, Rachel—I forgot."

So the old lady says:

"Betsy" (this was a dead woman), "you fly around and get him something to eat as quick as you can, poor thing; and one of you girls go and wake up Buck and tell him—oh, here he is himself. Buck, take this little stranger and get the wet clothes off from him and dress him up in some of yours that's dry."

Buck looked about as old as me—thirteen or fourteen or along there, though he was a little bigger than me. He hadn't on anything but a shirt, and he was very frowzy-headed. He came in gaping and digging one fist into his eyes, and he was dragging a gun along with the other one. He says:

"Ain't they no Shepherdsons around?"

They said, no, 'twas a false alarm.

"Well," he says, "if they'd a ben some, I reckon I'd a got one."

They all laughed, and Bob says:

"Why, Buck, they might have scalped us all, you've been so slow in coming."

"Well, nobody come after me, and it ain't right I'm always kept down; I don't get no show."

"Never mind, Buck, my boy," says the old man, "you'll have show enough, all in good time, don't you fret about that. Go 'long with you now, and do as your mother told you."

When we got up-stairs to his room he got me a coarse shirt and a roundabout and pants of his, and I put them on. While I was at it he asked me what my name was, but before I could tell him he started to tell me about a bluejay and a young rabbit he had catched in the woods day before yesterday, and he asked me where Moses was when the candle went out. I said I didn't know; I hadn't heard about it before, no way.

"Well, guess," he says.

"How'm I going to guess," says I, "when I never heard tell of it before?"

"But you can guess, can't you? It's just as easy."

"*Which* candle?" I says.

"Why, any candle," he says.

"I don't know where he was," says I; "where was he?"

"Why, he was in the *dark*! That's where he was!"

"Well, if you knowed where he was, what did you ask me for?"

"Why, blame it, it's a riddle, don't you see? Say, how long are you going to stay here? You got to stay always. We can just have booming times—they don't have no school now. Do you own a dog? I've got a dog—and he'll go in the river and bring out chips that you throw in. I got my own bunderlug, too. Does whatever I tells him. The best of the lot. Do you like to comb up Sundays, and all that kind of foolishness? You bet I don't, but ma she makes me. Confound these ole britches! I reckon I'd better put 'em on, but I'd ruther not, it's so warm. Are you all ready? All right. Come along, old hoss."

Cold corn-pone, cold corn-beef, butter and buttermilk—that is what they had for me down there, and there ain't nothing better that ever I've come across yet. Buck and his ma and all of them smoked cob pipes, except the dead woman, which was gone, and the two young women. They all smoked and talked, and I eat and talked. The baggers had been rounded up and put to a room all by themselves. I could hear 'em mumblin' and mutterin' through the wall. The young women had quilts around them, and their hair down their backs. They all asked me questions, and I told them how pap and me and all the family was living on a little farm down at the bottom of Arkansaw, and my sister Mary Ann run off and got married and never was heard of no more, and Bill went to hunt them and he warn't heard of no more, and Tom and Mort died, and then there warn't nobody but just me and pap left, and he was just trimmed down to nothing, on account of his troubles; so when he died I took what there was left, because the farm didn't belong to us, and started up the river, deck passage, and fell overboard; and that was how I come to be here. So they said I could have a home there as long as I wanted it. Then it was most daylight and everybody went to bed, and I went to bed with Buck, and when I waked up in the morning, drat it all, I had forgot what my name was. So I laid there about an hour trying to think, and when Buck waked up I says:

"Can you spell, Buck?"

"Yes," he says.

"I bet you can't spell my name," says I.

"I bet you what you dare I can," says he.

"All right," says I, "go ahead."

"G-e-o-r-g-e J-a-x-o-n—there now," he says.

"Well," says I, "you done it, but I didn't think you could. It ain't no slouch of a name to spell—right off without studying."

I set it down, private, because somebody might want *me* to spell it next, and so I wanted to be handy with it and rattle it off like I was used to it.

It was a mighty nice family, and a mighty nice house, too. I hadn't seen no house out in the country before that was so nice and had so much style. The room that was just to put the baggers in was bigger than what some families call a home. It didn't have an iron latch on the front door, nor a wooden one with a buckskin string, but a brass knob to turn, the same as houses in town. There warn't no bed in the parlor, nor a sign of a bed; but heaps of parlors in towns has beds in them. There was a big fireplace that was bricked on the bottom, and the bricks was kept clean and red by pouring water on them and scrubbing them with another brick; sometimes they wash them over with red water-paint that they call Spanish-brown, same as they do in town. They had big brass dog-irons that could hold up a saw-log. There was a clock on the middle of the mantel-piece, with a picture of a town painted on the bottom half of the glass front, and a round place in the middle of it for the sun, and you could see the pendulum swinging behind it. It was beautiful to hear that clock tick; and sometimes when one of these peddlers had been along and scoured her up and got her in good shape, she would start in and strike a hundred and fifty before she got tuckered out. They wouldn't took any money for her.

Well, there was a big outlandish parrot on each side of the clock, made out of something like chalk, and painted up gaudy. By one of the parrots was a cat made of crockery, and a crockery dog by the other; and when you pressed down on them they squeaked, but didn't open their mouths nor look different nor interested. They squeaked through underneath. There was a couple of big wild-turkey-wing fans spread out behind those things. On the table in the middle of the room was a kind of a lovely crockery basket that had apples and oranges and peaches and grapes piled up in it, which was much redder and yellower and prettier than real ones is, but they warn't real because you could see where pieces had got chipped off and showed the white chalk, or whatever it was, underneath.

This table had a cover made out of beautiful oilcloth, with a red and blue spread-eagle painted on it, and a painted border all around. It come all the way from Philadelphia, they said. There was some books, too, piled up perfectly exact, on each corner of the table. One was a big family Bible full of pictures. And there was the Julius Caesar book, about his wars and how the world was made up of three pieces. Another one was Pilgrim's Progress, about a man that left his family, it didn't say why. I read considerable in it now and then. The statements was interesting, but tough. Another was Friendship's Offering, full of beautiful stuff and poetry; but I didn't read the poetry. Another was Henry Clay's Speeches, and another was Dr. Gunn's Family Medicine, which told you all about what to do if a body was sick or dead. And there was a smaller book by Dr. Redman, cheaper lookin' and ratted around the edges, which talked about bunderlugs. Words like decomposition and aggression. It told how the dead was no more human than a stone or a dog, but could be put to good work depending on several factors. Things I mostly already knowed. There was a hymn book, too, and a lot of other books. And there was nice split-bottom chairs, and perfectly sound, too—not bagged down in the middle and busted, like an old basket.

They had pictures hung on the walls—mainly Washingtons and Lafayettes, and battles, and Highland Marys, and one called "Signing the Declaration." There was some that they called crayons, which one of the daughters which was dead and not come back made her own self when she was only fifteen years old. They was different from any pictures I ever see before—blacker, mostly, than is common. One was a woman in a slim black dress, belted small under the armpits, with bulges like a cabbage in the middle of the sleeves, and a large black scoop-shovel bonnet with a black veil, and white slim ankles crossed about with black tape, and very wee black slippers, like a chisel, and she was leaning pensive on a tombstone on her right elbow, under a weeping willow, and her other hand hanging down her side holding a white handkerchief and a reticule, and underneath the picture it said "Shall I Never See Thee More Alas." Another one was a young lady with her hair all combed up straight to the top of her head, and knotted there in front of a comb like a chair-back, and she was crying into a handkerchief and had a dead bird laying on its back in her other hand with its heels up, and underneath the picture it said "I Shall Never Hear Thy Sweet Chirrup More Alas." There was one where a young lady was at a window looking up at the moon, and tears running down her cheeks; and she had an open letter in one hand with black sealing wax showing on one edge of it, and she was mashing a locket with a chain to it against her mouth, and underneath the picture it said "And Art Thou Gone Yes Thou Art Gone Alas." And yet another what showed a man with a caved-in face and blank eyes, surely dead, an' he was holding a kettle, and underneath the picture it said "I Am Returned Unto You For A Time Alas." These was all nice pictures, I reckon, but I didn't somehow seem to take to them, because if ever I was down a little they always give me the fan-tods. Everybody was sorry she died, because she had laid out a lot more of these pictures to do, and a body could see by what she had done what they had lost. But I reckoned that with her disposition she was having a better time in the graveyard. She was at work on what they said was her greatest picture when she took sick, and every day and every night it was her prayer to be allowed to live till she got it done, but she never got the chance. It was a picture of a young woman in a long white gown, standing on the rail of a bridge all ready to jump off, with her hair all down her back, and looking up to the moon, with the tears running down her face, and she had two arms folded across her breast, and two arms stretched out in front, and two more reaching up towards the moon—and the idea was to see which pair would look best, and then scratch out all the other arms; but, as I was saying, she died before she got her mind made up, and now they kept this picture over the head of the bed in her room, and every time her birthday come they hung flowers on it. Other times it was hid with a little curtain. The young woman in the picture had a kind of a nice sweet face, but there was so many arms it made her look too spidery, seemed to me.

This young girl kept a scrap-book when she was alive, and used to paste obituaries and accidents and cases of patient suffering in it out of the Presbyterian Observer, and write poetry after them out of her own head. It was very good poetry. This is what she wrote about a boy by the name of Stephen Dowling Bots that fell down a well and was drownded:

Ode to Stephen Dowling Bots, Dec'd

And did young Stephen sicken, And did young Stephen die? And did the sad hearts thicken, And did the mourners cry?

No; such was not the fate of Young Stephen Dowling Bots; Though sad hearts round him thickened, 'Twas not from sickness' shots.

No whooping-cough did rack his frame, Nor measles drear with spots; Not these impaired the sacred name Of Stephen Dowling Bots.

Despised love struck not with woe That head of curly knots, Nor stomach troubles laid him low, Young Stephen Dowling Bots.

O no. Then list with tearful eye, Whilst I his fate do tell. His soul did from this cold world fly By falling down a well.

They got him out and emptied him; Alas it was too late; His spirit was gone for to sport aloft In the realms of the good and great.

If Emmeline Grangerford could make poetry like that before she was fourteen, there ain't no telling what she could a done by and by. Buck said she could rattle off poetry like nothing. She didn't ever have to stop to think. He said she would slap down a line, and if she couldn't find anything to rhyme with it would just scratch it out and slap down another one, and go ahead. She warn't particular; she could write about anything you choose to give her to write about just so it was sadful. Every time a man died, or come back, or a woman died, or come back, or a child died, or come back, she would be on hand with her "tribute" before he was cold. She called them tributes. The neighbors said it was the doctor first, then Emmeline, then the undertaker—the undertaker never got in ahead of Emmeline but once, and then she hung fire on a rhyme for the dead person's name, which was Whistler. She warn't ever the same after that; she never complained, but she kinder pined away and did not live long. Poor thing, many's the time I made myself go up to the little room that used to be hers and get out her poor old scrap-book and read in it when her pictures had been aggravating me and I had soured on her a little. I liked all that family, dead ones and all, and warn't going to let anything come between us. Poor Emmeline made poetry about all the dead people when she was alive, all the alive people who was dead, and it didn't seem right that there warn't nobody to make some about her now she was gone; so I tried to sweat out a verse or two myself, but I couldn't seem to make it go somehow. They kept Emmeline's room trim and nice, and all the things fixed in it just the way she liked to have them when she was alive, and nobody ever slept there. The old lady took care of the room herself, though there was plenty of baggers to do the work, and she sewed there a good deal and read her Bible there mostly.

Well, as I was saying about the parlor, there was beautiful curtains on the windows: white, with pictures painted on them of castles with vines all down the walls, and cattle coming down to drink. There was a little old piano, too, that had tin pans in it, I reckon, and nothing was ever so lovely as to hear the young ladies sing "The Last Link Is Broken" and play "The Battle of Prague" on it. The walls of all the rooms was plastered, and most had carpets on the floors, and the whole house was whitewashed on the outside.

It was a double house, and the big open place betwixt them was roofed and floored, and sometimes the table was set there in the middle of the day, and it was a cool, comfortable place. Nothing couldn't be better. And warn't the cooking good, and just bushels of it too!

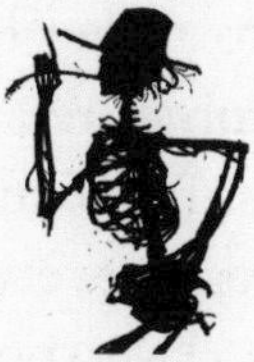

CHAPTER XVIII

Col. Grangerford was a gentleman, you see. He was a gentleman all over; and so was his family. He was well born, as the saying is, and that's worth as much in a man as it is in a horse, so the Widow Douglas said, and nobody ever denied that she was of the first aristocracy in our town; and pap he always said it, too, though he warn't no more quality than a mudcat himself. Col. Grangerford was very tall and very slim, and had a darkish-paly complexion, not a sign of red in it anywheres; he was clean shaved every morning all over his thin face, and he had the thinnest kind of lips, and the thinnest kind of nostrils, and a high nose, and heavy eyebrows, and the blackest kind of eyes, sunk so deep back that they seemed like they was looking out of caverns at you, as you may say. His forehead was high, and his hair was black and straight and hung to his shoulders. His hands was long and thin, and every day of his life he put on a clean shirt and a full suit from head to foot made out of linen so white it hurt your eyes to look at it; and on Sundays he wore a blue tail-coat with brass buttons on it. He carried a mahogany cane with a silver head to it. There warn't no frivolishness about him, not a bit, and he warn't ever loud. He was as kind as he could be—you could feel that, you know, and so you had confidence. Sometimes he smiled, and it was good to see; but when he straightened himself up like a liberty-pole, and the lightning begun to flicker out from under his eyebrows, you wanted to climb a tree first, and find out what the matter was afterwards. He didn't ever have to tell anybody to mind their manners—everybody was always good-mannered where he was. Everybody loved to have him around, too; he was sunshine most always—I mean he made it seem like good weather. When he turned into a cloudbank it was awful dark for half a minute, and that was enough; there wouldn't nothing go wrong again for a week.

When him and the old lady come down in the morning all the family got up out of their chairs and give them good-day, and didn't set down again till they had set down. Then Tom and Bob went to the sideboard where the decanter was, and mixed a glass of bitters and handed it to him, and he held it in his hand and waited till Tom's and Bob's was mixed, and then they bowed and said, "Our duty to you, sir, and madam;" and *they* bowed the least bit in the world and said thank you, and so they drank, all three, and Bob and Tom poured a spoonful of water on the sugar and the mite of whisky or apple brandy in the bottom of their tumblers, and give it to me and Buck, and we drank to the old people too.

Bob was the oldest and Tom next—tall, beautiful men with very broad shoulders and brown faces, and long black hair and black eyes. They dressed in white linen from head to foot, like the old gentleman, and wore broad Panama hats.

Then there was Miss Charlotte; she was twenty-five, and tall and proud and grand, but as good as she could be when she warn't stirred up; but when she was she had a look that would make you wilt in your tracks, like her father. She was beautiful.

So was her sister, Miss Sophia, but it was a different kind. She was gentle and sweet like a dove, and she was only twenty.

Each person had their own bagger to wait on them—Buck too, an' he believed his to be the smartest and best of all. My bagger had a monstrous easy time, because I warn't used to having anybody do anything for me, but Buck's was on the jump most of the time.

This was all there was of the family now, but there used to be more—three sons; they got killed; and Emmeline that died.

The old gentleman owned a lot of farms and over a hundred baggers. He freed all his negros on the very day the zomby legislation was past. He said he never felt none too good about workin' humans, no matter how dark they was, an' usin' the dead was the smartest idea anyone ever come up with. He said it would radicalize the whole future.

Sometimes a stack of people would come there, horseback, from ten or fifteen mile around, and stay five or six days, and have such junketings round about and on the river, and dances and picnics in the woods daytimes, and balls at the house nights. These people was mostly kinfolks of the family. The men brought their guns with them. It was a handsome lot of quality, I tell you.

There was another clan of aristocracy around there—five or six families—mostly of the name of Shepherdson. They was as high-toned and well born and rich and grand as the tribe of Grangerfords. The Shepherdsons and Grangerfords used the same steamboat landing, which was about two mile above our house; so sometimes when I went up there with a lot of our folks I used to see a lot of the Shepherdsons there on their fine horses.

One day Buck and me was away out in the woods hunting, and heard a horse coming. We was crossing the road. Buck says:

"Quick! Jump for the woods!"

We done it, and then peeped down the woods through the leaves. Pretty soon a splendid young man come galloping down the road, setting his horse easy and looking like a soldier. He had his gun across his pommel. I had seen him before. It was young Harney Shepherdson. I heard Buck's gun go off at my ear, and Harney's hat tumbled off from his head. He grabbed his gun and rode straight to the place where we was hid. But we didn't wait. We started through the woods on a run. The woods warn't thick, so I looked over my shoulder to dodge the bullet, and twice I seen Harney cover Buck with his gun; and then he rode away the way he come—to get his hat, I reckon, but I couldn't see. I only know Harney coulda had 'im, if he wanted.

I got a bad feelin' in my guts. I thought about that li'l bagger boy what I finished off. He warn't even alive no more. I couldn't imagine killin' a real live boy. I think I'd toss up my vittles an' never eat or sleep right ag'in.

We never stopped running till we got home. The old gentleman's eyes blazed a minute—'twas pleasure, mainly, I judged—then his face sort of smoothed down, and he says, kind of gentle:

"I don't like that shooting from behind a bush. Why didn't you step into the road, my boy?"

"The Shepherdsons don't, father. They always take advantage."

Miss Charlotte she held her head up like a queen while Buck was telling his tale, and her nostrils spread and her eyes snapped. The two young men looked dark, but never

said nothing. Miss Sophia she turned pale, but the color come back when she found the man warn't hurt.

Soon as I could get Buck down by the corn-cribs under the trees by ourselves, I says:

"Did you want to kill him, Buck?"

"Well, I bet I did."

"What did he do to you?"

"Him? He never done nothing to me."

"Well, then, what did you want to kill him for?"

"Why, nothing—only it's on account of the feud."

"What's a feud?"

"Why, where was you raised? Don't you know what a feud is?"

"Never heard of it before—tell me about it."

"Well," says Buck, "a feud is this way: A man has a quarrel with another man, and kills him; then that other man's brother kills *him*; then the other brothers, on both sides, goes for one another; then the *cousins* chip in—and by and by everybody's killed off, and there ain't no more feud. But it's kind of slow, and takes a long time."

"Has this one been going on long, Buck?"

"Well, I should *reckon*! It started thirty year ago, or som'ers along there. There was trouble 'bout something, and then a lawsuit to settle it; and the suit went agin one of the men, and so he up and shot the man that won the suit—which he would naturally do, of course. Anybody would."

"What was the trouble about, Buck?—land?"

"I reckon maybe—I don't know."

"Well, who done the shooting? Was it a Grangerford or a Shepherdson?"

"Laws, how do I know? It was so long ago."

"Don't anybody know?"

"Oh, yes, pa knows, I reckon, and some of the other old people; but they don't know now what the row was about in the first place."

"Has there been many killed, Buck?"

"Yes; right smart chance of funerals. But they don't always kill. Pa's got a few buckshot in him; but he don't mind it 'cuz he don't weigh much, anyway. Bob's been carved up some with a bowie, and Tom's been hurt once or twice."

"Has anybody been killed this year, Buck?"

"Yes; we got one and they got one. 'Bout three months ago my cousin Bud, fourteen year old, was riding through the woods on t'other side of the river, and didn't have no weapon with him, which was blame' foolishness, and in a lonesome place he hears a horse a-coming behind him, and sees old Baldy Shepherdson a-linkin' after him with his gun in his hand and his white hair a-flying in the wind; and 'stead of jumping off and taking to the brush, Bud 'lowed he could out-run him; so they had it, nip and tuck, for five mile or more, the old man a-gaining all the time; so at last Bud seen it warn't any use, so he stopped and faced around so as to have the bullet holes in front, you know, and the old man he rode up and shot him down. But he didn't git much chance to enjoy his luck, for inside of a week our folks laid *him* out."

"I reckon that old man was a coward, Buck."

"I reckon he *warn't* a coward. Not by a blame' sight. There ain't a coward amongst them Shepherdsons—not a one. And there ain't no cowards amongst the Grangerfords either. Why, that old man kep' up his end in a fight one day for half an hour against three Grangerfords, and come out winner. They was all a-horseback; he lit off of his horse and got behind a little woodpile, and kep' his horse before him to stop the bullets; but the Grangerfords stayed on their horses and capered around the old man, and peppered away at him, and he peppered away at them. Him and his horse both went home pretty leaky and crippled, but the Grangerfords had to be *fetched* home—and one of 'em was dead, and another died the next day. No, sir; if a body's out hunting for cowards he don't want to fool away any time amongst them Shepherdsons, becuz they don't breed any of that *kind*."

Next Sunday we all went to church, about three mile, everybody a-horseback. The men took their guns along, so did Buck, and kept them between their knees or stood them handy against the wall. The Shepherdsons done the same. It was pretty ornery preaching—all about

Judgment an' Damnation, and such-like tiresomeness; and how the fissythis was runnin' out of control an' the bunderlugs was agents of Satan who would shortly turn against mankind; but everybody said it was a good sermon, and they all talked it over going home, and had such a powerful lot to say about faith and good works and free grace and preforeordestination and anything to change the subject away from Judgment and Damnation, and I don't know what all, that it did seem to me to be one of the roughest Sundays I had run across yet.

We ate and the old gentleman said that the fissythis pox, like all poxes and all things, would 'ventually run its course and the world would right itself.

He said there had been ten years or better of fissythis an' I didn't realize it had been around such a long time. He said it started out as consumption, faraways back, and changed its disposition when it arrived in America. That information was in the books he owned, though he admitted there were not a few minds who were in disagreement over the whole thing.

"Either way, it'll pass."

I had to wonder what would become of the workforce if the fissythis really did go away. When all the baggers go back to Hell, who will folks buy and sell? They already set the negros free, so I supposed they'd have to get out there an' catch Chinamen or A-rabs to pick up the slack.

About an hour after dinner everybody was dozing

around, some in their chairs and some in their rooms, and it got to be pretty dull. Buck and a dog was stretched out on the grass in the sun sound asleep. I went up to our room, and judged I would take a nap myself. I found that sweet Miss Sophia standing in her door, which was next to ours, and she took me in her room and shut the door very soft, and asked me if I liked her, and I said I did; and she asked me if I would do something for her and not tell anybody, and I said I would. Then she said she'd forgot her Testament, and left it in the seat at church between two other books, and would I slip out quiet and go there and fetch it to her, and not say nothing to nobody. I said I would. So I slid out and slipped off up the road, and there warn't anybody at the church, except maybe a hog or two, for there warn't any lock on the door, and hogs likes a puncheon floor in summer-time because it's cool. If you notice, most folks don't go to church only when they've got to; but a hog is different.

Says I to myself, something's up; it ain't natural for a girl to be in such a sweat about a Testament. So I give it a shake, and out drops a little piece of paper with "*half-past two*" wrote on it with a pencil. I ransacked it, but couldn't find anything else. I couldn't make anything out of that, so I put the paper in the book again, and when I got home and upstairs there was Miss Sophia in her door waiting for me. She pulled me in and shut the door; then she looked in the Testament till she found the paper, and as soon as she read it she looked glad; and before a body could think she grabbed me and give me a squeeze, and said I was the best boy in the world, and not to tell anybody. She was mighty red in the face for a minute, and her eyes lighted up, and it made her powerful pretty. I was a good deal astonished, but when

I got my breath I asked her what the paper was about, and she asked me if I had read it, and I said no, and she asked me if I could read writing, and I told her "no, only coarse-hand," and then she said the paper warn't anything but a book-mark to keep her place, and I might go and play now.

I went off down to the river, studying over this thing, and pretty soon I noticed that my bagger was following along behind. Not Jim, but the one that was provided for me by the Grangerfords. I din' know what become of Jim. When this bagger was out of sight of the house he looked back and around a second, and then comes a-running, and says:

"Mars Jawge, if you'll come down into de swamp I'll show you a whole stack o' water-moccasins."

Thinks I, that's mighty curious; he said that yesterday. He oughter know a body don't love water-moccasins enough to go around hunting for them. What is he up to, anyway? So I says:

"All right; trot ahead."

I followed a half a mile; then he struck out over the swamp, and waded ankle deep as much as another half-mile. We come to a little flat piece of land which was dry and very thick with trees and bushes and vines, and he says:

"You shove right in dah jist a few steps, Mars Jawge; dah's whah dey is. I's seed 'm befo'; I don't k'yer to see 'em no mo'."

Then he slopped right along and went away, and pretty soon the trees hid him. I poked into the place a-ways and come to a little open patch as big as a bedroom all hung around with vines, and found a man laying there asleep—and, by jings, it was my old Jim!

I waked him up, and I reckoned it was going to be a

grand surprise to him to see me again, but it warn't. He nearly cried he was so glad, but he warn't surprised. Said he swum along behind me that night, and heard me yell every time, but dasn't answer, because he didn't want nobody to pick *him* up and take him into slavery again. Says he:

"I got sad a little, en couldn't swim fas', so I wuz a considable ways behine you towards de las'; when you landed I reck'ned I could ketch up wid you on de lan' 'dout havin' to shout at you, but when I see dat house I begin to go slow. I 'uz off too fur to hear what dey say to you—I wuz 'fraid o' de dogs; but when it 'uz all quiet agin I knowed you's in de house, so I struck out for de woods to wait for day. Early in de mawnin' some er de baggers come along, gwyne to de fields, en dey tuk me en showed me dis place, whah de dogs can't track me on accounts o' de water, en dey brings me truck to eat every night, en tells me how you's a-gitt'n along."

"Why didn't you tell my bunderlug to fetch me here sooner, Jim?"

"Well, 'twarn't no use to 'sturb you, Huck, tell we could do sumfn—but we's all right now. I ben doin' what I cain, en a-patchin' up de raf' nights when—"

"*What* raft, Jim?"

"Our ole raf'."

"You mean to say our old raft warn't smashed all to flinders?"

"No, she warn't. She was tore up a good deal—one en' of her was; but dey warn't no great harm done, on'y our traps was mos' all los'. Ef we hadn' dive' so deep en swum so fur under water, en de night hadn' ben so dark, en we warn't so sk'yerd, en ben sich punkin-heads, as de sayin' is, we'd a seed de raf'. But it's jis' as well we didn't, 'kase now she's all fixed up agin mos' as good as new, en we's got a new lot o' stuff, in de place o' what 'uz los'."

"Why, how did you get hold of the raft again, Jim—did you catch her?"

"How I gwyne to ketch her en I out in de woods? No; some er de zombys foun' her ketched on a snag along heah in de ben', en dey hid her in a crick 'mongst de willows, en dey wuz so much jawin' 'bout which un 'um she b'long to de mos' dat I come to heah 'bout it pooty soon, so I ups en settles de trouble by tellin' 'um she don't b'long to none uv um, but to you en me; en I ast 'm if dey gwyne to grab a young white genlman's propaty, en git a hid'n for it? Den I gin 'm ten cents apiece, en dey 'uz mighty well satisfied, en wisht some mo' raf's 'ud come along en make 'm rich agin. Dey's mighty good to me, dese baggers is, sma'test I ever did meet, en whatever I wants 'm to do fur me I doan' have to ast 'm twice, honey. Dat Jack's a good bagger, en pooty clever."

"Yes, he is. Grangerford money buys the best of the bunch. These almost as smart as you, Jim. But this bagger ain't ever told me you was here; told me to come, and he'd show me a lot of water-moccasins. If anything happens *he* ain't mixed up in it. He can say he never seen us together, and it'll be the truth."

I don't want to talk much about the next day. I reckon I'll cut it pretty short. I waked up about dawn, and was a-going to turn over and go to sleep again when I noticed how still it was—didn't seem to be anybody stirring. That warn't usual. Next I noticed that Buck was up and gone. Well, I gets up, a-wondering, and goes down stairs—nobody around; everything as still as a mouse. Just the same outside. Thinks I, what does it mean? Down by the wood-pile I comes across my bagger, and says:

"What's it all about?"

Says he:

"Don't you know, Mars Jawge?"

"No," says I, "I don't."

"Well, den, Miss Sophia's run off! 'deed she has. She run off in de night some time—nobody don't know jis' when; run off to get married to dat young Harney Shepherdson, you know—leastways, so dey 'spec. De fambly foun' it out 'bout half an hour ago—maybe a little mo'—en' I *tell* you dey warn't no time los'. Sich another hurryin' up guns en hosses *you* never see! De women folks has gone for to stir up de relations, en ole Mars Saul en de boys tuck dey guns en rode up de river road for to try to ketch dat young man en kill him 'fo' he kin git acrost de river wid Miss Sophia. I reck'n dey's gwyne to be mighty rough times."

"Buck went off 'thout waking me up."

"Well, I reck'n he *did*! Dey warn't gwyne to mix you up in it. Mars Buck he loaded up his gun en 'lowed he's gwyne to fetch home a Shepherdson or bust. Well, dey'll be plenty un 'm dah, I reck'n, en you bet you he'll fetch one ef he gits a chanst."

I took up the river road as hard as I could put. By and by I begin to hear guns a good ways off. When I came in sight of the log store and the woodpile where the steamboats lands I worked along under the trees and brush till I got to a good place, and then I clumb up into the forks of a cottonwood that was out of reach, and watched. There was a wood-rank four foot high a little ways in front of the tree, and first I was going to hide behind that; but maybe it was luckier I didn't.

There was four or five men cavorting around on their horses in the open place before the log store, cussing and yelling, and trying to get at a couple of young chaps that was behind the wood-rank alongside of the steamboat landing; but they couldn't come it. Every time one of them showed himself on the river side of the woodpile he got shot at. The two boys was squatting back to back behind the pile, so they could watch both ways.

By and by the men stopped cavorting around and yelling. They started riding towards the store; then up gets one of the boys, draws a steady bead over the wood-rank, and drops one of them out of his saddle. All the men jumped off of their horses and grabbed the hurt one and started to carry him to the store; and that minute the two boys started on the run. They got half way to the tree I was in before the men noticed. Then the men see them, and jumped on their horses and took out after them. They gained on the boys, but it didn't do no good, the boys had too good a start; they got to the woodpile that was in front of my tree, and slipped in behind it, and so they had the bulge on the men again. One of the boys was Buck, and the other was a slim young chap about nineteen years old.

The men ripped around awhile, and then rode away. As soon as they was out of sight I sung out to Buck and told him. He didn't know what to make of my voice coming out of the tree at first. He was awful surprised. He told me to watch out sharp and let him know when the men come in sight again; said they was up to some devilment or other—wouldn't be gone long. I wished I was out of that tree, but I dasn't come down. Buck begun to cry and rip, and 'lowed that him and his cousin Joe (that was the other young chap) would make up for this day yet. He said his father and his two brothers was killed, and two or three of the enemy. Said the Shepherdsons laid for them in ambush. Buck said his father and brothers ought to waited for their relations—the Shepherdsons was too strong for them. I asked him what was become of young Harney and Miss Sophia. He said they'd got across the river and was safe. I was glad of that; but the way Buck did take on because he didn't manage to kill Harney that day he shot at him—I hain't ever heard anything like it.

All of a sudden, bang! bang! bang! goes three or four guns—the men had slipped around through the woods and come in from behind without their horses! The boys jumped for the river—both of them hurt—and as they swum down the current the men run along the bank shooting at them and singing out, "Kill them, kill them!"

And things got much worse than that. Here come a terrible sound, like a crowd of angry hooligans shouting pure gibberish, and from the north comes a storm of teeth and limbs. These was bunderlugs, full-baggers, vicious and stoked with rage.

Where they come out of, I don't know. Somebody might think these zombys got themselves all together and hatched a scheme to cause a bunch of trouble; but someone else might incline to think it was a body's idea to catch n' corral 'em an' release 'em like a stampeding army at just the right moment.

So there was all this rage and viciousness going on. Men who was shooting on one another had to turn and shoot on the crazed baggers, some two-dozen strong. And it wasn't enough to kill a bagger by shooting him in the gut or in the chest. As I said, you got to get him in the brains, specific'ly at the trunk. You got to put him down by smashing his senses into jelly, otherwise he'll just keep comin' at you.

Well, what happened was an orgy of teeth and blood.

All those folks down there, no matter who they was or whose side they was on, they got themselves all tore up and ate by this throng of full-baggers.

It made me so sick I most fell out of the tree. I ain't a-going to tell *all* that happened—it would make me sick again if I was to do that. I wished I hadn't ever come ashore that night to see such things. I ain't ever going to get shut of them—lots of times I dream about them. Of these vicious men being outnumbered by even greater viciousness. Ever'thing Jim said 'bout feeling strange an' hungry was true. Them bunderlugs had a wicked taste for human flesh.

Only the devil could concoct such a thing.

I stayed in the tree till it begun to get dark, afraid to come down. There was no sound from a living person, only a few stray horses here and about. And when all that was left of the Shepherdsons and the Grangerfords was bones and steel, the baggers began to thin out, moving off into the bushes, yonder. They din' mark me. Their bellies was too full up to care anymore, I s'pect.

And there was all these piles of chewed meat, red and purple, which had passed through the baggers without being even a mite digested.

I saw another thing, too, which I will get to in a spell.

I was completely sickened and downhearted; so I made up my mind I wouldn't ever go anear that house again, because I reckoned I was to blame, somehow. I judged that that piece of paper meant that Miss Sophia was to meet Harney somewheres at half-past two and run off; and I judged I ought to told her father about that paper and the curious way she acted, and then maybe he would a locked her up, and this awful mess wouldn't ever happened.

When I got down out of the tree I crept along down

the river bank a piece, and found two bodies laying in the edge of the water, and tugged at them till I got them ashore; these ones wasn't eaten by zombys; then I covered up their faces, and got away as quick as I could. I cried a little when I was covering up Buck's face, for he was mighty good to me.

It was just dark now. I never went near the house, but struck through the woods and made for the swamp. Jim warn't on his island, so I tramped off in a hurry for the crick, and crowded through the willows, red-hot to jump aboard and get out of that awful country. The raft was gone! My souls, but I was scared! I couldn't get my breath for most a minute. Then I raised a yell. A voice not twenty-five foot from me says:

"Good lan'! is dat you, honey? Doan' make no noise."

It was Jim's voice—nothing ever sounded so good before. I run along the bank a piece and got aboard, and Jim he grabbed me and hugged me, he was so glad to see me. He says:

"Laws bless you, chile, I 'uz right down sho' you's dead agin. Bagger's been heah; he say he reck'n you's ben shot or ate up, kase you didn' come home no mo'; so I's jes' dis minute a startin' de raf' down towards de mouf er de crick, so's to be all ready for to shove out en leave soon as Jack comes agin en tells me for certain you IS dead. Lawsy, I's mighty glad to git you back again, honey."

I says:

"All right—that's mighty good; folks'll think I've been killed again, and chewed up or floated down the river—there's *lots* up there that 'll *surely* help them think so—so don't you lose no time, Jim, but just shove off for the big water as fast as ever you can. The woods is full up of monsters, more'n I coula 'magined."

I never felt easy till the raft was two mile below there and out in the middle of the Mississippi. Then we hung up our signal lantern, and judged that we was free and safe once more. I hadn't had a bite to eat since yesterday, an' I first wasn't sure thet I *could* eat but my stummick said it surely thought so, so Jim he got out some corn-dodgers and buttermilk, and pork and cabbage and greens—there ain't nothing in the world so good when it's cooked right—and whilst I eat my supper we talked and had a good time. I was powerful glad to get away from the death, and so was Jim to get away from the swamp. We said there warn't no home like a raft, after all. Other places do seem so cramped up and smothery, but a raft don't. You feel mighty free and easy and comfortable on a raft.

And the monsters cain't get you there. Not so easy.

CHAPTER XIX

Two or three days and nights went by; I reckon I might say they swum by, they slid along so quiet and smooth and lovely. Here is the way we put in the time. It was a monstrous big river down there—sometimes a mile and a half wide; we run nights, and laid up and hid daytimes; soon as night was most gone we stopped navigating and tied up—nearly always in the dead water under a towhead; and then cut young cottonwoods and willows, and hid the raft with them. Then we set out the lines. Next we slid into the river and had a swim, so as to freshen up and cool off; then we set down on the sandy bottom where the water was about knee deep, and watched the daylight come. Not a sound anywheres—perfectly still—just like the whole world was asleep, only sometimes the bullfrogs a-cluttering, maybe. The first thing to see, looking away over the water, was a kind of dull line—that was the woods on t'other side; you couldn't make nothing else out; then a pale place in the sky; then more paleness spreading around; then the river softened up away off, and warn't black any more, but gray; you could see little dark spots drifting along ever so far away—trading scows, and such things; and long black streaks—rafts; sometimes you could hear a sweep screaking; or jumbled up voices, it was so still, and sounds come so far; and by and by you could see a streak on the water which you know by the look of the streak that there's a snag there in a swift current which breaks on it and makes that streak look that way; and you see the mist curl up off of the water, and the east reddens up, and the river, and you make out a log-cabin in the edge of the woods, away on the bank on t'other side of the river, being a woodyard, likely, and piled by them cheats so you can throw a dog through it anywheres; then the nice breeze springs up, and comes fanning you from over there, so cool and fresh and sweet to smell on account of the woods and the flowers; but sometimes not that way, because they've left dead fish laying around, gars and such, and they do get pretty rank; and next you've got the full day, and everything smiling in the sun, and the song-birds just going it!

I had to ask Jim a thing. I says:

"You say you got the hunger, huh?"

"Aw yes," Jim says. "I got it alla time, like a pain inside me, but I knows betta than to act on it. I's yo' friend, Huck. I ain't never want to eat you up."

"When I saw them vicious full-baggers come eatin' on the Shepherdsons an' the Grangerfords, I saw other things, too."

"Like what, chile? Say."

"I saw some of the half-baggers thet worked the Grangerford house. I saw thet these ones was among the vicious ones, and they was doing just as much eating. It was like there was no diff'rence in disposition. Like they was the same, all claws an' teeth, even though they was docile just th' night before."

"That *is* something, Huck."

"I think so."

A little smoke couldn't be noticed now, so we would take some fish off of the lines and cook up a hot breakfast.

And afterwards we would watch the lonesomeness of the river, and kind of lazy along, and by and by lazy off to sleep. Wake up by and by, and look to see what done it, and maybe see a steamboat coughing along up-stream, so far off towards the other side you couldn't tell nothing about her only whether she was a stern-wheel or side-wheel; then for about an hour there wouldn't be nothing to hear nor nothing to see—just solid lonesomeness. Next you'd see a raft sliding by, away off yonder, and maybe a galoot on it chopping, because they're most always doing it on a raft; you'd see the axe flash and come down—you don't hear nothing; you see that axe go up again, and by the time it's above the man's head then you hear the *k'chunk*!—it had took all that time to come over the water. So we would put in the day, lazying around, listening to the stillness. Once there was a thick fog, and the rafts and things that went by was beating tin pans so the steamboats wouldn't run over them. A scow or a raft went by so close we could hear them talking and cussing and laughing—heard them plain; but we couldn't see no sign of them; it made you feel crawly; it was like spirits carrying on that way in the air. Jim said he believed it was spirits; but I says:

"No; spirits wouldn't say, 'Dern the dern fog.'"

Soon as it was night out we shoved; when we got her out to about the middle we let her alone, and let her float wherever the current wanted her to; then we lit the pipes, and dangled our legs in the water, and talked about all kinds of things—we was always naked, day and night, whenever the mosquitoes would let us—the new clothes Buck's folks made for me was too good to be comfortable, and besides I didn't go much on clothes, nohow.

Jim was a damn sight, naked. If you saw him without

his clothes, thar's no way you could mistake him for a living being. Aside from all his lesions and pocks and scars and 'brasions and holes, such as the spot where I cut his brand out, he was also grossly out of color in certain places. When he was alive, he was a negro of medium darkness, like powdered cocoa. But now that he was dead, having visited the devil, he was all sorts of colors and shades. His back, where the ribs showed through, was like a vibrant purple. His legs below the knees, down to his ankles, was coal black. His stummick was kinda blue and kinda green. He was something like a dark rainbow.

Sometimes we'd have that whole river all to ourselves for the longest time. Yonder was the banks and the islands, across the water; and maybe a spark—which was a candle in a cabin window; and sometimes on the water you could see a spark or two—on a raft or a scow, you know; and maybe you could hear a fiddle or a song coming over from one of them crafts. It's lovely to live on a raft. We had the sky up there, all speckled with stars, and we used to lay on our backs and look up at them, and discuss about whether they was made or only just happened. Jim he allowed they was made, but I allowed they happened; I judged it would have took too long to *make* so many. Jim said the moon could a *laid* them; well, that looked kind of reasonable, so I didn't say nothing against it, because I've seen a frog lay most as many, so of course it could be done. We used to watch the stars that fell, too, and see them streak down. Jim allowed they'd got spoiled and was hove out of the nest.

Jim says, "You trus' that I won' eat you, doncha, Huck?"

I says, "I trust *you*, Jim. But I don' think I trust none o' th' others, no matter how gentle they says they is."

"Only mattas what you trus' me, Huck."

"Well, I do, Jim."

Once or twice of a night we would see a steamboat slipping along in the dark, and now and then she would belch a whole world of sparks up out of her chimbleys, and they would rain down in the river and look awful pretty; then she would turn a corner and her lights would wink out and her powwow shut off and leave the river still again; and by and by her waves would get to us, a long time after she was gone, and joggle the raft a bit, and after that you wouldn't hear nothing for you couldn't tell how long, except maybe frogs or something.

After midnight the people on shore went to bed, and then for two or three hours the shores was black—no more sparks in the cabin windows. These sparks was our clock—the first one that showed again meant morning was coming, so we hunted a place to hide and tie up right away.

Jim said the bunderlugs woulda lay off me as long as I was with him. He said if any come along they'd reco'nize him as one o' their own an' not bother with me at all, no matter how fierce they was. I asked him how he could know such a thing for certain and he said it didn't *know* it, but *felt* it.

One morning about daybreak I found a canoe and crossed over a chute to the main shore—it was only two hundred yards—and paddled about a mile up a crick amongst the cypress woods, to see if I couldn't get some berries. Just as I was passing a place where a kind of a cowpath crossed the crick, here comes a couple of men tearing up the path as tight as they could foot it. I thought I was a goner, for whenever anybody was after anybody I judged it was *me*—or maybe Jim. An' I couldn't tell if these was baggers or not. I was about to dig out from there in a hurry, but they was pretty close to me then, and sung out and begged me to save their lives—said they hadn't been doing nothing, and was being chased for it—said there was men and dogs a-coming. They wanted to jump right in, but I says:

"Don't you do it. I don't hear the dogs and horses yet; you've got time to crowd through the brush and get up the crick a little ways; then you take to the water and wade down to me and get in—that'll throw the dogs off the scent."

They done it, and soon as they was aboard I lit out for our towhead, and in about five or ten minutes we heard the dogs and the men away off, shouting. We heard them come along towards the crick, but couldn't see them; they seemed to stop and fool around a while; then, as we got further and further away all the time, we couldn't hardly hear them at all; by the time we had left a mile of woods behind us and struck the river, everything was quiet, and we paddled over to the towhead and hid in the cottonwoods and was safe.

One of these fellows was about seventy or upwards, and had a bald head and very gray whiskers. He had an old battered-up slouch hat on, and a greasy blue woollen shirt, and ragged old blue jeans britches stuffed into his boot-tops, and home-knit galluses—no, he only had one. He had an old long-tailed blue jeans coat with slick brass buttons flung over his arm, and both of them had big, fat, ratty-looking carpet-bags.

The other fellow was about thirty, and dressed about as ornery. After breakfast we all laid off and talked, and the first thing that come out was that these chaps didn't know one another.

"What got you into trouble?" says the baldhead to t'other chap.

"Well, I'd been selling an article to take the tartar off the teeth—and it does take it off, too, and generly the enamel along with it—but I stayed about one night longer than I ought to, and was just in the act of sliding out when I ran across you on the trail this side of town, and you told me they were coming, and begged me to help you to get off. So I told you I was expecting trouble myself, and would scatter out *with* you. That's the whole yarn—what's yourn?

"Well, I'd ben a-runnin' a little temperance revival thar 'bout a week, and was the pet of the women folks, big and little, for I was makin' it mighty warm for the rummies, I *tell* you, and takin' as much as five or six dollars a night—ten cents a head, children and negros free—and business a-growin' all the time, when somehow or another a little report got around last night that I had a way of puttin' in my time with a private jug on the sly. A negro rousted me out this mornin', and told me the people was getherin' on the quiet with their dogs and horses, and they'd be along pretty soon and give me 'bout half an hour's start, and then run me down if they could; and if they got me they'd tar and feather me and ride me on a rail, sure. I didn't wait for no breakfast—I warn't hungry."

"Old man," said the young one, "I reckon we might double-team it together; what do you think?"

"I ain't undisposed. What's your line—mainly?"

"Jour printer by trade; do a little in patent medicines; theater-actor—tragedy, you know; take a turn to mesmerism and phrenology when there's a chance; teach singing-geography school for a change; sling a lecture sometimes—oh, I do lots of things—most anything that comes handy, so it ain't work. What's your lay?"

"I've done considerble in the doctoring way in my time.

Layin' on o' hands is my best holt—for cancer and paralysis, and sich things; and I k'n tell a fortune pretty good when I've got somebody along to find out the facts for me. Preachin's my line, too, and workin' camp-meetin's, and missionaryin' around."

Nobody never said anything for a while; then the young man hove a sigh and says:

"Alas!"

"What're you alassin' about?" says the bald-head.

"To think I should have lived to be leading such a life, and be degraded down into such company." And he begun to wipe the corner of his eye with a rag.

"Dern your skin, ain't the company good enough for you?" says the baldhead, pretty pert and uppish.

"Yes, it *is* good enough for me; it's as good as I deserve; for who fetched me so low when I was so high? I did myself. I don't blame *you*, gentlemen—far from it; I don't blame anybody. I deserve it all. Let the cold world do its worst; one thing I know—there's a grave somewhere for me. The world may go on just as it's always done, and take everything from me—loved ones, property, everything; but it can't take that. Some day I'll lie down in it and forget it all, and my poor broken heart will be at rest." He went on a-wiping.

"None of us will ever be at rest, I suspect, with the pox keeping us from going into our graves."

"That's a true sentiment, ain't it?"

"Drot your pore broken heart," says the baldhead; "what are you heaving your pore broken heart at *us* f'r? *We* hain't done nothing."

"No, I know you haven't. I ain't blaming you, gentlemen. I brought myself down—yes, I did it myself. It's right I should suffer—perfectly right—I don't make any moan."

"Brought you down from whar? Whar was you brought down from?"

"Ah, you would not believe me; the world never believes—let it pass—'tis no matter. The secret of my birth—"

"The secret of your birth! Do you mean to say—"

"Gentlemen," says the young man, very solemn, "I will reveal it to you, for I feel I may have confidence in you. By rights I am a duke!"

Jim's eyes bugged out when he heard that; and I reckon mine did, too. Then the baldhead says: "No! you can't mean it?"

"Yes. My great-grandfather, eldest son of the Duke of Bridgewater, fled to this country about the end of the last century, to breathe the pure air of freedom; married here, and died, leaving a son, his own father dying about the same time. The second son of the late duke seized the titles and estates—the infant real duke was ignored. I am the lineal descendant of that infant—I am the rightful Duke of Bridgewater; and here am I, forlorn, torn from my high estate, hunted of men, despised by the cold world, ragged, worn, heart-broken, and degraded to the companionship of felons on a raft!"

Jim pitied him ever so much, and so did I. We tried to comfort him, but he said it warn't much use, he couldn't be much comforted; said if we was a mind to acknowledge him, that would do him more good than most anything else; so we said we would, if he would tell us how. He said we ought to bow when we spoke to him, and say "Your Grace," or "My Lord," or "Your Lordship"—and he wouldn't mind it if we called him plain "Bridgewater," which, he said, was a title anyway, and not a name; and one of us ought to wait on him at dinner, and do any little thing for him he wanted done.

Well, that was all easy, so we done it. All through dinner Jim stood around and waited on him, and says, "Will yo' Grace have some o' dis or some o' dat?" and so on, and a body could see it was mighty pleasing to him.

The duke says, "Yer a fine bagger, ain't ya? Smart like I never met before, an' I have met me a whole pile o' baggers. Traded a few in my days. Good money once upon a time. Soon they'll be a nickel for six, I reckon. But I see you still got some sense rattling about in yer big, dead head. You just might appreciate in value."

An' Jim says, "Thanky, yo' grace."

But the old man got pretty silent by and by—didn't have much to say, and didn't look pretty comfortable over all that petting that was going on around that duke. He seemed to have something on his mind. So, along in the afternoon, he says:

"Looky here, Bilgewater," he says, "I'm nation sorry for you, but you ain't the only person that's had troubles like that."

"No?"

"No you ain't. You ain't the only person that's ben snaked down wrongfully out'n a high place."

"Alas!"

"No, you ain't the only person that's had a secret of his birth." And, by jings, *he* begins to cry.

"Hold! What do you mean?"

"Bilgewater, kin I trust you?" says the old man, still sort of sobbing.

"To the bitter death!" He took the old man by the hand and squeezed it, and says, "That secret of your being: speak!"

"Bilgewater, I am the late Dauphin!"

You bet you, Jim and me stared this time. Then the duke says:

"You are what?"

"Yes, my friend, it is too true—your eyes is lookin' at this very moment on the pore disappeared Dauphin, Looy the Seventeen, son of Looy the Sixteen and Marry Antonette."

"You! At your age! No! You mean you're the late Charlemagne; you must be six or seven hundred years old, at the very least."

"Trouble has done it, Bilgewater, trouble has done it; trouble has brung these gray hairs and this premature balditude. Yes, gentlemen, you see before you, in blue jeans and misery, the wanderin', exiled, trampled-on, and sufferin' rightful King of France."

Well, he cried and took on so that me and Jim didn't know hardly what to do, we was so sorry—and so glad and proud we'd got him with us, too. So we set in, like we done before with the duke, and tried to comfort *him*. But he said it warn't no use, nothing but to be dead and done with it all could do him any good; though he said it often made him feel easier and better for a while if people treated him according to his rights, and got down on one knee to speak to him, and always called him "Your Majesty," and waited on him first at meals, and didn't set down in his presence till he asked them. So Jim and me set to majestying him, and doing this and that and t'other for him, and standing up till he told us we might set down. This done him heaps of good, and so he got cheerful and comfortable. But the duke kind of soured on him, and didn't look a bit satisfied with the way things was going; still, the king acted real friendly towards him, and said the duke's great-grandfather and all the other Dukes of Bilgewater was a good deal thought of by *his* father, and was allowed to come to the palace considerable; but the duke stayed huffy a good while, till by and by the king says:

"Like as not we got to be together a blamed long time on this h-yer raft, Bilgewater, and so what's the use o' your bein' sour? It'll only make things oncomfortable. It ain't my fault I warn't born a duke, it ain't your fault you warn't born a king—so what's the use to worry? Make the best o' things the way you find 'em, says I—that's my motto. This ain't no bad thing that we've struck here—plenty grub and an easy life—come, give us your hand, duke, and le's all be friends."

The duke done it, and Jim and me was pretty glad to see it. It took away all the uncomfortableness and we felt mighty good over it, because it would a been a miserable business to have any unfriendliness on the raft; for what you want, above all things, on a raft, is for everybody to be satisfied, and feel right and kind towards the others.

It didn't take me long to make up my mind that these liars warn't no kings nor dukes at all, but just low-down humbugs and frauds. They 'uz always whispering to one another an' makin' suspicious eyes. An' also—I warn't borned just yesterday.

So I took Jim to the edge and started a whisperin' game of my own. I tells him the whole scene smells like pokey to me. I tells him:

"'They ain't no royalty. They's fixin' to fleece us somehow. Mebby knock us overboard an' truck off with the raft."

"Why," says Jim, "would a duke an' dolphin need to fleece *us*?"

"'Cause they ain't no duke an' dolphin, Jim. Lissen up to whut I'm tellin' you—these is conference men. *Bad* men. They're fixin' to swindle us good. I cain't devein the scheme, but sure as tootin' they's cookin' somethin' evil. An' we's just humiliatin' ourselves every time we kneel down."

"Bad men, huh, Huck?"

"*Bad* men. Hyuh!"

And then I gave them swindlers a hard look out of the corner of my eyes, an' I spit in the river so as to look stone. Din' wanna give away the giveaway.

CHAPTER XX

The royals asked us considerable many questions; wanted to know what we covered up the raft that way for, and laid by in the daytime instead of running—was Jim a runaway bagger? Says I:

"Goodness sakes! Aside from bein' a bagger he is also a negro, an' why would a runaway bag-negro run *south* of all places?"

No, they allowed he wouldn't. I had to account for things some way, so I says:

"My folks was living in Pike County, in Missouri, where I was born, and they all died off but me and pa and my brother Ike. Pa, he 'lowed he'd break up and go down and live with Uncle Ben, who's got a little one-horse place on the river, forty-four mile below Orleans. Pa was pretty poor, and had some debts; so when he'd squared up there warn't nothing left but sixteen dollars and our bagger, Jim, who was a livin' breathin' negro until he catched the fissythis. That warn't enough to take us fourteen hundred mile, deck passage nor no other way. Well, when the river rose pa had a streak of luck one day; he ketched this piece of a raft; so we reckoned we'd go down to Orleans on it. Pa's luck didn't hold out; a steamboat run over the forrard corner of the raft one night, and we all went overboard and dove under the wheel; Jim and me come up all right, but pa was drunk, and Ike was only four years old, so they never come up no more. Well, for the next day or two we had considerable trouble, because people was always coming out in skiffs and trying to take Jim away from me, saying they believed he was a runaway bagger. We don't run daytimes no more now; nights they don't bother us."

The duke says:

"Leave me alone to cipher out a way so we can run in the daytime if we want to. I'll think the thing over—I'll invent a plan that'll fix it. We'll let it alone for to-day, because of course we don't want to go by that town yonder in daylight—it mightn't be healthy."

Towards night it begun to darken up and look like rain; the heat lightning was squirting around low down in the sky, and the leaves was beginning to shiver—it was going to be pretty ugly, it was easy to see that. So the duke and the king went to overhauling our wigwam, to see what the beds was like. My bed was a straw tick better than Jim's, which was a corn-shuck tick; there's always cobs around about in a shuck tick, and they poke into you and hurt; and when you roll over the dry shucks sound like you was rolling over in a pile of dead leaves; it makes such a rustling that you wake up. Well, the duke allowed he would take my bed; but the king allowed he wouldn't. He says:

"I should a reckoned the difference in rank would a sejested to you that a corn-shuck bed warn't just fitten for me to sleep on. Your Grace'll take the shuck bed yourself."

Jim and me was in a sweat again for a minute, being afraid there was going to be some more trouble amongst them; so we was pretty glad when the duke says:

"'Tis my fate to be always ground into the mire under the iron heel of oppression. Misfortune has broken my once haughty spirit; I yield, I submit; 'tis my fate. I am alone in the world—let me suffer; can bear it."

I was still dreamin' up a scheme to rid ourselves of these jokers, but so-far I haidn't come up with nothin' much. An' Jim was keepin' pretty mum.

The king comes over an' says, "I knows yer a runnin' zomby 'cause I seen the sign at the print shop. Y'ain't foolin' me, Jim. I knows precisely what's goin' on here, an' I also knows there be a reward fo' yo' capture, too. You jest keep thet in mind. You jest rememba' it's not you two what calls the shots on dis river."

An' I thought about lettin' out a string o' cuss-words, just then, but Jim pat me on th' shoulder as to say to let it pass.

Them royals seemed to be holdin' all the face cards.

We got away as soon as it was good and dark. The king told us to stand well out towards the middle of the river, and not show a light till we got a long ways below the town. We come in sight of the little bunch of lights by and by—that was the town, you know—and slid by, about a half a mile out, all right. When we was three-quarters of a mile below we hoisted up our signal lantern; and about ten o'clock it come on to rain and blow and thunder and lighten like everything; so the king told us to both stay on watch till the weather got better; then him and the duke crawled into the wigwam and turned in for the night. It was my watch below till twelve, but I wouldn't a turned in anyway if I'd had a bed, because a body don't see such a storm as that every day in the week, not by a long sight. My souls, how the wind did scream along! And every second or two there'd come a glare that lit up the white-caps for a half a mile around, and you'd see the islands looking dusty through the rain, and the trees thrashing around in the wind; then comes a *h-whack*!—bum! bum!

bumble-umble-um-bum-bum-bum-bum—and the thunder would go rumbling and grumbling away, and quit—and then *rip* comes another flash and another sockdolager. The waves most washed me off the raft sometimes, but I hadn't any clothes on, and didn't mind. We didn't have no trouble about snags; the lightning was glaring and flittering around so constant that we could see them plenty soon enough to throw her head this way or that and miss them.

I had the middle watch, you know, but I was pretty sleepy by that time, so Jim he said he would stand the first half of it for me; he was always mighty good that way, Jim was. He come out an' his lips looked to be dark and wet, but I couldn' tell for sure in the night. So I crawled into the wigwam and beheld a right dreadful sight.

The king and the duke was deader 'n hell.

The one fella's eyes was all bugged out an' starin' into eternity, and the other was a terr'ble bloody mess. Lookt to me like Jim'd strangled one fella with one hand and mebby gouged the' other to death with a pick. There wasn't much about that one to identify him, 'cept I could see the wide-eyed fella was the king so this one had to be the duke, by my deduction.

I come out an' tells Jim to explain himself and tell about what happened. Jim says:

"They was *bad* men, Huck. You says so yo'self."

I says, "So you din' hafta *kill* 'em for it."

"But I jes' wanted to hab me a li'l taste. I don' wan' do wrong, Huck. I's lookin' out fo' you. An' fo' me. An' I knowed those two was gonna mess it all up fo' us. I jus' had to take a li'l taste an' satisfy my innerds."

"You had to go an' eat that fella's face? You couldn't stop yourself?"

"Wall, I reckon I coulda, but I d'cided not to."

'Bout then the dark sky opened up an' the rain come down. I laid down on the deck an' just let it wash over me, an' it was peaceful.

I didn't mind the rain, because it was warm, and the waves warn't running so high now. About two they come up again, though, and Jim was going to *roust* me; but he changed his mind, because he reckoned they warn't high enough yet to do any harm; but he was mistaken about that, for pretty soon all of a sudden along comes a regular ripper and washed me overboard. It most *re*-killed Jim a-laughing. He was the easiest bagger to laugh that ever was, anyway.

An' when we got me back on the raft, Jim decides it's time to get rid of the royalty, and so we dumps the king and the duke over the side an' waves goodbye to 'em. I din' feel too bad about it. I reckoned I shoulda felt worse, but I didn't. Mebby somethin' was hard'ning inside me. Or soft'ning, too.

I took the watch, and Jim he laid down and snored away; and by and by the storm let up for good and all; and the first cabin-light that showed I rousted him out, and we slid the raft into hiding quarters for the day. Me an' Jim ate breakfast, an' Jim looked mighty pleased of himself. I says:

"You sure did chew that fella good."

An' Jim boasted, "I coulda et lots more, too, but I din' wan' seem a glutton. I jus' wanted to fix the sitchyashun, is all. You did say they 'uz *bad* men, an' I knowed they was fixin' to harm us."

"Yah, you did good."

"Thanky, Huck."

There was a little one-horse town about three mile down

the bend, and we was out of coffee, so Jim said I better go along in the canoe and get some.

When I got there there warn't nobody stirring; streets empty, and perfectly dead and still, like Sunday. I found a sick negro sunning himself in a back yard. He was all fancy an' free an' livin' like a white man, 'xcept he was dyin'; and he said everybody that warn't too young or too sick or too old was gone to camp-meeting, about two mile back in the woods. An' that wasn't too many people either, on account o' most folks were boilin' up with pox, shut into their homes.

The negro said, "So many dyin', dey won't be no one left to bag *us*."

I had some smoke and then lit out for the camp-meeting.

I got there in about a half an hour fairly dripping, for it was a most awful hot day. There was as much as a thousand people there, far more than the dyin' negro figured, but also most of 'em come from twenty mile around. The woods was full of teams and wagons, hitched everywheres, feeding out of the wagon-troughs and stomping to keep off the flies. There was sheds made out of poles and roofed over with branches, where they had lemonade and gingerbread to sell, and piles of watermelons and green corn and such-like truck.

The preaching was going on under the same kinds of sheds, only they was bigger and held crowds of people. The benches was made out of outside slabs of logs, with holes bored in the round side to drive sticks into for legs. They didn't have no backs. The preachers had high platforms to stand on at one end of the sheds. The women had on sunbonnets; and some had linsey-woolsey frocks, some gingham ones, and a few of the young ones had on calico. Some of the young men was barefooted, and some of the children didn't have on any clothes but just a tow-linen shirt. Some of the old women was knitting, and some of the young folks was courting on the sly. A few folks brought their baggers along, and these just stood out at the perimeter, stupidly, and stunk all th' way to Heaven.

The first shed I came to the preacher was lining out a hymn. He lined out two lines, everybody sung it, and it was kind of grand to hear it, there was so many of them and they done it in such a rousing way; then he lined out two more for them to sing—and so on. The people woke up more and more, and sung louder and louder; and towards the end some begun to groan, and some begun to shout, and even some of the baggers at the back began to sway, like they wasn't afraid of Hell no more. Then the preacher begun to preach, and begun in earnest, too; and went weaving first to one side of the platform and then the other, and then a-leaning down over the front of it, with his arms and his body going all the time, and shouting his words out with all his might; and every now and then he would hold up his Bible and spread it open, and kind of pass it around this way and that, shouting, "It's the brazen serpent in the wilderness! Look upon it and live!" And people would shout out, "Glory!—*a*-a-*men*!" And so he went on, and the people groaning and crying and saying amen:

"Oh, come to the mourners' bench! come, black with sin! (*amen*!) come, sick and sore! (*amen*!) come, lame and halt and blind! (*amen*!) come, pore and needy, sunk in shame! (*a-a-men*!) come, all that's worn and soiled and suffering!—come with a broken spirit! come with a contrite heart! come in your rags and sin and dirt! the waters that cleanse is free, the door of heaven stands open—oh, enter in and be at rest!" (*a-a*-men! *glory, glory hallelujah*!)

And then he talked about the fissythis that was takin' more folks 'n ever before, an' how ever'one had to pray harder to right the situation; an' if you lost someone an' they come back, you was s'posed to keep prayin' for them so the devil would let go of their tortured souls.

Then came more singin'.

And so on. You couldn't make out what the preacher said any more, on account of the shouting and crying. Folks got up everywheres in the crowd, and worked their way just by main strength to the mourners' bench, with the tears running down their faces; and when all the mourners had got up there to the front benches in a crowd, they sung and shouted and flung themselves down on the straw, just crazy and wild.

Well, somethin' got a-hold of me, and I raised my little voice up so you could hear me over everybody; and next I went a-charging up on to the platform, and the preacher he begged me to speak to the people, and I done it.

I told them the same story I told the royals, but with a few alt'rations that I added as I went along, which is how most storytellin' goes, anyway. I talked about livin' in Pike County, an' how ever'one died but me an' pap an' a brother named Ike. I talked about poorness and debt and pap's drinkin' and gamblin'; an' how I was orphaned and kidnapped; an' how I excaped; and how me an my Uncle Ben was on a raft, headed for a new life in the South; an' how a steamboat run over the forrard corner of the raft last night, and we both went overboard and dove under the wheel; and how I almost drowned comin' ashore 'cause I barely knowed how to swim.

And then I busted into tears, and so did everybody. Then

somebody sings out, "Take up a collection for him, take up a collection!" Well, a half a dozen made a jump to do it, but somebody sings out, "Let *him* pass the hat around!" Then everybody said it, the preacher too.

So I went all through the crowd with my hat swabbing my eyes, and blessing the people and praising them and thanking them for being so good to the poor orphans of the world; and every little while the prettiest kind of girls, with the tears running down their cheeks, would up and ask me would I let them kiss me for to remember me by; and I always done it, even though it made me want to squirm outta my own skin—and I was invited to stay a week; and everybody wanted me to live in their houses, and said they'd think it was an honor; but I said I was headin' overland to try to make contact with an older sister that was my sole livin' relative an' I hadn't time to waste.

I had to duck away and lose myself under the crowd 'fore I could get away from there.

When I got back to the raft and I come to count up, I found I had collected eighty-seven dollars and seventy-five cents. And then I had fetched away a bag o' coffee and a three-gallon jug of whisky that I found on the back of a wagon, too, for Jim. I told him about the poster I saw at the post office:

"There was a picture of a runaway bagger with flies buzzin' around his head, and a two-hundred-dollar reward under it. The reading was all about you, and just described you to a dot. It said you run away from St. Jacques' plantation, forty mile below New Orleans, last winter, and likely went north, and whoever would catch you and send him back he could have the reward and expenses."

Jim said, “Sho’ ’nuff, dat’s what de royals was fixin’ to do. It warn’t no bluff, was it, Huck? Folks is a-huntin’ fo’ me now.”

“Seems mebby, Jim.”

We laid low and kept still, and never shoved out till nearly ten o’clock; then we slid by, pretty wide away from the town, and didn’t hoist our lantern till we was clear out of sight of it.

When Jim called me to take the watch at four in the morning, he says:

“Huck, does you reck’n we gwyne to run acrost any mo’ kings on dis trip?”

“No,” I says, “I reckon not.”

“Well,” says he, “dat’s all right, den. I reckon I doan’ like kings.”

I found Jim saying some mumbo-jumbo which he said was some voodoo, just in case the ghosts of the royals be followin’ after us. I agreed that was probably a sound idea.

CHAPTER XXI

It was after sun-up now, an' we tied up at a sheltered spot under a tall forest. Jim went in the water to scrub off some of the rot, but he didn't go very deep. He said he didn't feel very float-worthy, nowadays. Said he gave up on breathin' a long time ago and maybe there weren't no air left in him.

After breakfast I took a seat on the corner of the raft, and rolled up my britches, and let my legs dangle in the water, so as to be comfortable, and I lit a smoke, and went to enjoying the day. An' it wasn't minutes before another someone come traipsing along to get into our affairs.

This fella introduced hisself as Bert Hock, but Jim heard it as Birdock and that's what we ended up callin' him ever after.

Birdock *said* he was just freshly dead, a brand-new bagger, and would we mind if he rode along with us so's he could sell himself on the market yonder. Jim said:

"I neva heard o' no bagger sellin' himself. You is dead now. The only one who kin sell you is some'un other than you'self."

"Jus' 'cause somethin' ain't been done before," Birdock said, "it don't mean it can't be done at all. An' why cain't a bunderlug sell his own self? I knows of wimmen who sells themselves all time."

That din' sit right with ol' Jim.

Myself, I couln' see a thing about Bert Hock thet would make me believe he was back from Hell. He didn't look the least bit dead, except for a patch of bumps on 'is face, but those was beet red an' full of fresh blood. He had no black parts or blue parts or yellow parts and, aside from being dirty, he shore din' look ill t'me.

He said he was an actor, back when he was alive.

Jim said, "Mebby you be actin' now."

"No sir," says Birdock. "I'm as dead as they come. Pinch me—"

I reached out an' gave the flesh of his arm a good twist and he shrieked like a fancy school girl. This, he said, was due to instinct more 'n anything, and he hadn't actually felt a damn thing. Wall, not even Jim believed that.

Birdock made himself a longsword out of oak laths and called himself Richard III.; and the way *he* pranced around the raft was grand to see. Bagger Jim said Birdock was crazy like a turd-house squirrel. But by and by *he* tripped and fell overboard, and after that he took a rest, and talked about all kinds of adventures he'd had in other times along the river, back when he was an actor, and alive.

After dinner he says:

"Well, friends, I do a first-class show, you know, not all just dancin' and swordplay, so I guess I *kin* add a little more to it. I can do Hamlet's soliloquy like the back o' my hand."

"Hamlet's which?"

"Hamlet's soliloquy, you know; the most celebrated thing in Shakespeare. Ah, it's sublime, sublime! I know it as surely as I know the Lord's prayer."

So he went to marching up and down, thinking, and

frowning horrible every now and then; then he would hoist up his eyebrows; next he would squeeze his hand on his forehead and stagger back and kind of moan; next he would sigh, and next he'd let on to drop a tear. It was beautiful to see him. By and by he got it. He told us to give attention. Then he strikes a most noble attitude, with one leg shoved forwards, and his arms stretched away up, and his head tilted back, looking up at the sky; and then he begins to rip and rave and grit his teeth; and after that, all through his speech, he howled, and spread around, and swelled up his chest, and just knocked the spots out of any acting ever I see before. This is the speech—I learned it, easy enough, while he was learning it to Jim:

To be, or not to be; that is the bare bodkin That makes calamity of so long life; For who would fardels bear, till Birnam Wood do come to Dunsinane, But that the fear of something after death Murders the innocent sleep, Great nature's second course, And makes us rather sling the arrows of outrageous fortune Than fly to others that we know not of. There's the respect must give us pause: Wake Duncan with thy knocking! I would thou couldst; For who would bear the whips and scorns of time, The oppressor's wrong, the proud man's contumely, The law's delay, and the quietus which his pangs might take, In the dead waste and middle of the night, when churchyards yawn In customary suits of solemn black, But that the undiscovered country from whose bourne no traveler returns, Breathes forth contagion on the world, And thus the native hue of resolution, like the poor cat i' the adage, Is sicklied o'er with care, And all the clouds that lowered o'er our housetops, With this regard their currents turn awry, And lose the name of action.

'Tis a consummation devoutly to be wished. But soft you, the fair Ophelia: Ope not thy ponderous and marble jaws, But get thee to a nunnery—go!

Well, the crazy old man he liked that speech, and he mighty soon got it so he could do it first-rate. It seemed like he was just born for it; and when he had his hand in and was excited, it was perfectly lovely the way he would rip and tear and rair up behind when he was getting it off.

Birdock boasted he ought to git some showbills printed; and then, for two or three days as we floated along, the raft was a most uncommon lively place, for there warn't nothing but sword fighting and rehearsing—as *Birdock* called it—going on all the time. Jim was mostly awestruck by the one-man spectacle. One morning, when we was pretty well down the State of Arkansaw, we come in sight of a little one-horse town in a big bend; so we tied up about three-quarters of a mile above it, in the mouth of a crick which was shut in like a tunnel by the cypress trees, and both of us but Jim took the canoe and went down there to see if there was any chance in that place for this Hamlet show.

We struck it mighty lucky; there was going to be a circus there that afternoon, and the country people was already beginning to come in, in all kinds of old shackly wagons, and on horses. The circus would leave before night, so Birdock figured his one-man show would have a pretty good chance. He said he'd like to hire the courthouse. He said it would be a grand thing.

He was all talk and talk and talk.

He said we should get them bills printed up.

He made it sound so exciting, this show that he'd probably never get to perform. He described exactly what the new showbills would say:

Shaksperean Revival!!!
Wonderful Attraction!
For One Night Only!

The world renowned tragedian, Birdock the Younger, now deceased, of Drury Lane Theatre London, and the Royal Continental Theatres, in his sublime Shaksperean Spectacle entitled

The Balcony Scene in Romeo and Juliet!!!

Romeo . . . . *Birdock*
Juliet . . . . *Birdock*

Assisted by the whole strength of the company!
New costumes, new scenes, new appointments!
Also: The thrilling, masterly, and blood-curdling Broad-sword conflict in Richard III, performed by one man!!!

Richard III . . . . *Birdock*
Richmond . . . . *Birdock*

Also: (by special request)
Hamlet's Immortal Soliloquy!!
By The Illustrious Birdock! Done by him 300 consecutive nights in Paris!
For One Night Only, On account of imperative European engagements!
Admission 25 cents; children and servants, 10 cents.

Well, I had to tell it to him that no one was going to allow no bagger to hire a courthouse an' put on a show. An' I know he weren't really no bagger, but he didn't seem to know it for himself. And eventually he jus' gave up on the notion of gettin' to perform. I was mostly just hoping to see bits of the circus.

Birdock showed me his methods fer pickin' pockets, an' we got a few more dollars from that. I told him I ne'er heard of no bagger gettin' such urges as to steal. But he told me he was just havin' pangs of his former life.

He suggested we take our dollars an' get a hotel room, and sleep a proper sleep on a soft mattress, bunked together for comfort. Wall, I sure din' feel like goin' back to sleep already. I said,

"You is a bagger, so you says, and you ain't needin' to be worryin' about comforts 'cause you got no feelins left."

"I got habits," he said. "Ain't broke 'em yet."

"You jus' make it up as you go, don't ya?"

"Mebby some of it, Huck. For certain."

"I want sweets. An' some tabacky, too."

"Yeah, Huck."

Then we went loafing around town. The stores and houses was most all old, shackly, dried up frame concerns that hadn't ever been painted; they was set up three or four foot above ground on stilts, so as to be out of reach of the water when the river was over-flowed. The houses had little gardens around them, but they didn't seem to raise hardly anything in them but jimpson-weeds, and sunflowers, and ash piles, and old curled-up boots and shoes, and pieces of bottles, and rags, and played-out tinware. The fences was made of different kinds of boards, nailed on at different times; and they leaned every which way, and had gates that didn't generly have but one hinge—a leather one. Some of the fences had been white-washed some time or another, but *Birdock* said it was in Clumbus' time, like enough. There was generly hogs in the garden, and people driving them out.

All the stores was along one street. They had white domestic awnings in front, and the country people hitched their horses to the awning-posts. There was empty drygoods boxes under the awnings, and loafers roosting on them all day long, whittling them with their Barlow knives; and chawing tobacco, and gaping and yawning and stretching—a mighty ornery lot. They generly had on yellow straw hats most as wide as an umbrella, but didn't wear no coats nor waistcoats, they called one another Bill, and Buck, and Hank, and Joe, and Andy, and talked lazy and drawly, and used considerable many cuss words. There was as many as one loafer leaning up against every awning-post, and he most

always had his hands in his britches-pockets, except when he fetched them out to lend a chaw of tobacco or scratch. What a body was hearing amongst them all the time was:

"Gimme a chaw 'v tobacker, Hank."

"Cain't; I hain't got but one chaw left. Ask Bill."

Maybe Bill he gives him a chaw; maybe he lies and says he ain't got none. Some of them kinds of loafers never has a cent in the world, nor a chaw of tobacco of their own. They get all their chawing by borrowing; they say to a fellow, "I wisht you'd len' me a chaw, Jack, I jist this minute give Ben Thompson the last chaw I had"—which is a lie pretty much everytime; it don't fool nobody but a stranger; but Jack ain't no stranger, so he says:

"*You* give him a chaw, did you? So did your sister's cat's grandmother. You pay me back the chaws you've awready borry'd off'n me, Lafe Buckner, then I'll loan you one or two ton of it, and won't charge you no back intrust, nuther."

"Well, I *did* pay you back some of it wunst."

"Yes, you did—'bout six chaws. You borry'd store tobacker and paid back nigger-head."

Store tobacco is flat black plug, but these fellows mostly chaws the natural leaf twisted. When they borrow a chaw they don't generly cut it off with a knife, but set the plug in between their teeth, and gnaw with their teeth and tug at the plug with their hands till they get it in two; then sometimes the one that owns the tobacco looks mournful at it when it's handed back, and says, sarcastic:

"Here, gimme the *chaw*, and you take the *plug*."

All the streets and lanes was just mud; they warn't nothing else *but* mud—mud as black as tar and nigh about a foot deep in some places, and two or three inches deep in *all* the places. The hogs loafed and grunted around everywheres.

You'd see a muddy sow and a litter of pigs come lazying along the street and whollop herself right down in the way, where folks had to walk around her, and she'd stretch out and shut her eyes and wave her ears whilst the pigs was milking her, and look as happy as if she was on salary. And pretty soon you'd hear a loafer sing out, "Hi! *so* boy! sick him, Tige!" and away the sow would go, squealing most horrible, with a dog or two swinging to each ear, and three or four dozen more a-coming; and then you would see all the loafers get up and watch the thing out of sight, and laugh at the fun and look grateful for the noise. Then they'd settle back again till there was a dog fight. There couldn't anything wake them up all over, and make them happy all over, like a dog fight—unless it might be putting turpentine on a stray dog and setting fire to him, or tying a tin pan to his tail and see him run himself to death.

On the river front some of the houses was sticking out over the bank, and they was bowed and bent, and about ready to tumble in, the people had moved out of them. The bank was caved away under one corner of some others, and that corner was hanging over. People lived in them yet, but it was dangersome, because sometimes a strip of land as wide as a house caves in at a time. Sometimes a belt of land a quarter of a mile deep will start in and cave along and cave along till it all caves into the river in one summer. Such a town as that has to be always moving back, and back, and back, because the river's always gnawing at it.

One thing I did notice was a considerable lack of baggers hangin' about, like these folks din' have much use for 'em, and that didn't make no sense to me 'cause this was territory where folks traditionally enjoyed havin' slaves.

The nearer it got to noon that day the thicker and thicker

was the wagons and horses in the streets, and more coming all the time. Families fetched their dinners with them from the country, and eat them in the wagons. There was considerable whisky drinking going on, and I seen three fights. By and by somebody sings out:

"Here comes old Boggs!—in from the country for his little old monthly drunk; here he comes, boys!"

All the loafers looked glad; I reckoned they was used to having fun out of Boggs. One of them says:

"Wonder who he's a-gwyne to chaw up this time. If he'd a-chawed up all the men he's ben a-gwyne to chaw up in the last twenty year he'd have considerable ruputation now."

Another one says, "I wisht old Boggs'd threaten me, 'cuz then I'd know I warn't gwyne to die for a thousan' year."

Boggs comes a-tearing along on his horse, whooping and yelling like an Injun, and singing out:

"Cler the track, thar. I'm on the waw-path, and the price uv coffins is a-gwyne to raise."

He was drunk, and weaving about in his saddle; he was over fifty year old, and had a very red face. Everybody yelled at him and laughed at him and sassed him, and he sassed back, and said he'd attend to them and lay them out in their regular turns, but he couldn't wait now because he'd come to town to kill old Colonel Sherburn, and his motto was, "Meat first, and spoon vittles to top off on."

He see me, and rode up and says:

"Whar'd you come f'm, boy? You prepared to die?"

Then he rode on. I was scared, but a man says:

"He don't mean nothing; he's always a-carryin' on like that when he's drunk. He's the best naturedest old fool in Arkansaw—never hurt nobody, drunk nor sober."

Boggs rode up before the biggest store in town, and

bent his head down so he could see under the curtain of the awning and yells:

"Come out here, Sherburn! Come out and meet the man you've swindled. You're the houn' I'm after, and I'm a-gwyne to have you, too!"

And so he went on, calling Sherburn everything he could lay his tongue to, and the whole street packed with people listening and laughing and going on. By and by a proud-looking man about fifty-five—and he was a heap the best dressed man in that town, too—steps out of the store, and the crowd drops back on each side to let him come. He says to Boggs, mighty ca'm and slow—he says:

"I'm tired of this, but I'll endure it till one o'clock. Till one o'clock, mind—no longer. If you open your mouth against me only once after that time you can't travel so far but I will find you."

Then he turns and goes in. The crowd looked mighty sober; nobody stirred, and there warn't no more laughing. Boggs rode off blackguarding Sherburn as loud as he could yell, all down the street; and pretty soon back he comes and stops before the store, still keeping it up. Some men crowded around him and tried to get him to shut up, but he wouldn't; they told him it would be one o'clock in about fifteen minutes, and so he *must* go home—he must go right away. But it didn't do no good. He cussed away with all his might, and throwed his hat down in the mud and rode over it, and pretty soon away he went a-raging down the street again, with his gray hair a-flying. Everybody that could get a chance at him tried their best to coax him off of his horse so they could lock him up and get him sober; but it warn't no use—up the street he would tear again, and give Sherburn another cussing. By and by somebody says:

"Go for his daughter!—quick, go for his daughter; sometimes he'll listen to her. If anybody can persuade him, she can."

So somebody started on a run. I walked down street a ways and stopped. In about five or ten minutes here comes Boggs again, but not on his horse. He was a-reeling across the street towards me, bare-headed, with a friend on both sides of him a-holt of his arms and hurrying him along. He was quiet, and looked uneasy; and he warn't hanging back any, but was doing some of the hurrying himself. Somebody sings out:

"Boggs!"

I looked over there to see who said it, and it was that Colonel Sherburn. He was standing perfectly still in the street, and had a pistol raised in his right hand—not aiming it, but holding it out with the barrel tilted up towards the sky. The same second I see a young girl coming on the run, and two men with her. Boggs and the men turned round to see who called him, and when they see the pistol the men jumped to one side, and the pistol-barrel come down slow and steady to a level—both barrels cocked. Boggs throws up both of his hands and says, "Don't shoot!" Bang! goes the first shot, and he staggers back, clawing at the air—bang! goes the second one, and he tumbles backwards on to the ground, heavy and solid, with his arms spread out. That young girl screamed out and comes rushing, and down she throws herself on her father, crying, and saying, "Oh, he's killed him, he's killed him!" The crowd closed up around them, and shouldered and jammed one another, with their necks stretched, trying to see, and people on the inside trying to shove them back and shouting, "Back, back! give him air, give him air!"

Colonel Sherburn he tossed his pistol on to the ground, and turned around on his heels and walked off.

They took Boggs to a little drug store, the crowd pressing around just the same, and the whole town following, and I rushed and got a good place at the window, where I was close to him and could see in. They laid him on the floor and put one large Bible under his head, and opened another one and spread it on his breast; but they tore open his shirt first, and I seen where one of the bullets went in. He made about a dozen long gasps, his breast lifting the Bible up when he drawed in his breath, and letting it down again when he breathed it out—and after that he laid still; he was dead. Then they pulled his daughter away from him, screaming and crying, and took her off. She was about sixteen, and very sweet and gentle looking, but awful pale and scared.

Well, pretty soon the whole town was there, squirming and scrouging and pushing and shoving to get at the window and have a look, but people that had the places wouldn't give them up, and folks behind them was saying all the time, "Say, now, you've looked enough, you fellows; 'tain't right and 'tain't fair for you to stay thar all the time, and never give nobody a chance; other folks has their rights as well as you."

There was considerable jawing back, so I slid out, thinking maybe there was going to be trouble. The streets was full, and everybody was excited. Everybody that seen the shooting was telling how it happened, and there was a big crowd packed around each one of these fellows, stretching their necks and listening. One long, lanky man, with long hair and a big white fur stovepipe hat on the back of his head, and a crooked-handled cane, marked out the places on the ground where Boggs stood and where Sherburn stood, and the people following him around from one place to t'other and watching everything he done, and bobbing their heads to show they understood, and stooping a little and resting their hands on their thighs to watch him mark the places on the ground with his cane; and then he stood up straight and stiff where Sherburn had stood, frowning and having his hat-brim down over his eyes, and sung out, "Boggs!" and then fetched his cane down slow to a level, and says "Bang!" staggered backwards, says "Bang!" again, and fell down flat on his back. The people that had seen the thing said he done it perfect; said it was just exactly the way it all happened. Then as much as a dozen people got out their bottles and treated him.

Well, by and by somebody said Sherburn ought to be lynched. An' somebody else said it weren't enough for the fissythis to be takin' from us all our best people, an' even some of our worst, but that ain't enough, an' men got to kill one another just to hurry things along. And then another person was agreein' about how Sherburn ought to be lynched, and directly. In about a minute everybody was saying it; so away they went, mad and yelling, and snatching down every clothes-line they come to to do the hanging with.

CHAPTER XXII

They swarmed up towards Sherburn's house, a-whooping and raging like Injuns, and everything had to clear the way or get run over and tromped to mush, and it was awful to see. Children was heeling it ahead of the mob, screaming and trying to get out of the way; and every window along the road was full of women's heads, and there was *young* boys in every tree, and old-timers looking over every fence; and as soon as the mob would get nearly to them they would break and skaddle back out of reach. Lots of the women and girls was crying and taking on, scared most to death.

They swarmed up in front of Sherburn's palings as thick as they could jam together, and you couldn't hear yourself think for the noise. It was a little twenty-foot yard. Some sung out "Tear down the fence! tear down the fence!" Then there was a racket of ripping and tearing and smashing, and down she goes, and the front wall of the crowd begins to roll in like a wave.

Just then Sherburn steps out on to the roof of his little front porch, with a double-barrel gun in his hand, and takes his stand, perfectly ca'm and deliberate, not saying a word. The racket stopped, and the wave sucked back.

Sherburn never said a word—just stood there, looking down. The stillness was awful creepy and uncomfortable.

Sherburn run his eye slow along the crowd; and wherever it struck the people tried a little to out-gaze him, but they couldn't; they dropped their eyes and looked sneaky. Then pretty soon Sherburn sort of laughed; not the pleasant kind, but the kind that makes you feel like when you are eating bread that's got sand in it.

Then he says, slow and scornful:

"The idea of *you* lynching anybody! It's amusing. The idea of you thinking you had pluck enough to lynch a *man*! Because you're brave enough to tar and feather poor friendless cast-out women that come along here, did that make you think you had grit enough to lay your hands on a *man*? Why, a *man's* safe in the hands of ten thousand of your kind—as long as it's daytime and you're not behind him.

"Do I know you? I know you clear through was born and raised in the South, and I've lived in the North; so I know the average all around. The average man's a coward. In the North he lets anybody walk over him that wants to, and goes home and prays for a humble spirit to bear it. In the South one man all by himself, has stopped a stage full of men in the daytime, and robbed the lot. Your newspapers call you a brave people so much that you think you are braver than any other people—whereas you're just *as* brave, and no braver. Why don't your juries hang murderers? Because they're afraid the man's friends will shoot them in the back, in the dark—and it's just what they *would* do.

"So they always acquit; and then a *man* goes in the night, with a hundred masked cowards at his back and lynches the rascal. Your mistake is, that you didn't bring a man with you; that's one mistake, and the other is that you didn't come in the dark and fetch your masks. You brought *part* of a man—Buck Harkness, there—and if you hadn't had him to start you, you'd a taken it out in blowing.

"You didn't want to come. The average man don't like trouble and danger. *You* don't like trouble and danger. But if only *half* a man—like Buck Harkness, there—shouts 'Lynch him! lynch him!' you're afraid to back down—afraid you'll be found out to be what you are—*cowards*—and so you raise a yell, and hang yourselves on to that half-a-man's coat-tail, and come raging up here, swearing what big things you're going to do. The pitifulest thing out is a mob; that's what an army is—a mob; they don't fight with courage that's born in them, but with courage that's borrowed from their mass, and from their officers. But a mob without any *man* at the head of it is *beneath* pitifulness. Now the thing for *you* to do is to droop your tails and go home and crawl in a hole. If any real lynching's going to be done it will be done in the dark, Southern fashion; and when they come they'll bring their masks, and fetch a *man* along. Now *leave*—and take your half-a-man with you"—tossing his gun up across his left arm and cocking it when he says this.

The crowd washed back sudden, and then broke all apart, and went tearing off every which way, and Buck Harkness he heeled it after them, looking tolerable cheap. I could a stayed if I wanted to, but I didn't want to.

I told Birdock I wanted to have a look at the circus and that sounded just fine to him, bein' that he was half out of his mind and thought he might perform a bit o' *Hamlet* for the crowd. I told him it would be best just to stifle it. People was already agitated enough.

And there was a woman wandering 'round an' through the tents callin' out for her son, calling him by name. He was Joseph and he was but five years old. She went around callin' and callin' out for him, but there weren't no response.

It was such a noisy and riotous place to be. No one woulda heard Birdock's *Hamlet* anyhow, even if he stood on the deck an' yelled it through a drum.

In the big tent I could see a bit of what was going on:

It was a real bully circus. It was the splendidest sight that ever was when they all come riding in, two and two, a gentleman and lady, side by side, the men just in their drawers and undershirts, and no shoes nor stirrups, and resting their hands on their thighs easy and comfortable—there must a been twenty of them—and every lady with a lovely complexion, and perfectly beautiful, and looking just like a gang of real sure-enough queens, and dressed in clothes that cost millions of dollars, and just littered with diamonds. It was a powerful fine sight; I never see anything so lovely. And then one by one they got up and stood, and went a-weaving around the ring so gentle and wavy and graceful, the men looking ever so tall and airy and straight, with their heads bobbing and skimming along, away up there under the tent-roof, and every lady's rose-leafy dress flapping soft and silky around her hips, and she looking like the most loveliest parasol.

And then faster and faster they went, all of them dancing, first one foot out in the air and then the other, the horses leaning more and more, and the ringmaster going round and round the center-pole, cracking his whip and shouting "Hi!—hi!" and the clown cracking jokes behind him; and by and by all hands dropped the reins, and every lady put her knuckles on her hips and every gentleman folded his arms, and then how the horses did lean over and hump themselves! And so one after the other they all skipped off into the ring, and made the sweetest bow I ever see, and then scampered out, and everybody clapped their hands and went just about wild.

And then Birdock took me by the scruff of my shirt and pulled me aside. He said we best be leaving now. Said he had a right terrible feeling in the bottom of his guts. I said, "How can you have a feeling in your guts if you dead, Birdock?"

"I don't rightly know," he said, "but there's an awful commotion yonder, and it strikes me that we should get to going while the going is good."

And then comes a yippin' and a hootin' and all kinds of hollering, and it was a sound like I'd only heard one time before. A most dreadful sound.

Someone said, "Baggers."

And that was enough for my ears. I knowed from what I already seen what was really going on. Folks was getting' tore up and eaten by the dead, like what happened to the Grangerfords. I sure didn't care to see such a sight again.

I took Birdock by the hand and begun to run. Didn't put no thought to it at all, just ran. All the way back to the river. And the whole way I could hear that the carnage was out of hand. Screams an' snarls an' just the worst kind of commotion.

See, those folks musta thought their baggers just up and wandered off, but it was more like they was regrouping in the forest, formulatin' a scheme to eat.

And when we come down to the raft to push off an' get clear, ol' Jim has his face buried in the entrails of a li'l blond boy, eatin' like he was just famished. I says,

"Jim! What the devil is into you?" And Jim says,

"I sorry, Huck. I got hungry and careless, and done let

my instink get th' betta of me. I knowed it was wrong before I did it, but I jus' couldn' help maself."

And Birdock's face twisted up in disgustedness an' fear. I says,

"It's a damn feast back there, Jim. We gotta shove off."

An' Jim composed hisself an' wiped his face and kicked the little boy into the river and we hove out. Birdock still din' know what to make of things as we floated away from the massacre. He din' look to know whether he was safer here, with Jim, or back there with all them hungry baggers. Mebby just a wee bit of his sense was shining through.

Birdock weren't dead. He was just nuts.

He got all fidgety an' nervous and started singing out like a loon:

At the Court House! For 3 Nights Only!
The World-Renowned Tragedian
Birdock the Younger!
Of the London and
Continental Theatres,
In his Thrilling Tragedy of
The King's Cameleopard,
Or the Royal Nonesuch!!!
Admission 50 cents.

Jim looked at me like he din' know what to make of it, but I was cross about what Jim done and showed him my angriest frown. He couldn't muster the nerve to look my way for the rest of the evening. That was something akin to shame, I reckon.

Things was all messed up.

I says to Birdock, "If'n you is a zomby, like you say you

is, why don't you go on an' tell me why even these tame baggers are suddenly risin' up an' eatin' their masters, huh?"

Birdock shrugged. "Mebby I can't figger it."

"Mebby you dilluted in the brain."

"Mebby I ain't."

"My guess is you're jus' playin' dead 'cause you in some kind of trouble. Maybe you stole some un's horse or kist his wife. I dunno, but I know for sure this is a ruse. You're summonin' yer actin' abilities, hopin' to come off as a dead man, but it ain't workin' on me. No, sir. You a fraud. You don' know nothin."

Zomby Jim just held his tongue.

CHAPTER XXIII

In the mornin' Birdock was still fast asleep, twitterin' about poetry an' scratchin' himself, but me an' Jim was awake and we had ourselves a talk about things.

He said he feared the worst for me, bein' that baggers from all over, half-baggers and full-baggers alike, fresh and rotten, was now givin' in to their urges to eat. He said it was happenin' more than I knew, an' that he could hear the wickedness in the calm of night.

"Jus' lyin' still I kin hear 'em all over, hungered as ever, frothin' an' growlin' up a storm."

I told 'im he had to get leverage on his own wicked instincts. I said it wouldn't be long 'fore someone come along and konked his head off for eatin' kids. "You know as well as I do thet folks don' tolerate eatin' kids." Jim said,

"Naw. I shore reckon they don't."

An' that day was pretty unadventurous, 'cept for a part when Birdock got to performin' and fell in the river again. Me an' Jim wondered between us if we should jus' leave him behind, but it didn't seem right to me in the end.

Mostly it was a day for quiet an' reflection.

I went to sleep, and Jim didn't call me when it was my turn. He often done that. When I waked up just at daybreak he was sitting there with his head down betwixt his knees, moaning and mourning to himself. I didn't take notice nor let on. I knowed what it was about. He was thinking about his wife and his children, wherever they was, and he was low and homesick; because he hadn't ever been away from home before in his life. Or his death. He was often moaning and mourning that way nights, when he judged I was asleep, and saying, "Po' little 'Lizabeth! po' little Johnny! it's mighty hard; I spec' I ain't ever gwyne to see you no mo', no mo'!" He was a mighty good bagger, Jim was, when he wasn't eatin' folks.

But this time I somehow got to talking to him about his wife and young ones. When he was alive he was a brute. By and by he says:

"What makes me feel so bad dis time 'uz bekase I hear sumpn over yonder on de bank like a whack, er a slam, while ago, en it mine me er de time I treat my little 'Lizabeth so ornery. She warn't on'y 'bout fo' year ole, en she tuck de sk'yarlet fever, en had a powful rough spell; but she got well, en one day she was a-stannin' aroun', en I says to her, I says:

"'Shet de do'.'

"She never done it; jis' stood dah, kiner smilin' up at me. It make me mad; en I says agin, mighty loud, I says:

"'Doan' you hear me? Shet de do'!'"

"She jis stood de same way, kiner smilin' up. I was a-bilin'! I says:

"'I lay I *make* you mine!'

"En wid dat I fetch' her a slap side de head dat sont her a-sprawlin'. Den I went into de yuther room, en 'uz gone 'bout ten minutes; en when I come back dah was dat do' a-stannin' open *yit*, en dat chile stannin' mos' right in it, a-lookin' down and mournin', en de tears runnin' down. My, but I *wuz* mad! I was a-gwyne for de chile, but jis' den—it was a do' dat open innerds—jis' den, 'long come de wind en slam it to, behine de chile, ker-*blam*!—en my lan', de chile never move'! My breff mos' hop outer me; en I feel so—so—I doan' know *how* I feel. I crope out, all a-tremblin', en crope aroun' en open de do' easy en slow, en poke my head in behine de chile, sof' en still, en all uv a sudden I says *pow*! jis' as loud as I could yell. She never budge! Oh, Huck, I bust out a-cryin' en grab her up in my arms, en say, 'Oh, de po' little thing! De Lord God Amighty fogive po' ole Jim, kaze he never gwyne to fogive hisself as long's he live!' Oh, she was plumb deef en dumb, Huck, plumb deef en dumb—en I'd ben a-treat'n her so!"

But then I wondered aloud if Zomby Jim could forgive himself *now*, bein' that he wasn't alive no more. I said,

"Bein' dead ought to be liberatin' of such things."

Jim nodded his head slowly and said, "It sho' ought to be."

Birdock woke up and he was listening to our conversation an' he couldn't resist the urge to throw his own two cents in. He started to say what ways death had liberated him from certain painful memories, but Jim told him to shet his mouth tight. Jim said,

"You ain't no bagger. You a con man o' some kind. I don' know what yo' game be, but you either out o' yo' mind or you be playin' de angles. Yo don' know nuttin' 'bout bein' dead, fool."

And that chafed Birdock good. He said he been all the way down to Hell an' saw the devil himself, and it weren't to no man to say otherwise. And Jim said,

"Did you see de lady wit' de red dress?"

An' before no time at all Birdock answered, "Of course I did. I saw her at the devil's right hand, an' she was equal parts beautiful an' wicked, both at once."

At this, Jim could only laugh 'cause he was just blowin' wind. There was no red lady in Hell, not one that ol' Jim knew of. An' he told Birdock he was just barkin' out his own backside, an' I had to laugh about it, too.

Next day, towards night, we laid up under a little willow towhead out in the middle, where there was a village on each side of the river, and ol' Birdock was still fixin' to sell himself as a hardworkin' bagger. Me, I didn't mind 'cause we needed to hustle up some more supplies and such, even d'spite the fact that the world was becomin' a pretty dangerous place t'be. Jim he said he hoped it wouldn't take but a few hours, because it got mighty heavy and tiresome to him when he had to lay all day in the wigwam tied with the rope. You see, we had to tie him, because I could no more trust him to not eat the passers-by. An' Jim was pretty acceptin' of that. He obeyed pretty much ever'thing I told him.

But then I figured I didn't want anyone to stumble along and find him tied up like that and think to turn him in for the reward, neither, so I told Birdock we had to come up with some kinda ruse.

He wasn't too bright, that Birdock, but he soon struck it. We gave Jim some slack so he could walk about an' amuse himself. Jim was already ten shades of blue from bein' dead, an' it was hard to judge his original race. Birdock figgered he could pass for an Oriental, perhaps, 'specially one of them Mohammedans. So he made up a sign. The sign said,

Sick Arab—but harmless when not out of his head. *Keep away.*

And he nailed that shingle to a lath, and stood the lath up four or five foot in front of the wigwam. We was satisfied. Jim said it was a sight better than lying tied a couple of years every day. Birdock told him to make himself free and easy, and if anybody ever come meddling around, he must hop out of the wigwam, and carry on a little, and fetch a howl or two like a wild beast, and he reckoned they would light out and leave him alone. Which was sound enough judgment; but you take the average man, and he wouldn't wait for him to howl. Why, he didn't only look like he was dead, he looked considerable more than that.

Now me an' Birdock went into town an' I picked a couple pockets while he went and quizzed folks about who's like to buy him, being that he was such a fine specimen and could cook an' clean as good as any living servant, and the whole scene was quite ridiculous 'cause there wasn't no one who took Birdock fer a dead man.

But also there was talk trickling through; 'bout how the fissythis was worse than ever and folks were comin' back rabid and not peaceful like before. An' even the peaceful ones was turnin' mean, as if a switch had been throwed.

And then there was talk about the things which I'd seen with my own eyes, or heard with my ears, 'bout whole bands of baggers who swept into towns and et up ever'one who resided there. And those stories just made my stomach turn over 'cause I knew it to be true. A fella says,

"It's a curse from the b'yond. New Yawk City is no'n but a graveyard. The whole world is goin' straight t' Hell, which is how Beelzebubby planned it."

An' I got the goosebumps again and told Birdock it was time to mosey on. He weren't getting' any takers, anyhow. Most folks looked at him like he was out of his head, anyhow. The ones who didn't was all reluctant to own a bagger 'cause of all the stories goin' 'round. Birdock says,

"I bet I'm worth a pretty penny in Buffalo."

He was optimistic like that.

We hadn' even got to leave town 'fore someone started yellin' about the Devil's Army movin' in from the East.

CHAPTER XXIV

The news was all over town in two minutes, and you could see the people tearing down on the run from every which way, some of them putting on their coats as they come. Pretty soon we was in the middle of a crowd, and the noise of the tramping was like a soldier march. The windows and dooryards was full; and every minute somebody would say, over a fence:

"Is it *them*?"

And somebody trotting along with the gang would answer back and say:

"You bet it is."

And it was the same as before, 'cept that men had weapons a-ready and was bandin' to make the best of things. Women an' children were shuffled away for safe hiding, and tame baggers was beheaded where they stood—just in case they had any plans on mutinying.

Birdock was sensible enough to be right terrified. He'd saw what I'd saw, after all, and despite all his crazy talk he knowed deep down that he weren't one of the Devil's Army.

So we run all the way back to the river.

Jim calls out, "I hear it, yes I does. I hear de commotion. I hear it in de wind, Huck. It be getting' bad, bad, bad."

We shoved off an' I said we best stick to the river forever; never go ashore again. That's how it was getting' to be. I knowed it wasn't gonna change any. It was only gonna get worse. Miles worse. The dead was a mean, hungry bunch.

An' so we stayed on the raft three days, long as we could hold out, an' we just went with the current. I couldn't think o' anywhere we had to get to anytime soon. Jim had himself a good ear for his kind, and he telled me whenever he could hear 'em on the wind. He could tell if they was in droves, or jus' small groups, or even just two at a time.

We dasn't stop again at any town for days and days; kept right along down the river. We was down south in the warm weather now, and a mighty long ways from home. We begun to come to trees with Spanish moss on them, hanging down from the limbs like long, gray beards. It was the first I ever see it growing, and it made the woods look solemn and dismal.

It was good havin' Jim nearby. I wonder'd how come he could keep hisself from eatin' me all up, but I put it down to frien'ship. That don' explain why he din' eat thet damn Birdock, though.

Ever'thing that came out of Birdock's mouth was loonacy. He told a story 'bout how a couple Italians went to have dinner with a fella named Tremble Ickle, and the wine was the best anyone ever tasted, and the banquet was like magic; an' if you cut into a leg of pork you might find a stuffed quail; an' if you spooned open the quail, you'd find yourself with an oyster. And that story took him a blasted long time to tell, an' it was all about food, more 'n anything, and me 'n Jim gave up listening long b'fore Birdock was even half finished tellin' it.

We passed a village where a man stood on the dock and waved us on, holdin' up a sign that said Quarantine. I got the impression that fissythis was hittin' pretty hard there, but mebby it was jus' rabies.

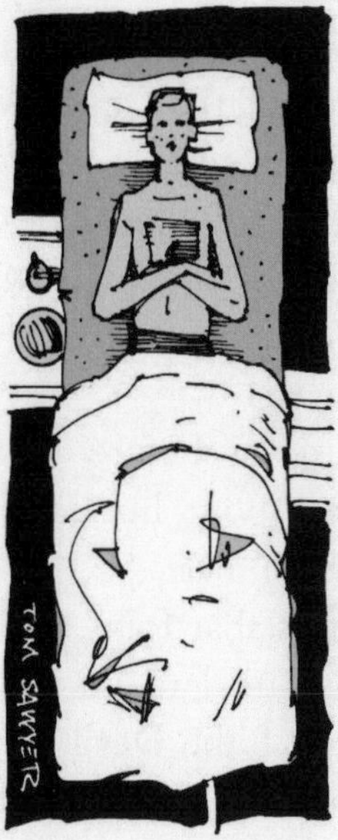

An' then a steamboat come by and it was stuiffed right to the gills with passengers; so many they seemed to be hangin' over the sides, and Jim figgered it was maybe a million folks onboard. He said a million was the biggest number imaginable. I don't think it was quite *that* many folks, but it shore was a lot of 'em. And then I figgered for myself they was getting' out of the north in droves, getting' away from the zombys what war eatin' everyone up.

That sent shivers up an' down my spine.

Anyway, on th' morn' of the fourth day I couldn't stand it no more. Had to stretch my legs an' get some grub. An' Birdock was only too eager to get himself onto dry land. He said,

"I'll fetch a pretty penny for myself, just you wait an' see, an' I won't no more hafta live like this." He was all squirrel-eyed an' fidgety.

So Jim says he ain't heard no bagger activity in quite a spell, an' figgers it might be safe to go ashore. He said mebby we was outrunnin' the Devil's Army, p'haps jus' by a few miles, but he seemed sure we was ahead o' th' carnage.

That sounded fine to me, an' especially to Birdock, an' we put to shore at the very next town what come along. This was Steadman, an' it seemed peaceful enough, an' there was a funeral in progress.

We done the same as before, which was to give Jim enough slack to move about, but not enough thet he could go chasin' after a human meal.

First good sign was that folks was still keepin' baggers and those baggers seemed to be b'havin' themselves. So maybe we was ahead of the Devil's Army after all. Maybe things was peterin' out the further we drifted.

I thought about pickin' through some pockets at the funeral, but somethin' felt wrong in my guts about that an' I kept my hands to myself.

After the funeral, along about noon-time, a couple of baggger traders come along, and Birdock went to talk to them about sellin' himself. All I could hear was laughter. One o' them traders as't Birdock if'n he was drunk. I was sure hopin' they'd take him. An' while they talked, I went down to the dry goods store to buy some licorice an' mebby see if there was any talk about bagger hordes.

Mebby I wasted too much time lollin' about. Things was quiet an' peaceful an' ordinary. I saw a matron walkin' with her bagger an' he was carryin' her things an' that made me feel good about things.

Some time passes an' I can't find that loon Birdock anywhere; an' it crosses my mind thet mebby he managed to sell himself to them traders, after all. So I head back down to the river with my pockets full up of candy an' vittles an' I yells out,

"Set her loose, Jim! we're all right now! Birdock's sold!"

But there warn't no answer, and nobody come out of the wigwam. Jim was gone! I set up a shout—and then another—and then another one; and run this way and that in the woods, whooping and screeching; but it warn't no use—old Jim was gone. Then I set down and cried; I couldn't help it. But I couldn't set still long. Pretty soon I went out on the road, trying to think what I better do, and I run across a boy walking, and asked him if he'd seen a strange bagger dressed so and so, and he says:

"Yes."

"Whereabouts?" says I.

"Down to Silas Phelps' place, two mile below here. He's a runaway bagger, and they've got him. Was you looking for him?"

"You bet I ain't! I run across him in the woods about an hour or two ago, and he said if I hollered he'd *eat* my livers out—and told me to lay down and stay where I was; and I done it. Been there ever since; afeard to come out."

"Well," he says, "you needn't be afeard no more, becuz they've got him. They getting' all the wayward baggers, 'cause word from the north is that they've all gone frizzy."

"*Yeah*, frizzy. It's a good job they got him."

"Well, I *reckon*! There's two hunderd dollars reward on him. He's not just a wayward bagger, but he's a bagger with a price on 'im, too. It's like picking up money out'n the road."

"Yes, it is—and I could a had it if I'd been big enough; I see him *first*. Who nailed him?"

"It was an old fellow—a stranger—and he sold out his chance in him for a hunnert dollars."

"A hunnert, huh?"

"He was a troubled fella. All crazy eyes an' panick. Mebby he don' even know whut a hunnert dollars is wo'th. Say, gimme a chaw tobacker, won't ye?"

I didn't have none, so he left. I went to the raft, and set down in the wigwam to think. But I couldn't come to nothing. I thought till I wore my head sore, but I couldn't see no way out of the trouble. After all this long journey, and after all we'd done for that Birdock, here it was all come to nothing, everything all busted up and ruined, because he could have the heart to serve Jim such a trick as that, and make him a slave again all his death, and amongst strangers, too, for a hunnert dirty dollars.

That's what crazy men are like. There's no sense t'be found in it.

Once I said to myself it would be a thousand times better for Jim to be a bagger-slave at home where he was *from*, as long as he'd *got* to be a bagger-slave, and so I'd better write a letter to Tom Sawyer and tell him to tell Miss Watson where he was. But I soon give up that notion for two things: she'd be mad and disgusted at his rascality and ungratefulness for leaving her, and so she'd sell him straight down the river again; and if she didn't, everybody naturally despises an ungrateful *or* dead-brained bagger, and they'd make Jim feel it all the time, and so he'd feel ornery and disgraced. And then think of *me*! It would get all around that Huck Finn helped a bagger to get his freedom; and if I was ever to see anybody from that town again I'd be ready to get down and lick his boots for shame. That's just the way: a person does a low-down thing, and then he don't want to take no consequences of it. Thinks as long as he can hide, it ain't no disgrace. That was my fix exactly. The more I studied about this the more my conscience went to grinding me, and the more wicked and low-down and ornery I got to feeling. And at last, when it hit me all of a sudden that here was the plain hand of Providence slapping me in the face and letting me know my wickedness was being watched all the time from up there in heaven, whilst I was stealing a poor old woman's *bagger* that hadn't ever done me no harm, and now was showing me there's One that's always on the lookout, and ain't a-going to allow no such miserable doings to go only just so fur and no further, I most dropped in my tracks I was so scared. Well, I tried the best I could to kinder soften it up somehow for myself by saying I was brung up wicked, and so I warn't so much to blame; but something inside of me kept saying, "There was the Sunday-school, you could a gone to it; and if you'd a done it they'd a learnt you there that people that acts as I'd been acting about that bagger goes back to the everlasting fire and stays there."

It made me shiver. And I about made up my mind to pray, and see if I couldn't try to quit being the kind of a boy I was and be better. So I kneeled down. But the words wouldn't come. Why wouldn't they? It warn't no use to try and hide it from Him. Nor from *me*, neither. I knowed very well why they wouldn't come. It was because my heart warn't right; it was because I warn't square; it was because I was playing double. I was letting *on* to give up sin, but away inside of me I was holding on to the biggest one of all. I was trying to make my mouth *say* I would do the right thing and the clean thing, and go and write to that bagger's owner and tell where he was; but deep down in me I knowed it was a lie, and He knowed it. You can't pray a lie—I found that out.

So I was full of trouble, full as I could be; and didn't

know what to do. At last I had an idea; and I says, I'll go and write the letter—and then see if I can pray. Why, it was astonishing, the way I felt as light as a feather right straight off, and my troubles all gone. So I got a piece of paper and a pencil, all glad and excited, and set down and wrote:

> *Miss Watson, your runaway bagger Jim is down here a mile above Steadman, and traders has got him and maybe they will give him up for the reward if you send.*
>
> *Huck Finn.*

I felt good and all washed clean of sin for the first time I had ever felt so in my life, and I knowed I could pray now. But I didn't do it straight off, but laid the paper down and set there thinking—thinking how good it was all this happened so, and how near I come to being lost and going to hell. And went on thinking. And got to thinking over our trip down the river; and I see Jim before me all the time: in the day and in the night-time, sometimes moonlight, sometimes storms, and we a-floating along, talking and singing and laughing. But somehow I couldn't seem to strike no places to harden me against him, but only the other kind. I'd see him standing my watch on top of his'n, 'stead of calling me, so I could go on sleeping; and see him how glad he was when I come back out of the fog; and when I come to him again in the swamp, up there where the carnage was; an' how he wouldn't never bring hisself to eat me no matter how bad the urge got; and such-like times; and would always call me honey, and pet me and do everything he could think of for me, and how good he always was; and how he smelled not so terrible fer a dead man, not as bad as some o' the others; and then I happened to look around and see that paper.

It was a close place. I took it up, and held it in my hand. I was a-trembling, because I'd got to decide, forever, betwixt two things, and I knowed it. I studied a minute, sort of holding my breath, and then says to myself:

"All right, then, I'll *go* to Hell"—and tore it up.

It was awful thoughts and awful words, but they was said. And I let them stay said; and never thought no more about reforming. I shoved the whole thing out of my head, and said I would take up wickedness again, which was in my line, being brung up to it, and the other warn't. And for a starter I would go to work and steal Jim out of bag-slavery again; and if I could think up anything worse, I would do that, too; because as long as I was in, and in for good, I might as well go the whole hog.

Then I set to thinking over how to get at it, and turned over some considerable many ways in my mind; and at last fixed up a plan that suited me. So then I took the bearings of a woody island that was down the river a piece, and as soon as it was fairly dark I crept out with my raft and went for it, and hid it there, and then turned in. I slept the night through, and got up before it was light, and had my breakfast, and put on my store clothes, and tied up some others and one thing or another in a bundle, and took the canoe and cleared for shore. I landed below where I judged was Phelps's place, and hid my bundle in the woods, and then filled up the canoe with water, and loaded rocks into her and sunk her where I could find her again when I wanted her, about a quarter of a mile below a little steam sawmill that was on the bank.

Then I struck up the road, and when I passed the mill I

see a sign on it, "Phelps's Sawmill," and when I come to the farm-houses, two or three hundred yards further along, I kept my eyes peeled, but didn't see nobody around, though it was good daylight now. But I didn't mind, because I didn't want to see nobody just yet—I only wanted to get the lay of the land. According to my plan, I was going to turn up there from the village, not from below. So I just took a look, and shoved along, straight for town. Well, the very first man I see when I got there was that dang Birdock.

"Hel-*lo*! Where'd *you* come from?" Then he says, kind of glad and eager, "Where's the raft?—got her in a good place?"

I says:

"Why, that's just what I was going to ask you."

Then he didn't look so joyful, and says:

"What was your idea for asking *me*?" he says.

"Well," I says, "I let time slip away yesterday; so I went a-loafing around town to hear what folks are sayin'. A man up and offered me ten cents to help him pull a skiff over the river and back to fetch a sheep, and so I went along; but when we was dragging him to the boat, and the man left me a-holt of the rope and went behind him to shove him along, he was too strong for me and jerked loose and run, and we after him. We didn't have no dog, and so we had to chase him all over the country till we tired him out. We never got him till dark; then we fetched him over, and I started down for the raft. When I got there and see it was gone, I says to myself, 'They've got into trouble and had to leave; and they've took my bagger, which is the only bagger I've got in the world, and now I'm in a strange country, and ain't got no property no more, nor nothing, and no way to make my living;' so I set down and cried. I slept in the woods all night. But what *did* become of the raft, then?—and Jim—poor Zomby Jim!"

"Blamed if I know—that is, what's become of the raft. I got me a hundred dollars for Jim and nothin' for myself. These fellas took a listen to my heartbeats and declared that I'm still alive. And when I got home late last night and found the raft gone, I said, 'That little rascal has stole our raft and shook *me*, and run off down the river.'"

"I wouldn't shake my bagger, would I?—the only bagger I had in the world, and the only property."

"I never thought of that. Fact is, I reckon I'd come to consider him *our* bagger; yes, I did consider him so—goodness knows we had trouble enough for him. An' you know it's all for 'is own good, don' you? They is roundin' up these wayward zombys so they don't get in no trouble like in the north. That Jim is a danger an' a liability an' I done you a favor, Huck."

I told that Birdock what I really thought about him. I called him a loon and a low-down dirty bastard.

That didn't bother him none, he was so crazed. He just went twirlin' off like a drunk or a dancer, recitin' his stories to the air.

Somebody nearby says, "They're takin' all them extra baggers an' puttin' 'em to the executioner—except for the particularly good ones."

I begun to cry. I says, "Jim's a good enough bagger, all right. He's got most of himself an' he's smart an' he kin talk. More'n that, I know he'd never so much as take a nip at me." The stranger says,

"You got to talk to the man who deals with the bagger traders. A farmer by the name of Silas Phelps. He draws a lot of water 'round these parts."

So I left, and struck for the back country. I went straight out in the country and made my way through the woods towards Phelps'. I reckoned I better start in on *a* plan straight off without fooling around, because I wanted to stop the blade from comin' down on Jim's neck.

CHAPTER XXV

When I got there it was all still and Sunday-like, and hot and sunshiny; the bunderlugs and hands was gone to the fields; and there was them kind of faint dronings of bugs and flies in the air that makes it seem so lonesome and like everybody's dead and gone; and if a breeze fans along and quivers the leaves it makes you feel mournful, because you feel like it's spirits whispering—spirits that's been dead ever so many years—and you always think they're talking about you. As a general thing it makes a body wish he was dead, too, and done with it all.

Phelps' was one of these little one-horse cotton plantations, and they all look alike. A rail fence round a two-acre yard; a stile made out of logs sawed off and up-ended in steps, like barrels of a different length, to climb over the fence with, and for the women to stand on when they are going to jump on to a horse; some sickly grass-patches in the big yard, but mostly it was bare and smooth, like an old hat with the nap rubbed off; big double log-house for the white folks—hewed logs, with the chinks stopped up with mud or mortar, and these mud-stripes been whitewashed some time or another; round-log kitchen, with a big broad, open but roofed passage joining it to the house; log smoke-house back of the kitchen; three little log bagger-runs in a row t'other side the smoke-house; one little hut all by itself away down against the back fence, and some outbuildings down a piece the other side; ash-hopper and big kettle to bile soap in by the little hut; bench by the kitchen door, with bucket of water and a gourd; hound asleep there in the sun; more hounds asleep round about; about three shade trees away off in a corner; some currant bushes and gooseberry bushes in one place by the fence; outside of the fence a garden and a watermelon patch; then the cotton fields begins, and after the fields the woods.

I went around and clumb over the back stile by the ash-hopper, and started for the kitchen. When I got a little ways I heard the dim hum of a spinning-wheel wailing along up and sinking along down again; and then I knowed for certain I wished I was dead—for that *is* the lonesomest sound in the whole world.

I went right along, not fixing up any particular plan, but just trusting to Providence to put the right words in my mouth when the time come; for I'd noticed that Providence always did put the right words in my mouth if I left it alone.

When I got half-way, first one hound and then another got up and went for me, and of course I stopped and faced them, and kept still. And such another powwow as they made! In a quarter of a minute I was a kind of a hub of a wheel, as you may say—spokes made out of dogs—circle of fifteen of them packed together around me, with their necks and noses stretched up towards me, a-barking and howling; and more a-coming; you could see them sailing over fences and around corners from everywheres.

A black woman come tearing out of the kitchen with a rolling-pin in her hand, singing out, "Begone *you* Tige! you Spot! begone sah!" and she fetched first one and then another of them a clip and sent them howling, and then the rest followed; and the next second half of them come back, wagging their tails around me, and making friends with me. There ain't no harm in a hound, nohow.

And behind the woman comes a little black girl and two little black boys without anything on but tow-linen shirts, and they hung on to their mother's gown, and peeped out from behind her at me, bashful, the way they always do. An' I thought to myself this was how it musta been before the fissythis, when folks was still usin' dark folks as slaves; and it seemed very strange to me. You know—humans ownin' living humans. And here comes the white woman running from the house, about forty-five or fifty year old, bareheaded, and her spinning-stick in her hand; and behind her comes her little white children, acting the same way the other kids was going. She was smiling all over so she could hardly stand—and says:

"It's *you*, at last!—*ain't* it?"

I out with a "Yes'm" before I thought.

She grabbed me and hugged me tight; and then gripped me by both hands and shook and shook; and the tears come in her eyes, and run down over; and she couldn't seem to hug and shake enough, and kept saying, "You don't look as much like your mother as I reckoned you would; but law sakes, I don't care for that, I'm so glad to see you! It's the worst kind of news we've been getting down here. Dear, dear, I am so pleased that none of those monsters were able to eat you up! Children, it's your cousin Tom!—tell him howdy."

But they ducked their heads, and put their fingers in their mouths, and hid behind her. So she run on:

"Lize, hurry up and get him a hot breakfast right away—or did you get your breakfast on the boat?"

I said I had got it on the boat. So then she started for the house, leading me by the hand, and the children tagging after. When we got there she set me down in a split-bottomed chair, and set herself down on a little low stool in front of me, holding both of my hands, and says:

"Now I can have a *good* look at you; and, laws-a-me, I've been hungry for it a many and a many a time, all these long years, and it's come at last! We been expecting you a couple of days and more. What kep' you?—boat get aground?"

"Yes'm—she—"

"Don't say yes'm—say Aunt Sally. Where'd she get aground?"

I didn't rightly know what to say, because I didn't know whether the boat would be coming up the river or down. But I go a good deal on instinct; and my instinct said she would be coming up—from down towards Orleans. That didn't help me much, though; for I didn't know the names of bars down that way. I see I'd got to invent a bar, or forget the name of the one we got aground on—or—Now I struck an idea, and fetched it out:

"It warn't the grounding—that didn't keep us back but a little. We blowed out a cylinder-head."

"Good gracious! anybody hurt?"

"Killed a Chinaman."

"Well, it's lucky; because sometimes people do get hurt. Two years ago last Christmas your uncle Silas was coming up from Newrleans on the old Lally Rook, and she blowed out a cylinder-head and crippled a man. And I think he died afterwards. He was a Baptist. Your uncle Silas knowed a family in Baton Rouge that knowed his people very well. Yes, I remember now, he *did* die. Mortification set in, and they had to amputate him. But it didn't save him. Yes, it was mortification—that was it. He turned blue all over, and died in the hope of a glorious eternity. But he must be thankin' the Lord he din' have to come back as slave-dead, now, like so many others, poor souls. They say he was a sight to look at. Your uncle's been up to the town every day to fetch you. And he's gone again, not more'n an hour ago; he'll be back any minute now. You must a met him on the road, didn't you?—oldish man, with a—"

"No, I didn't see nobody, Aunt Sally. The boat landed just at daylight, and I left my baggage on the wharf-boat and went looking around the town and out a piece in the country, to put in the time and not get here too soon; and so I come down the back way."

"Who'd you give the baggage to?"

"Nobody."

"Why, child, it'll be stole!"

"Not where I hid it I reckon it won't," I says.

"How many were on the boat?"

It was kinder thin ice, but I says:

"I reckon a million or more."

I was getting so uneasy I couldn't listen good. I had my mind on the children all the time; I wanted to get them out to one side and pump them a little, and find out who I was. But I couldn't get no show, Mrs. Phelps kept it up and run on so. Pretty soon she made the cold chills streak all down my back, because she says:

"But here we're a-running on this way, and you hain't told me a word about Sis, nor any of them, or what's become of them. These are devilish times. I can only pray that ever'one gets evacuated before the worst sets in. Now I'll rest my works a little, and you start up yourn; just tell me *everything*—tell me all about 'm all every one of 'm; and how they are, and what they're doing, and what they told you to tell me; and every last thing you can think of."

Well, I see I was up a stump—and up it good. Providence had stood by me this fur all right, but I was hard and tight aground now. I see it warn't a bit of use to try to go ahead—I'd got to throw up my hand. So I says to myself, here's another place where I got to resk the truth. I opened my mouth to begin; but she grabbed me and hustled me in behind the bed, and says:

"Here he comes! Stick your head down lower—there, that'll do; you can't be seen now. Don't you let on you're here. I'll play a joke on him. Children, don't you say a word."

I see I was in a fix now. But it warn't no use to worry; there warn't nothing to do but just hold still, and try and be ready to stand from under when the lightning struck.

I had just one little glimpse of the old gentleman when he come in; then the bed hid him. Mrs. Phelps she jumps for him, and says:

"Has he come?"

"No," says her husband.

"Good-*ness* gracious!" she says, "what in the warld can have become of him?"

"I can't imagine," says the old gentleman; "and I must say it makes me dreadful uneasy."

"Uneasy!" she says; "I'm ready to go distracted! He *must* a come; and you've missed him along the road. I *know* it's so—something tells me so."

"Why, Sally, I *couldn't* miss him along the road—*you* know that."

"But oh, dear, dear, what *will* Sis say! He must a come! You must a missed him. He—"

"Oh, don't distress me any more'n I'm already distressed.

I don't know what in the world to make of it. I'm at my wit's end, and I don't mind acknowledging 't I'm right down scared. But there's no hope that he's come; for he *couldn't* come and me miss him. Sally, it's terrible—just terrible—something's happened to the boat, sure! An' we got these other issues to deal with—"

"Why, Silas! Look yonder!—up the road!—ain't that somebody coming?"

He sprung to the window at the head of the bed, and that give Mrs. Phelps the chance she wanted. She stooped down quick at the foot of the bed and give me a pull, and out I come; and when he turned back from the window there she stood, a-beaming and a-smiling like a house afire, and I standing pretty meek and sweaty alongside. The old gentleman stared, and says:

"Why, who's that?"

"Who do you reckon 't is?"

"I hain't no idea. Who *is* it?"

"It's Tom Sawyer!"

By jings, I most slumped through the floor! But there warn't no time to swap knives; the old man grabbed me by the hand and shook, and kept on shaking; and all the time how the woman did dance around and laugh and cry; and then how they both did fire off questions about Sid, and Mary, and the rest of the tribe.

But if they was joyful, it warn't nothing to what I was; for it was like being born again, I was so glad to find out who I was. Well, they froze to me for two hours; and at last, when my chin was so tired it couldn't hardly go any more, I had told them more about my family—I mean the Sawyer family—than ever happened to any six Sawyer families. And I explained all about how we blowed out a cylinder-head at the mouth of White River, and it took us three days to fix it. Which was all right, and worked first-rate; because *they* didn't know but what it would take three days to fix it. If I'd a called it a bolthead it would a done just as well. An' how there was a million of us onboard, so many that we was hangin' over the edges, and it was the best evac'ation I ever experienced.

Now I was feeling pretty comfortable all down one side, and pretty uncomfortable all up the other. Being Tom Sawyer was easy and comfortable, and it stayed easy and comfortable till by and by I hear a steamboat coughing along down the river. Then I says to myself, s'pose Tom Sawyer comes down on that boat? And s'pose he steps in here any minute, and sings out my name before I can throw him a wink to keep quiet?

Well, I couldn't *have* it that way; it wouldn't do at all. I must go up the road and waylay him. So I told the folks I reckoned I would go up to the town and fetch down my baggage. The old gentleman was for going along with me, but I said no, I could drive the horse myself, and I druther he wouldn't take no trouble about me.

An' that worked out good for him, too, 'cause he had all this business with the traders an' the wayward baggers; and they was still debatin' on the best way to deal with things, trying to circle-vent a zomby uprising like what was happenin' in the north. I says,

"You killin' them dirty zombys, yet?" And he says,

"Nut fer a spell, I reckon. Some folks think it's money into the dirt. Others say it's fer the best. Y'all knows I cain't even make my own mind about it."

And that made me smile inside, knowin' there was still time to save Jim.

CHAPTER XXVI

So I started for town in the wagon, and when I was half-way I see a wagon coming, and sure enough it was Tom Sawyer, and I stopped and waited till he come along. I says "Hold on!" and it stopped alongside, and his mouth opened up like a trunk, and stayed so; and he swallowed two or three times like a person that's got a dry throat, and then says:

"I hain't never thought you'd come back a bagger."

I says:

"I hain't come back a bagger—I hain't even *died*."

When he heard my voice it righted him up some, but he warn't quite satisfied yet. He says:

"Don't you play nothing on me, because I wouldn't on you. Honest injun, you ain't a bagger or a ghost?"

"Honest injun, I ain't," I says. "I din' catch no pox for surely."

"Well, that ought to settle it, of course; but I can't somehow seem to understand it no way. Looky here, warn't you ever sick or murdered or eaten at all?"

"No. I warn't ever, not at all—I played it on them. You come in here and smell me if you don't believe it."

So he done it, had a sniff; and it satisfied him; and he was that glad to see me again he didn't know what to do. And he wanted to know all about it right off, because it was a grand adventure, and mysterious, and so it hit him where he lived. But I said, leave it alone till by and by; and told his driver to wait, and we drove off a little piece, and I told him the kind of a fix I was in, and what did he reckon we better do? He said, let him alone a minute, and don't disturb him. So he thought and thought, and pretty soon he says:

"It's all right; I've got it. Take my trunk in your wagon, and let on it's your'n; and you turn back and fool along slow, so as to get to the house about the time you ought to; and I'll go towards town a piece, and take a fresh start, and get there a quarter or a half an hour after you; and you needn't let on to know me at first."

I says:

"All right; but wait a minute. There's one more thing—a thing that *nobody* don't know but me. And that is, there's a bagger here that I'm a-trying to rescue, and his name is *Jim*—old Miss Watson's Jim."

He says:

"What! Why, Jim is—"

He stopped and went to studying. I says:

"I know what you'll say. You'll say it's dirty, low-down business; but what if it is? I'm low down; and I'm a-going to steal him, and I want you keep mum and not let on. Will you?"

His eye lit up, and he says:

"I'll *help* you steal him!"

Well, I let go all holts then, like I was shot. It was the most astonishing speech I ever heard—and I'm bound to say Tom Sawyer fell considerable in my estimation. Only I couldn't believe it. Tom Sawyer a bagger-stealer!

"Oh, shucks!" I says; "you're joking."

"I ain't joking, either."

"Well, then," I says, "joking or no joking, if you hear anything said about a runaway zomby, don't forget to remember that *you* don't know nothing about him, and I don't know nothing about him."

Then we took the trunk and put it in my wagon, and he drove off his way and I drove mine. But of course I forgot all about driving slow on accounts of being glad and full of thinking; so I got home a heap too quick for that length of a trip. The old gentleman was at the door, and he says:

"Why, this is wonderful! Whoever would a thought it was in that mare to do it? I wish we'd a timed her. And she hain't sweated a hair—not a hair. It's wonderful. Why, I wouldn't take a hundred dollars for that horse now—I wouldn't, honest; and yet I'd a sold her for fifteen before, and thought 'twas all she was worth."

That's all he said. He was the innocentest, best old soul I

ever see. But it warn't surprising; because he warn't only just a farmer, he was a preacher, too, and had a little one-horse log church down back of the plantation, which he built it himself at his own expense, for a church and schoolhouse, and never charged nothing for his preaching, and it was worth it, too. There was plenty other farmer-preachers like that, and done the same way, down South. But he made most of his money off the exchange of baggers, an' it was a considerable weight on his conscience that they was havin' to round up these zombys just to finish 'em off so cruel-like. He said,

"Sometimes I think they still a bit human inside."

"Yes," I said. "I reckon they seem that way to me sometimes, too."

"But it's Armageddon comin' down the pike. An' you know that as well as anyone, don't ya, Tom? I'm sure you've seen awful sights."

"Yes sir."

An' deep inside, I knowed this man was right. I saw them dead hordes for myself. Saw 'em an' heard 'em and smelt 'em. But still I couldn't let Jim go down like that. I said,

"Das you check 'em all for brands?"

"Don't matter," he told me. "Brands don't matter no more. Whether they got 'em or don't, it don't change the situation at all."

In about half an hour Tom's wagon drove up to the front stile, and Aunt Sally she see it through the window, because it was only about fifty yards, and says:

"Why, there's somebody come! I wonder who 'tis? Why, I do believe it's a stranger. Jimmy" (that's one of the children) "run and tell Lize to put on another plate for dinner."

Everybody made a rush for the front door, because, of

course, a stranger don't come *every* year, and so he lays over the yaller-fever, for interest, when he does come. Tom was over the stile and starting for the house; the wagon was spinning up the road for the village, and we was all bunched in the front door. Tom had his store clothes on, and an audience—and that was always nuts for Tom Sawyer. In them circumstances it warn't no trouble to him to throw in an amount of style that was suitable. He warn't a boy to meeky along up that yard like a sheep; no, he come ca'm and important, like the ram. When he got a-front of us he lifts his hat ever so gracious and dainty, like it was the lid of a box that had butterflies asleep in it and he didn't want to disturb them, and says:

"Mr. Archibald Nichols, I presume?"

"No, my boy," says the old gentleman, "I'm sorry to say 't your driver has deceived you; Nichols's place is down a matter of three mile more. Come in, come in."

Tom he took a look back over his shoulder, and says, "Too late—he's out of sight."

"Yes, he's gone, my son, and you must come in and eat your dinner with us; and then we'll hitch up and take you down to Nichols's."

"Oh, I *can't* make you so much trouble; I couldn't think of it. I'll walk—I don't mind the distance."

"But we won't *let* you walk—it wouldn't be Southern hospitality to do it. Come right in."

"Oh, *do*," says Aunt Sally; "it ain't a bit of trouble to us, not a bit in the world. You must stay. It's a long, dusty three mile, and we can't let you walk. Not in these uncertain times. And, besides, I've already told 'em to put on another plate when I see you coming; so you mustn't disappoint us. Come right in and make yourself at home."

So Tom he thanked them very hearty and handsome, and let himself be persuaded, and come in; and when he was in he said he was a stranger from Hicksville, Ohio, and his name was William Thompson—and he made another bow.

Well, he run on, and on, and on, making up stuff about Hicksville and everybody in it he could invent, an' about how pret' near ever'one in town got all gobbled up by rovin' bunderlugs, and I getting a little nervious, and wondering how this was going to help me out of my scrape; and at last, still talking along, he reached over and kissed Aunt Sally right on the mouth, and then settled back again in his chair comfortable, and was going on talking; but she jumped up and wiped it off with the back of her hand, and says:

"You owdacious puppy!"

He looked kind of hurt, and says:

"I'm surprised at you, m'am."

"You're s'rp— Why, what do you reckon I am? I've a good notion to take and— Say, what do you mean by kissing me?"

He looked kind of humble, and says:

"I didn't mean nothing, m'am. I didn't mean no harm. I—I—thought you'd like it."

"Why, you born fool!" She took up the spinning stick, and it looked like it was all she could do to keep from giving him a crack with it. "What made you think I'd like it?"

"Well, I don't know. Only, they—they—told me you would."

"*They* told you I would. Whoever told you's *another* lunatic. I never heard the beat of it. Who's *they*?"

"Why, everybody. They all said so, m'am."

It was all she could do to hold in; and her eyes snapped,

and her fingers worked like she wanted to scratch him; and she says:

"Who's 'everybody'? Out with their names, or there'll be an idiot short."

He got up and looked distressed, and fumbled his hat, and says:

"I'm sorry, and I warn't expecting it. They told me to. They all told me to. They all said, kiss her; and said she'd like it. They all said it—every one of them. But I'm sorry, m'am, and I won't do it no more—I won't, honest."

"You won't, won't you? Well, I sh'd *reckon* you won't!"

"No'm, I'm honest about it; I won't ever do it again—till you ask me."

"Till I *ask* you! Well, I never see the beat of it in my born days! I lay you'll be the Methusalem-numskull of creation before ever I ask you—or the likes of you."

"Well," he says, "it does surprise me so. I can't make it out, somehow. They said you would, and I thought you would. But—" He stopped and looked around slow, like he wished he could run across a friendly eye somewheres, and fetched up on the old gentleman's, and says, "Didn't *you* think she'd like me to kiss her, sir?"

"Why, no; I—I—well, no, I b'lieve I didn't."

Then he looks on around the same way to me, and says:

"Tom, didn't *you* think Aunt Sally'd open out her arms and say, 'Sid Sawyer—'"

"My land!" she says, breaking in and jumping for him, "you impudent young rascal, to fool a body so—" and was going to hug him, but he fended her off, and says:

"No, not till you've asked me first."

So she didn't lose no time, but asked him; and hugged him and kissed him over and over again, and then turned him over to the old man, and he took what was left. And after they got a little quiet again she says:

"Why, dear me, I never see such a surprise. We warn't looking for *you* at all, but only Tom. Sis never wrote to me about anybody coming but him."

"It's because it warn't *intended* for any of us to come but Tom," he says; "There's a lotto to see who gets on which boat an' it was just Tom what did on the first one, as you know. But one feller died before he got his spot an' I begged and begged, and at the last minute I was let to come, too; so, coming down the river, me and Tom thought it would be a first-rate surprise for him to come here to the house first, and for me to by and by tag along and drop in, and let on to be a stranger. But it was a mistake, Aunt Sally. This ain't no healthy place for a stranger to come."

"No—not impudent whelps, Sid. You ought to had your jaws boxed; I hain't been so put out since I don't know when. But I don't care, I don't mind the terms—I'd be willing to stand a thousand such jokes to have you here. Well, to think of that performance! I don't deny it, I was most putrified with astonishment when you give me that smack."

We had dinner out in that broad open passage betwixt the house and the kitchen; and there was things enough on that table for seven families—and all hot, too; none of your flabby, tough meat that's laid in a cupboard in a damp cellar all night and tastes like a hunk of old cold cannibal in the morning. Uncle Silas he asked a pretty long blessing over it, said all kinda things about plague and Judgment an' death an' forgiveness, but it was worth it; and it didn't cool it a bit, neither, the way I've seen them kind of interruptions do lots of times. There was a considerable good deal of talk all the afternoon, and me and Tom was on the lookout all the time;

but it warn't no use, they didn't happen to say nothing about the rounded-up baggers, an' where they was bein' corralled, and we was afraid to try to work up to it. But at supper, at night, one of the little boys says:

"Pa, mayn't Tom and Sid and me go to the show when it comes?"

"No," says the old man, "I reckon it's gonna be gruesome, an' you young fellas—though I know it you already seen a lot—you shore don't need to be seein' what's comin'. We had fifty penned out at Cobb Field, an' there's bound to be more . . ."

So there it was!—but I couldn't help it. Tom and me was to sleep in the same room and bed; so, being tired, we bid good-night and went up to bed right after supper, and clumb out of the window and down the lightning-rod, and shoved for the town.

On the road Tom he told me all about how it was reckoned I was murdered, and how pap disappeared pretty soon, and didn't come back no more, and what a stir there was when Jim run away; and I told Tom all about our li'l adventures, 'bout the King an' the Duke an' thet crazed Birdock, and as much of the raft voyage as I had time to; and as we struck into the town and up through the—here comes a raging rush of people with torches, and an awful whooping and yelling, and banging tin pans and blowing horns; and we jumped to one side to let them go by; and as they went by I see they had Birdock astraddle of a rail—that is, I knowed it *was* Birdock, though he was all over tar and feathers, and didn't look like nothing in the world that was human—just looked like a monstrous big soldier-plume. Well, it made me sick to see it; and I was sorry for that poor pitiful fool, it seemed like I couldn't ever feel any hardness against him any more in the world. It was a dreadful thing to see. Human beings *can* be awful cruel to one another.

Someone said he was caught touchin' a young feller, most inappropriate.

I heard 'bout men like him before. I wunnert if'n he been sizin' me up like that all along. That whole bit about pretendin' to be a bagger jus' some kinda ruse to seem least like a threat. Mebby not, mebby so. But it was a good thing Jim was most always nearby.

We see we was too late—couldn't do no good. We asked some stragglers about it, and they said they was going to toss Birdock into the gulch an' burn him alive. Birdock yelled,

"Huck! I is caught in a bad way!"

But what could I do for him?

All I could muster was a wave as they carted him past.

An' thet's southern justice for ya.

We went to where Tom figgered Cobb Field was, and it was, and we could see that so many baggers had been put into a corral, 'cept it was dark and we'd hafta get good an' close to see if Jim was in with 'em.

They was all bein' presided over by one of them traders, plus two fellas in tall hats. Some baggers was groaning and some was mumbling and some was talkin' low, an' all of them seemed perfectly well heeled, in my opinion. Tom said,

"You bes' watch an' be shore, Huck. They look tame enough, but I seen what happens when the change comes. It's a sore sight. Whole big groups of 'em just go mad."

"I seen it, too," I says. "Don't ferget that. But I know Jim ain't like the others; an' if Hell comes to Earth, ol' Jim will stan' by me."

And then Tom had a laugh 'cause he was rememberin'

playin' tricks on the old fella. An' I laughed, too, and soon we was both laughin' to beat the band. I said,

"I'm shore glad you're here, Tom."

Tom nodded and smiled an' I could see his nose was runnin' yella.

I never said nothing; but I knowed mighty well it weren't a good thing.

And it warn't.

That bagger trader come over and told us to scoot; to get goin' home before he got th' urge to whack us good.

So we did. An' on the way back to the Phelpses Tom told me he had a plan, and I see in a minute it was worth fifteen of mine for style, and would make Jim just as free a zomby as any of mine would, and maybe get us all killed besides. So I was satisfied, and said we would waltz in on it on the 'morrow.

We poked along back home, and I warn't feeling so gay as I was before, but kind of ornery, and humble, and to blame, somehow—though I hadn't done nothing. But that's always the way; it don't make no difference whether you do right or wrong, a person's conscience ain't got no sense, and just goes for him anyway. If I had a yaller dog that didn't know no more than a person's conscience does I would piss on him.

CHAPTER THE LAST

No need to say what was Tom's good idea, 'cause it didn't get to pan out, anyway. But it *was* a good one. Tom was a fox for schemes.

Come dawn, he was a-hackin' and coughin' and his eyes were movin' unnatural, rollin' back in his skull one minute and normal the next. We was bunkin' together an' I was the first t'notice him like that.

Aunt Sally come along and she was still callin' him Sid; and that tweaked at me 'cause I knew Tom could pass, an' he would pass with his aunt thinkin' he was somebody who he wasn't. And for a moment I thought about Tom buried under a headstone with th' wrong name, but then sense grabbed me an' I realized he'd be comin' back as a bagger; so I wouldn't *really* be losin' my good friend, no how.

In a clear moment, Tom as't if Silas would come an' talk to him, but Sally said Silas was gone to the field, bein' that word had come of some kinda commotion. My stomach near jumped up into my mouth, and I asked her,

"Are they killin the baggers already?"

"Don't rightly know," she said. "It sounded like some other kind of business. But don't you fret about all that. We got to get a poultice on Sid right directly. That an' some cool water might hold him a spell."

Well, I was stuck.

There was Jim I had to rescue, somehow; an' here was Tom Sawyer, prob'ly gonna die b'fore the day ended, maybe sooner.

Aunt Sally went off to get them comfort items, and then Tom jumped into a moment o' clarity an' grabbed me by the scruff of my shirt. He says,

"Cain't go home, Huck. Thar ain't nothin' left. It was hell bad. Bad enough thet I don't rightly 'spect to see any familiar faces if another boat comes along."

"Don't be sayin' that, Tom," I said. "We'll see lots o' folks again, you can be shore of that."

"Miss Watson's gone. I din' wanna say."

"She passed?"

"She passed an' come back, but she was a vicious one. An' it was only in time to join in with th' rest of the baggers, and it was a terrible show. An' I didn't see how it all ended up, 'cause I ran. Had to run all the way down to Hockett to get onto that boat. It weren't no lotto, like I said. It was every Tom for hisself. An' I din' even tell Aunt Sally 'bout Aunt Polly an' all the rest who all was gone."

"You gonna?"

"Don't rightly know."

That's all he said, and that's all I said. It warn't no use to say any more. But I couldn't make out how he was willing to go out of this world; so I just let it go, and never bothered no more about it. If he was bound to have it so, I couldn't help it.

I felt powerful sad, now. I thought about all th' folks we knowed, an' how it was all done with, an' my eyes'd never see 'em again.

Aunt Sally come back with a tray an' she shooed me out of the room. I told Tom I'd come back an' see him just as soon as I could, but both of us knew it weren't goin' to go that way. Just like Tom's great scheme to free Jim. It's a good thing to believe, even though you suspect it won't go thet way.

It takes up more room than all the rest of a person's insides, and yet ain't no good, nohow. Tom Sawyer, he knows the same.

The door closed behind me and that was truly the last I ever saw of Tom Sawyer.

Ayyy-men.

I ran all th' way to Cobb Field, an' went through the crick, too, hopin' to shave some time.

I weren't happy that Miss Watson was gone, but I found relief knowin' that it meant Jim was a free bagger. That or he belonged to me for *real*, an' that was just the same as bein' free.

An' I remember that the air was thick and the ground was damp and I could taste my own spit so powerful it was like havin' a mouthful of blood.

An' then there was gunfire. An' more gunfire.

And the screamin come, too.

First thing I thought was all them penned baggers was bein' gunned down, but the closer I got the more I unnerstood what was really happening. It was like before. And the time before that, too. An' it was clear to me now that the Devil's Army was like a neverendin' stream of red army ants.

They come from the north, like fire, an' there was a million.

All the men what could be mustard was present, all armed, an' firin' at a wave of bodies that was hardly slowed by bullets.

Here I was at the opposite end of Cobb Field. All that

horror was mebby a mile across the grass, on t'other side of the bunderlug coop. I know fear and sense shoulda made turnabout and bolted for the way I come, but it was a voice that steeled me up. Jim hollers,

"Get yo'self gone, Huck! Run away! Run away, honey!"

An' I was so pleased to hear 'is voice that the smile what crossed my face made my cheeks ache.

"Go won, Huck! Go won now!"

There was at least fifty baggers in that pen, an' Jim was pressed right to the edge, pointed south with a long dead arm through the slats, pointin' the way I oughted t'be goin'.

And all that shootin' and hissin' and growlin' and screamin' kept rollin' over the field like a wave outta my worst nightmares; but before I know what I'm doin' I'm at the gate an' I'm untyin' it. An' it struck me how docile these rounded-up half-baggers really was, 'cause most of 'em ought to have 'ad the sense to let theirselves out, but chose not to for bein' soft-mannered and tamed.

Yes, they was like a pack of tired hounds, not in any rush to go anywheres or do anything atall. Zomby Jim hadta push his way through the mass to get to me at th' gate. If those had been livin' people, or full-bag biters, it woulda been a stampede. But it was not so. I says,

"Jim, c'mon! We got to git!"

He was darker and a little more rotted than when I last saw him. Or maybe I'd been so accustomed to him thet I hardly noticed. That little time apart made me realize how crackly and peeled he was becomin'. He says,

"We goan back to da raft, Hyuck! Ol' Jim will git you safe."

An' by this time, so many of those armed men were on the ground, getting' chewed up and feasted on, an' there wasn't hardly no more gunfire goin' off. And here comes the bagger horde, thunderin' across the plain to feast on me an' anyone else who might come along. All dead eyes, brown skin and yella teeth.

Jim scooped me up like I was a bagga flour and threw me on his shoulder. And then he starts a-takin' giant runnin' strides and I feel like one of them Arabs perched high upon a racin' elephant. I kin see backwards an' I see that when the Devil's Army gets close to the corral, the tame baggers inside began thrashin' and clawin' around, like a 'coon turned on a penny from rabies.

Seemed to me they mus' all be sharin' thoughts—and when a bad one gets close to a not-bad one, their ideas become the same. Just as when one duck starts flyin' away across the pond, the rest of 'em go, too. And that's what happened when the horde neared the pen. Pretty quick it was all chompin' teeth.

A million crazed baggers and a million chompin' teeth.

Pretty soon I had to close my eyes. I kept 'em shut tight and it was a dark and ankshis trip, goin' up an' down and up an' down as Jim hurled through the bushes and over the hills and down to the river. And always right in front of my closed eyes I knowed we was bein' pursued, and closely, too.

But here is me tellin' this story, so y'all know I din' die.

Wall, we got fairly clear. Comin' past the Phelps place, I reckon, them zombys turned to feast on Aunt Sally and whoever else might be nearby; and me n' Jim just kept on hurlin'.

I don't hardly remember showin' Jim where the raft was, nor castin' off, nor fallin' dead asleep from fright, nor none o' that. It was Jim what took care of ever'thing. It was Jim what got us clear and free and safe. And I'll bet I didn't wake up until it was a whole new morning.

That was how we went. Back on the river.

And things wasn't good nowhere. Good baggers was turnin' bad all the ways across the nation, and their numbers grew, and they swept into towns like sheet lightning and consumed ever'thing that breathed. All the way from Buffalo to N'Orlins to Mexico to wherever.

An' me and Jim just kept goin' with th' river, thinkin' mebby we'll get to England or the South Pole with our hides intact. Well, with *my* hide intact. Jim's hide was much like a rotten potato. But he knowed what I knowed: That Napoleon had killed the fissythis in Europe, so there couln' possibly be bagger hordes over there.

Mebby we din' know much.

We drifted an' drifted and I thought about all those million folks who perished. Most of 'em I didn't know, but I concentrated real hard on the ones I did. Thought about ever'one I ever met, at least once. I thought about Miss Watson an' I thought about pap, too. I thought about how I'd never really know which folks got eaten up, and which ones was doin' th' eating.

I hoped Tom Sawyer was doin' th' eatin'. It coulda gone either way. If he passed before the horde arrived, he woulda come back. If not, wall, I knowed he must be in a better place now, with the big Lord, like th' others. Jim said,

"We sho' das got a long way to go, Huck."

"Yuh," I says. "But we come a long ways, too."

"Ain't dat da truf!"

"It is, Jim. It shorely is."

"Byootyful day."

"Yuh. I wonder if pap is out there somewhere. He be a vicious one even if he ain't dead."

Jim says, kind of solemn:

"He ain't a-comin' back no mo', Huck."

I says:

"I know it, Jim."

"For sho' he ain't. Hunnert pa cent."

"How you so shore?"

"Nemmine why, Huck—but he ain't comin' back no mo."

But I kept at him; so at last he says:

"Doan' you 'member de house dat was float'n down de river, en dey wuz a mad bagga in dah, crazed, en I went in en delivered him and didn' let you come *close*? Well, den, you kin tank yo' stahs, kase dat wuz him."

That made me feel nice an' warm inside.

I wanted to make Jim feel the same way, down in his dead heart.

I told him he was a *free* bagger. No more bounty or rules or nothin'. It was all beside th' point, o'course, since there wasn't no more bagger trade, nor traders, nor reward, nor owners, nor nuttin' else; but he liked knowin' his freedom was completely official, anyhow. Sorta made it taste better, I reckon.

I din' know the name of the town we come to next, but we drifted right on by it.

When I think about these dead folks turnin' and eatin' on each other, I sometimes wonder if we've lost anything at all.

About the Authors

Mark Twain was born **Samuel Clemens** in Florida, Missouri, in 1835. The complete list of his literary work is extensive, but he is most famous for penning *The Adventures of Tom Sawyer* and *Adventures of Huckleberry Finn.* According to William Faulkner, Twain is *The Father of American literature.*

In 1909, he told a friend, "I came in with Halley's Comet in 1835. It is coming again next year, and I expect to go out with it. It will be the greatest disappointment of my life if I don't go out with Halley's Comet. The Almighty has said, no doubt: 'Now here are these two unaccountable freaks; they came in together, they must go out together.'"

He died in 1910, in Connecticut.

He has no email address.

W. Bill Czolgosz has written fewer books than Mark Twain, and none of them nearly as competently. His own personal favorite is *Eat @t Zero's*, published by Coscom Entertainment in 2005 and currently out of print. His latest project is a graphic novel called *Zombifrieze,* illustrated by **Sean Simmans**, a frequent collaborator.

Czolgosz lives in Proud Lake, Saskatchewan, with his two children and three cats, just a mile down the street from his on-again/off-again ladyfriend, who has not yet called the police.

He can be contacted by the angry, the insane, the melancholy, and the desperate at wbczolgosz@gmail.com.

About the Author

[illegible]

[illegible]

[illegible]

[illegible]

[illegible]